Mia's Journey

By John Rebell & Zee Ryan

An Erotic Thriller

This is a work of fiction. Any resemblance to characters, companies, or organizations is purely coincidental and a creation of the author's imagination.

ISBN-10: 0-9824182-2-1
ISBN-13: 978-0-9824182-2-2

To get free updates on this book as well as free chapters for this book as well as upcoming novels, please go to :

http://JohnRebell.com

You can contact the author from the website with any comments or criticisms and will receive a personal reply as long you're polite.

Other books by this author:

Three Pagoda Pass (Kindle Edition: $2.99)
Bad Karma (Kindle Edition $2.99)

Dedication

To Lennon. You are the best part of me. You make it all worthwhile.
To Blake: With love.

Mia's Journey

An Erotic Thriller

Prologue

"It's going to cost you twenty-five thousand dollars, and that's cash, up front," said the lawyer.

The lawyer looked at the man across from him. He brought his teenage daughter in with him. *Probably hoping I wouldn't be a prick, in front of her, just for her sake,* he thought. *What an idiot.*

"I don't have twenty-five thousand dollars," said the man.

"Then you shouldn't have been diddling little girls. Because you know what they say…"

The man looked at him; no reply was necessary.

"Life sucks, then you go to jail," said the lawyer.

The man was working class. Maybe a welder or something. Something manual. The lawyer could smell the dried sweat from across the desk. The girl was sixteen or so, maybe seventeen. It was hard to tell.

She was looking all around the room, wide-eyed, when she thought no one was looking. All the other times she kept her eyes down. She wore third-hand, hand me downs. Her dress was getting thin in places from being washed too many times, and fraying around the edges of the hem.

She had small, but full breasts. He thought he could see her nipples poking through, but he wasn't sure. Her hair was dirty. She rubbed her hands across his leather chairs. They left sweat marks behind. Her palms were sweaty. She was nervous. *I'll have to wipe it down with disinfectant after she leaves*, thought the lawyer.

The man had been caught by police after they had received a tip that he was inviting young girls into his trailer in the middle of the afternoon. After questioning the girls it appeared he wanted to get "friendly." The man seemed to gravitate towards the ten to twelve-year-old variety. Likes the budding titties, does he? Not that the lawyer blamed him, who doesn't? But shit, man, at least have the good sense not to get caught. The lawyer wondered if the man diddled his own daughter too. Probably. Didn't they all?

"Well, if you don't have the money, there isn't much I can do. Your arraignment is tomorrow and bail, in this situation, is going to be difficult. If you can avoid jail time, which I doubt, you'll be a registered sex offender for the rest of your life. By the way, I wouldn't expect an easy time in the joint either. Murderers have daughters, too."

"There must be somethin' you can do."

"How much money have you got?"

"I got five hundred on me."

"For five hundred, I'll be happy to show you a nice public defender who won't give a shit."

"Wait….I got somethin' worth a lot more than twenty-five thousand."

"I don't do barter."

"Hear me out."

"OK, whataya got?"

"Her," pointing at his daughter. "She's trained."

The lawyer looked at the man. Was he serious? This just got interesting.

"It's illegal in this state to marry a minor," he said, testing the water.

"She's eighteen."

"She doesn't look any older than sixteen."

"What can I say? Maybe she was a late bloomer. Wanna see her birth certificate?"

The lawyer thought he'd played the guy when the guy had been playing him all along. He hadn't brought her to the meeting so the lawyer would "act nice." He had been planning on selling her all along.

"There are people in this world, like law enforcement, who would consider that human trafficking."

"Is that what the feebs are calling marriage these days? Human trafficking? Well, they sure do have a way with big words, now don't they?"

"And just how would you see this working?"

"Easy. You get the ball rollin' on your end. And we'll start sending out invitations to the big happy occasion on ours. I'm sure you can postpone this, and delay that, until after the wedding day. Once it's official, I'll expect you to keep your end of the bargain. Or there could be some frontier justice in your future."

"You wearing a wire?" asked the lawyer.

"Nope. Take a look." The man stood up, lifted his shirt, and turned around. The lawyer could see a line of dirt and brown grime around his waistline.

The lawyer waved him back down into the chair.

The girl all this time kept her eyes down as the men talked about her. She didn't even let on she was hearing them.

"What do you mean 'she's trained'? Is she a virgin?"

"Of course not. But who wants one of them? Crying and cater-wauling all the time. Trust me when I tell you, a cherry isn't worth the aggravation."

The lawyer figured he *could* trust the man for knowing that much.

The father reached over and slapped the girl upside the head, causing her dirty hair to fall over her face. She stood up without a word and dropped her dress. She wasn't wearing a bra or panties. She covered her sex with her hands.

"Take a look at that ass, she's as tight as a twelve-year-old. Mia, get over there and suck your future husband's cock like a good little whore." Mia obediently walked over to the lawyer and dropped to her knees.

Part One

Ten Years Later

"It is my feeling that Time ripens all things; with
Time all things are revealed; Time is the father of truth."

Francois Rabelais

"The struggle of my life created empathy - I could relate to pain, being abandoned, having people not love me."

Oprah Winfrey

Chapter 1

Mia's husband picked her up by the hair, and slammed her into the bedroom wall.

"Well Mia, you've done it again. Thanks to your monumental fuckin' stupidity I have no more clean shirts. Once again, all you had to do was one simple thing…turn on the fucking washer. No matter what it is, it is always too much to ask."

Mia bounced off the wall, and directly into the open hand slap of her husband, rocking her head backwards as she slipped onto the floor. Blood started trickling from a split lip.

"Oh no, little cunt. It's not going to go that easy for you. Not by a long shot."

The lawyer booted her while she was on the floor carefully, placing the kick just right. Some bruising, yes, but broken bones, no. She wasn't going to get the satisfaction of going into the emergency room where some do-gooder liberal doctor might start noticing a pattern. She could take it. He'd seen his father deal out a lot worse to his mother over the years.

He picked Mia up by the hair again, this time coming away with a handful of brunette hair, including the roots. He threw her on the bed. Mia stayed on the bed, arms protecting her breasts, silently, eyes tightly shut. She knew better than to say anything.

Her husband took off his belt. He wanted her to see what was coming.

"Open your eyes." He waited for Mia to open her lids. "Here is the decision before us. You know perfectly well you were supposed to start the washer before we left this morning. You knew if you didn't, then you would be punished. With me so far, Low Life?"

Mia just looked at him and said nothing.

"Silence is to be taken for assent," said the lawyer, quoting legal scripture. "Ergo, you must want to be punished." He made a show of wrapping the belt around his hand. "You know, when I bought your worthless ass from your father ten years ago, he told me you liked being beaten. That you intentionally did things so you could get hurt, and that made your cunt water. I didn't believe him. However, he was right. You do. So I'm going to beat you to within an inch of your life, and we'll see how you like that. Stand up and take your clothes off."

Mia stood up with her eyes down. She could see her husband's hard-on tent his pants at the thought of tonight's fun. She had only known two men throughout her life, and they both got stiff cocks from beating their women. She was resigned. Her's was a life spent in hell. She knew it. Maybe they were right. It's what she deserved, because it was certainly all she got.

The belt snapped and cracked against her upper thighs.

"You aren't moving quickly enough, dear. Your loving husband awaits."

Her dress was new, one of her best, and she didn't want it ruined so she hurried up, trying to slip it off her shoulders. Her husband grabbed it, and simply ripped it down her front, the zipper in back, shredding her skin.

"Arms up!"

Mia raised her arms, and a rope came down from the ceiling on a pulley with a pair of handcuffs attached to it. Her husband put the handcuffs on, making sure they were too tight and biting into the skin and bone at her wrist. Mia whimpered, and he raised the rope and strung her up in front of a mirror.

The lawyer walked out of the bedroom then, and she could hear him opening and slamming cabinet doors. He returned with a bottle of whiskey, which he opened with his teeth. He took a long swig of it, wiped his mouth on the back of his hand, and set it down. Whiskey always made him mean. He unzipped his pants, and adjusted his boxers so his cock came free, swinging in the breeze. He walked over, looked at himself in the mirror, staring at Mia trussed up in the background, and took another swig. He started stroking his cock.

"I'm going to tell you what I'm going to do now so that you can ap-

"In the middle of the journey of my life I came to myself within a dark wood where the straight way was lost."

Dante Alighieri

Chapter 2

The man sat alone in a well-furnished den, hitting one note, a G flat, on a Yamaha grand piano, over and over.

He was slumped against the keyboard, his elbow resting against the end corner. In the reflective shine of the highly polished black wood, he could see his sideburns turning gray. His head was cocked as he listened to the same note again and again. *Something is wrong,* he thought to himself. *Is it me, or is that note off?* He hit the key a few more times. *That note is definitely off,* he thought.

A little boy, hearing the sound, came and stood at the doorway, silently watching his father. His two-front teeth had just fallen out, giving him a gap-tooth smile. He walked over and casually put his elbow on his father's shoulder.

"That note sounds funny, Daddy."

"Think so, Big Bear?"

"I think so. Hit it a few more times."

The man hit the note three more times; head cocked, looking at the little boy.

"What do you think?"

"It's off."

"I think so too. What do you think we ought to do about it?"

"What can we do about it?"

"Nothing. Right now anyway."

"Then I wouldn't worry about it."

"You're a smart kid, you know that?"

"Yeah, I know," he said, totally secure in the love of his father.

"Play me a song, Daddy?"

"What do you want to hear?"

"Some Rock and Roll."

The father's right hand reached out and hit the high note on the right side of the keyboard with his little finger, held it, then switched over to his middle finger. In one fast, smooth motion drew his finger all the way up the keyboard to the left-hand bass notes, then all the way back down to the right high notes again. All ten fingers of his left and right hand moving rapidly on the keys in the high note section. It sounded like hard rain tinkling on a tin roof as he punched into the song's intro. The Yamaha boomed, like a wild animal released from its cage. He chose an early Rock and Roll song.

"Sing, Daddy."

"Darkness is callin' now,
I'm havin' trouble seeing.
I've never been able to tell her,
how I'm feelin'.
From out of the darkness,
she walks like a dream.
She makes me feel crazy,
she makes me wanna scream."

The little boy starts moving perfectly to the beat; eyes closed, snapping his fingers in time to the music as he slips out of his body, and his musical Muse takes over. He starts dancing to the music.

"Nothin' gonna help you,
from a love that's blind.
It'll cause you to stumble,
you'll doubt your own mind."

"It's on the light side, baby, oh yeah."

The father comes off the piano stool, and both father and son start dancing about the room, the piano silent, but the music filling their heads all the same.

"Listen close, right here...The sax is coming."

"I can hear it, Daddy."

A high-pitched tenor sax fills both their heads at the same time in the silent room, going into a two minute long solo.

The man slips back onto the stool and picks up right at the moment the sax fades out, both hands slamming the keyboard so hard and loud, the windows rattle.

"I need some beat. Gimme some beat, Big Bear."

The little boy steps up to the table, head cocked, looking at his father.

"OK, take her on down, Big Bear. Right...Now!"

The boy starts a tattoo drum beat with his fingers completely in time with his father's piano. The Man kicks the song into high gear.

"Darkness is callin' now,
I'm havin' trouble seeing.
I've never been able to tell her,
how I'm feelin'.
From out of the darkness,
she walks like a dream.
She makes me feel crazy,
she makes me wanna scream."

"Nothin' gonna help you,
from a love that's blind.
It'll cause you to stumble,
you'll doubt your own mind."

"It's on the light side, baby, oh yeah.
You'll find me on the light side, baby, oh yeah."

The man hit the last note with his little finger, and the chord faded to silence. The boy and his father stood looking at each other, smiling goofily.

"I love it when that happens," said the little boy.

"I do too," said the man.

A woman stood watching from another room, not understanding their connection and slightly jealous of it. She shook her head, gathered up her purse, and left the house, not saying a word of goodbye. The door shut quietly.

The father and son, didn't notice, they could still hear the music playing their heads.

"The ultimate tragedy is not the oppression and cruelty by the bad people but the silence over that by the good people."

Martin Luther King, Jr.

Chapter 3

"Hey Trailer Trash, are you about ready?" yelled Mia's Husband, standing near the door.

Mia had been putting the final brushes of base around the side of her head where there was bruising, so it wouldn't show at work.

Her husband, a rising star in a local law firm, glanced at his Rolex. *That little cunt was going to make me late,* he thought.

"I'll give you until the count of three, Mia. Then you'll have another bruise you can spend all day trying to cover up. One…two…"

"I'm here," said Mia, coming into the room, standing on one foot, trying to put her black pumps on.

"I don't get it. You *KNOW* it takes you a certain amount of time to do something, why can't you get up early enough to take care of it? Lazy, cunt. Come on, let's go. I'm already late because of you." He stuffed Mia's coat into her arms and shoved her out the door.

The lawyer locked the house, slapped a wide smile on his face for the world to see, and walked his wife to the Lexus, holding her elbow, like the loving husband he was. A neighbor was getting their mail out of the mailbox across the street.

"How you doing, Jack," he waved, "how about them Cyclones, uh?"

"They're unstoppable this year, for sure," yelled the neighbor back.

"We getting together for a game and some beer this weekend?"

"Sure. Your house or mine?"

"Let's do yours. We did mine last weekend."

"No problem. See at one p.m. on Saturday."

Mia kept her eyes down, and waited for her husband to open the door for her. He gave a jaunty wave goodbye, opened the car door, and pushed her into the front seat.

Their neighborhood was upper-middle class, as befitted a young attorney on the way up. Most of his neighbors either worked at the banks or insurance companies downtown as upper or mid-level executives. It was a well-polished street, a family neighborhood, of white picket fences, and well trimmed lawns. The lawyer backed down their driveway, gave a final toot on the horn at his neighbor, and they were on their way.

The lawyer dropped Mia off at the school entrance. "I'll be here to pick you up at three forty-five. Don't make me wait on you again, Mia."

"I won't," she said. He watched her getting out of the car, absently thinking he might rape her ass later tonight if the mood struck him. Something about the thought of hearing her cries of pain and wiping the blood off his cock after always got him in the mood. He watched as she walked toward the building. One of the male teachers was also on his way in, smiled, and opened the door for her. She smiled thank you, kept her eyes down, and kept walking.

Mia walked into the office and checked her mail cubby. She wasn't full time, so she didn't get benefits like the regular staff. While the staff was polite and professional, they treated her as an afterthought.

She saw a note from the principal to come to his office after her last period class. Fear immediately thumped, falling like a large rock into her stomach. What had she done wrong?

Mia walked into the classroom slowly. Dread creeping up her throat the whole way. The kids were loud and rambunctious. Since she was a substitute, they knew they didn't have to listen to her. She walked into class and on the secret wavelength that kids shared, they took one look at her, and knew today was going to be a vacation. She tried calling them to order and taking attendance. Most of the boys ignored her. The girls just looked at her with feminine disdain.

Mia finished her day at three o'clock and walked slowly to the principal's office. The dread had been building all day. She knew she was going to get fired. She also knew that would mean a beating from her husband. She noticed the blinds were drawn over the office windows, not a good sign. She knocked softly, and waited for a response.

"Come on in, Mia," came the reply. He sounded friendly, so

maybe it wouldn't be too bad after all.

Mia entered. There were books and papers piled on both the visitor's chairs, so she had nowhere to sit.

"Sorry, it's been a busy day," he said. He came from behind the desk, smiling, and leaned against the edge.

"You wanted to see me?" Eyes down.

"Yes, I did. I hear you've been having a hard time controlling some of the kids in your class."

"No. They're just kids being kids."

"Well sometimes kids need to be punished. Especially, the girls. Girls need a nice hard spank every now and then."

"Excuse me, Sir? You know I can't lay a hand on a child."

"You're absolutely right, Mia. However, I can."

He grabbed Mia's wrist and pinned it behind her back. Using the leverage of his weight, he angled the arm up her shoulder until Mia was forced downward. He then steered her toward the desk and bent her over it.

"No, don't…please."

He pulled her dress up and with his other hand started laying hard smacks against her backside, on her small, smooth ass. One slap after another fell, each one getting more vicious. Mia just lay there and took it. Eyes closed, trying not to sob so she wouldn't make him even angrier. She could feel her ass getting red, and the burning stings from his hand. When his hand started to hurt, he stopped, shook the pain out, and then he stuck his fingers into her panties, and probed into her vagina.

"Like I said, the little bitches like a nice hard spank occasionally." He released her and pulled her up, taking the opportunity to feel her tits, and roughly pinch her nipples.

"Be a good little bitch and get out of her before I make you suck my cock."

Mia hurried out of his office, wiping her eyes, hoping no one saw her.

Mia's husband was outside in the parking lot waiting for her, just like he said he would be when his cell phone rang.

"Yeah?"

"You're right. A good beating does make her pussy wet," said the principal. "I might like to sample that some more."

"She's a submissive little slut, isn't she?"

"What else does she do?"

"Whatever you want...I'll let you beat the shit out of her for three hundred," said the lawyer, watching Mia walk towards the car with her eyes down, snapping the cell phone shut.

"Loneliness is never more cruel than when it is felt in close propinquity with someone who has ceased to communicate."

Germaine Greer

Chapter 4

The man walked downstairs to his home office, with a cup of coffee in his hand and flipped on the computer. He opened his email and casually clicked through the business correspondence. He had a number of Internet businesses he made money from, so he could take care of his entire life by computer. There wasn't very much of interest and no pressing customer orders that needed his attention.

He checked his online planners, and he was still well ahead of the curve. There was nothing pressing he needed to do that he hadn't planned for.

He had written eight books on alternative energy subjects, some of which were quite well received. As such, he usually had a number of speaking engagements as well as consulting work waiting for him if he wanted it. He had just completed his first fiction novel as well and was going over the final edits with his editor.

He was also working on a sequel to the one he just finished. He sat down to write. He had a goal of writing one thousand words a day. It always pleased him when his Muse sat down with him and he could write more.

He picked up his plot outline, mentally adjusted to where he was, and started writing. He looked up again, and two hours had passed. He had no conception of where the time went. To him, it felt like no more than ten minutes. He noted the word count and saw he wrote three thousand words. It was ten-thirty in the morning, and he was done for the day with a clear conscience.

He sat back in his chair, and thought about what to do for the rest of the day. He had a MeetUp Group meeting at three p.m.

A few months before, he had started "Meetup group" in his town for fiction writers. He didn't know why he did it. Maybe it was just the loneliness. Seven years of full time writing on your own will do it to you. Living completely inside his head, day in and day out. He needed to get out more.

The Meetup group was fun. No more than a couple of people showed up at any given time. But he knew it wasn't something he really wanted to continue after the three-month trial period.

There was an email reminder in his inbox saying he had to renew his dues, or they would cancel the group. Instead, he went to his account and canceled it himself. He would still attend today. After all, it was a bakery, and he liked the fresh bagels.

The sound on his computer went off alerting him to a new email. He looked at the "From" line, but didn't recognize the name. He felt something, but couldn't place it, so he dismissed it. He clicked on the email.

```
    I would appreciate any advice or feedback
you have to give.  I have no writer friends,
and I am very new to all of this.  I wrote a
romance novel and have just started a second.
I have amassed a small pile of rejection let-
ters, so I am thinking about self- publishing.
I am unsure and nervous about it, however,
since I don't know anyone who has done it be-
fore.
    Thanks,
    Mia
```

He thought about inviting her to the final MeetUp Group, but she had sent the email through them, so she must already know about it. It didn't appear like she was going to go. Nor did he feel like taking on another angst-ridden, insecure puppy who didn't know the difference between "your" and "you're." He stared at the writing again. He couldn't tell how old she was. Even so, she wasn't a puppy. There was a certain style and grace to her words. He thought he could hear music in them. And there was that nagging feeling again. A soft voice way in the back of his mind. What was the voice trying to say? He decided to answer.

Hello Mia,

Self-publishing is easy once you get the hang of it. About the best place is (Amazon) for paperbacks, and Kindle KDP (Amazon) for e-books. It is like anything else; it has its pros and cons. The biggest thing to consider with self-publishing is all the hats you'll have to wear yourself. That means, editor, proofreader, formatter, and most important, marketer, of your work. If you're willing to learn those things, then self-publishing is the way to go. If you're "technologically challenged," then it might not be.

I hope this helps,

He hit the send button and figured that would be the last he would ever hear from her.

"Online communities are an expression of loneliness."

Joanne Harris

Chapter 5

"Mia, you really are a totally useless little cunt, you know that?"

Mia shied away from the blow. She knew it was coming, and it came. It was an open-handed slap this time at least. He hit her high in the head, so her hair would hide any bruising. It rocked her backwards, and she fell off her chair.

"I just asked you to do one…simple…little…thing." Her husband drew the words out. "And you can't even get that right without fucking the whole thing up."

The lawyer knew full well Mia had been spanked and manhandled by her boss a few hours before. The thought made is cock thicken. He liked the idea that other men wanted to stick their cocks into what he owned. He could understand perfectly why a pimp would want to send his girls out to service other men. The lawyer hadn't been sure he could trust the father ten years ago when he bought her, but she had proven a good sexual investment.

Is there anything better than owning your own bitch? he thought.

Of course, after fucking the same wench for ten years he was tired of her. Which made her perfect for the entertainment he craved now.

Mia knew better than to offer an explanation. So she kept her head down and didn't say a word.

"Do me a favor Mia? Clean this shit up and then, do us both a favor and go commit suicide."

She was sitting in the middle of the mess of her dinner all over the floor. She picked herself up off the floor, as her husband turned and stomped out of the kitchen. He didn't even tell her what she had done wrong.

She heard the TV come on, and pop/phitz as he opened a beer, and turned on the game. He threw the pop top back into the kitchen for her to clean up. It twirled on the floor and came to rest at her feet.

Mia picked it up, throwing it in the trash and started cleaning her dinner off the floor. She could feel the side of her head as it started to swell. She hoped her makeup would hide it since she had to work in the morning. She was a substitute teacher, and kids picked up on stuff not said.

"Hey, Mia!"

"Yes?" she said, scared, walking back into the living room.

Her husband was holding a letter, addressed to her. He had already opened it.

"Your publisher got back to you. They rejected that cringe-worthy story of yours…again." He sneered and threw the opened envelope and letter at her. "Not that that is any surprise."

She picked up the letter, reading it.

"We regret to inform you that at this time…" and walked back to the bedroom, sat down at the computer and turned it on. *Who am I kidding? It probably is drivel,* she thought. *Even if I don't get accepted for publication, I can always self-publish,* she thought. *Why bother? Who's going to read it?*

She opened her email and there was a message from the organizer of the Meetup group she had thought about joining, if her husband let her.

He was helpful and supportive, but not all together interested. She sent him another email back.

```
Yes, thank you.  Amazon was what I had
thought about checking out.  It seems that most
of the time technology has a beef with me, but
hopefully I can be a fast learner.

Two questions --if I have overstayed my wel-
come on your email, please just ignore this
message, and I will stop bothering you  :)
```

Do I need to worry about copyrighting my work?

Does KDP have stock cover art for use?

Thanks for your time,

This time she got an almost immediate reply back. He must have been sitting at his computer.

Technically speaking, any time an author creates an original work and publishes it, it is considered "copyrighted." The question comes in to what degree of PROTECTION the copyright gives you. The highest degree of protection is if you make it official and copyright it with the government. You can look at this roughly the same as if two people live together, or they have a valid marriage license. Both are considered married under common law, but an official marriage license gives both parties more legal benefits.

They have a "Cover creator" you can use, which will turn out a half-way decent cover for you. I create my own in PhotoShop so I have never used it, but I've seen it when I've put my books up. (Covers are important…don't underestimate them)

I hope this helps,

He seemed like he was thawing out towards her at least. He didn't mind that she was asking questions. She didn't have anyone to talk to about her writing. No one she could get advice from, and she had all these questions. There was a ton of information online but nothing that seemed specific to her situation.

"Mia!"

Mia got up and walked back into the living room to see what her husband wanted.

"Yes?"

He stood up, unzipped his pants, pulling out his cock. He held it in his hand. It was thickening as she watched. The beer put a cruel streak into his eyes.

"Get on your hands and knees and do the only thing you have the slightest bit of talent for, you little slut."

"There is no loneliness like that of a failed marriage."

Alexander Theroux

Chapter 6

The man walked into his house; it smelled like Asian cooking. His wife must be home. His son was sitting at the table eating 'Hop Lit Low,' a kind of Vietnamese duck egg with a fully formed duck embryo still in the shell, beak, feathers, and all. He hated the smell of them. His son loved them.

"Hi, Daddy."

"Hi, Big Bear."

"You want to know what happened at day care today?"

"Sure."

"A fire truck came."

"Really? Was there a fire?"

"Of course not. They let us play on the truck."

"So you didn't put out any fires? Or save any kittens?"

"Of course not, Daddy. They let me sit in the driver's seat though and turn on the siren."

His wife came to the table then and sat down. She was still pretty in the timeless way of Asian women. She picked up some chopsticks and stirred them around in the rice and vegetables.

"Where have you been?" she asked.

"Out."

"You weren't working late?"

"No, I wasn't."

"I think I'm going back to Vietnam. I need to see my family."

"OK."

"I'm going to bring the boy with me."

He's got a name, he thought silently. "He just needs to be back before school starts, that's all. But we can talk about it later."

They finished the meal with the man talking to his son about his day. His wife was silent. She didn't offer to make him anything to eat, and he didn't ask.

He walked upstairs and into his bedroom after putting his son down for the night and reading him a story. His wife was already there. She was sitting up in bed watching a Vietnamese soap opera on the home theater system. It was all singing and dancing with some comedy thrown in. She never watched anything else, and he didn't understand a word of it.

"I wasn't joking when I said I wanted to go to Vietnam." Not even bothering to ask if he wanted to come with them.

"I know."

"You don't care if I take the boy with me?"

"Of course I care. But he should see his grandparents, or more importantly, his grandparents need to see him. It's been awhile."

"I'm thinking maybe he should go to school there for a while."

"I'm thinking maybe you're wrong," said the man.

"Why?"

"For one, the schools suck in Vietnam. Two, he lives here. This is where his home and friends are, and three, I don't want him too."

"You say that like you have a say in the matter."

"You say that like I don't."

"How long has it been since we've made love?" she asked changing the subject before it could go too far.

"Over three years."

"There isn't much left to us."

"No, there isn't."

"What's left?"

"Emptiness, and loneliness," said the man.

"It wasn't always that way."

"No, it wasn't."

"What happened to us?"

He looked at her. He remembered a time when he helped her escape a Communist country. He spent three long years in Bangkok planning it.

He remembered another time when they almost got shot by Malaysian police at a border crossing at Hat Yai.

He remembered when the Vietnamese government revoked her passport and citizenship when they figured it out two years later and left her stateless, without a passport and nowhere to go. He remembered getting her to the American Embassy and declaring political asylum for her.

He remembered being so much in love with her, his own life would have been a pleasurable price to pay. When they met, she couldn't even speak English.

He remembered bringing her to America, and her wide-eyed wonder at this huge, beautiful country.

He remembered bringing her to the Grand Canyon for the first time. He blindfolded her, and led her carefully right up to the edge of the South Rim and took off the blindfold. She almost collapsed at the beauty of one of this country's greatest natural masterpieces, her breath, literally taken away.

He remembered when she returned to Vietnam after the Vietnamese government granted her amnesty, and she could return. He remembered her joy, the tears running down her face, at seeing her family after almost ten years in exile.

He remembered starting a business for her in Vietnam, then having the government steal it from them, after it was successful. He remembered how they had started over from nothing.

He remembered sitting in a shabby Vietnamese hospital, luxurious by Vietnamese standards, when his son was born in Saigon, and his life began again through the eyes of his son.

Eighteen, long years of turbulent, one-of-a-kind memories. Almost his entire adult life.

Now they no longer made love, and she didn't even want to look at him. Now he looked at her and wondered what he did wrong.

"I think we have just done everything we were meant to do. That's all."

"I'll always love you, you know. You're the only man I've ever known."

"I know. I'll always love you too. Go to Vietnam and have a good time with your family. But Big Bear has to be back before school starts. If you want to stay, that's fine."

Crushed by the sadness that the love of his entire life, went wrong. And he didn't know why.

> "Find a place inside where there's joy,
> and the joy will burn out the pain."
>
> Joseph Campbell

Chapter 7

Mia found a pen pal in an unlikely place outside the hell of her daily existence. When she wrote, he replied.

She couldn't go to work and could barely sit down. Blood was still seeping from her ass from last night's ordeal. She sat down at her computer and saw his latest reply and wrote back.

```
    Thanks for the info and advice.  As you can
probably tell, I have recently just 'fallen'
into writing.  I never had it on my radar as
something for me, but I jumped in and now I
really enjoy it a lot.  Again, I'm not sure if
I'm doing it correctly but enjoying what you
do is half the battle - right?  Well, making
money would be nice too.  I am a person who
fears making a mistake so this seems like a
big scary venture.

    Thanks,

    Mia
```

Again, the reply was almost instant. He seemed to take an interest in her. He also seemed to know her feelings, how she felt about her writing. She just wasn't writing in an empty space anymore, her words were reaching someone. Someone understood the loneliness and frustration of writing.

OK, I need to get a better handle on you, so I know how to tailor advice because I don't know at what stage of development you're at.

So please permit me to ask some questions. What is your age? Education? Past work experience? How many years have you been writing? What genres are you interested in cracking into?

As far as fear goes, we all deal with it all the time. It's a constant companion. Fear of rejection, fear of failure, fear of criticism, fear of publishing, you name it. Been there, done that.

It isn't about making money in the beginning. It is about getting people to read, and like your work and want more of it. To build a fan base, to get people talking about your books. Money comes later, maybe even, much later. If you're starting out, don't even consider it. Especially if you're writing fiction.

This is a marathon. If you enjoy writing, then it isn't work. It's a release. It's something you HAVE to do in order to keep your own sanity.

Try to get it to flow, but if it doesn't, write anyway. Write every single day. Write a journal, if nothing else. The goal should be 500-1000 words, every day. Don't worry about anything else. Don't worry about punctuation, misspellings, or trying to make it perfect. Just write.

I hope this helps,

The man finished writing his message back to Mia and hit the send button. What was it about this girl? Something about her made him curious. It was undeniable. He wasn't sexually interested in the slightest, having given up on American women decades ago.

He hadn't bothered to screw an American woman in over 20 years, and he had no intention of starting now.

He reached up inside his head and decided to explore it. He'd just take a peek. Just to see if she was worth bothering with or another spoiled American brat. He sent his intention out with the email and was immediately slammed backwards as it hit a big, black wall.

What the fuck...

Mia looked at his email and started to get suspicious, why did he care? Of course she knew he probably just wanted to fuck her, or maybe he was an Internet predator. She'd heard about those as well. What if her husband found out she was talking to someone online? Plus he was getting too close. It felt like he was getting into her mind. Her defenses shot up immediately.

At the same time, she didn't feel any threat from him. Just interest. Was that possible? That someone was interested in just me? She decided to reply, but not too much. Then, she felt something like a small caress, almost as if someone whispered, "It's OK," and she opened up.

```
    It is great to hear someone say the things
that are rattling around inside my head!  I
think I told you, I don't know any other writ-
ers.
    I am in my late twenties.  I have a Bach-
elor's Degree in education and am currently a
substitute teacher.  I write on days I'm not
subbing.  I have been writing for only about a
year.  I really am into Romance novels, ones
that lean towards more 'adult' themes.  As I
mentioned before, I wrote a 70,000+ story and
am about 1/3 of the way done with a second.  I
read a lot, which is what got me interested in
writing.
    I think my stories sound good, but I don't
know if that is just because they came from
my head!  I average about 800- 1000 words on
days I can write.  Some days the words seem to
```

write themselves and other days I have to stop
and think often. Sometimes it feels like the
story is eating my brain, and I can't wait to
get it out! Does that sound crazy? :)

  As for fear, I am the person that always
over thinks things. I never put myself too
far out there because it is safer not to try.
Does that make sense? Writing is the only
thing that has made me not want not to pull
back. That is part of the reason why I don't
want to stop.
  Geez, I sound like I am in therapy.

  Thanks,
  Mia

The man sat back and read her email. Feeling it, tasting it. He suddenly realized what the feeling was. He liked her. The thought took him totally by surprise.

Why? He asked himself. It wasn't sexual. Then another feeling hit him just as hard. She's me, years and years ago. So long, it might as well have been another lifetime.

The man recognized himself in the reflective beauty of her words.

"Love is something far more than desire for sexual intercourse; it is the principal means of escape from the loneliness which afflicts most men and women throughout the greater part of their lives."

Bertrand Russell

Chapter 8

The prostitute knocked on the hotel room door, and the man opened it.

She was pretty, probably a co-ed, bleached-blond hair, but it didn't look bad. She was no more than twenty-three. She wasn't dressed like a whore at least. She wore very little make-up, she didn't need to, and a gym outfit.

She looked like a young soccer mom. Maybe she was.

"Hi. Can I come in?"

"Sorry. Sure."

She walked past the man, and he checked out her ass. Not bad. She continued walking into the room, checking things out as she did. She was looking around for some clue as to who this John was. The man didn't bring any personal items with him, so good luck with that one.

"Did they tell you on the phone how much I charge?"

"I seem to remember they didn't forget that part."

"Well...?

The man gave her the money. The transaction finished, she unzipped her top and took it off. The man looked at her. She had nice tits. He had gotten the "mom" part of the soccer mom right anyway. She took off her sweatpants as well and stood in her underwear, waiting for a cue from the man.

"So what are you into?"

"I wish I knew," said the man.

"Huh?"

"Nothing. What's your name?"

"Candy, what's yours?"

Yeah, right.

"You can call me 'That Guy.'"

She giggled. "Is that your first, or last name?"

"Both. My parents were simple people. You see, their last name was Guy and they only referred to me as 'That.'"

"You're putting me on, right?"

"Probably."

"OK, That Guy, it's your money and you paid for an hour, but the clock is ticking."

He looked at her eyes and could see the hardness just starting to creep into them. He decided to move his mind up a plane and see what he could see in them. He slipped the mental gear into place. He noticed his lower mind was carrying on the conversation and putting her at ease. Good.

He stared at her eyes. They were bright blue. *Fake contacts*, he thought, then slipped behind them. There was blackness and rot gnawing at the edges of her soul. She wasn't lost, but she soon would be if she carried on her current mode of thinking. He slipped out of her and went back to his lower mind.

"…of course, you can't expect him to understand that."

"No, they never do," he heard himself say. "Most men are assholes."

"Yes, they are. You know, you're different. I kind of like you. I'll let you fuck my ass for fifty dollars more. I know you like it."

"I have a better idea."

"Oh? What's that?" Hint of suspicion in her voice.

"How about if you just take the money I just gave you, and here,- here's fifty more,- we call it a night, and you spend it on your child?"

"How did you know I have a child?" Suspicion real now. She started putting her clothes back on in a hurry.

"I don't. Lucky guess. I figured it was 50-50, I'd be right."

"OK," slightly mollified.

"Do you have kids?"

"Yes, I do.

"Boy or girl?"

"A boy."

"'Trust me, you don't want a daughter."

"I don't?"

"No. For one, they are only interested in their daddies. And their daddies are usually assholes."

"OK, thanks. I'll keep it in mind. But seriously, I think I want to be alone."

"Yeah, you said that already. So why'd you call then?"

"I don't know. Desperate, I guess. Or maybe just stupid."

"But after seeing me naked, you're not as desperate or as stupid, huh?" She zipped her top up, and started putting on her track shoes.

"No, really, it isn't like that. You're gorgeous. It's me."

"It's your money. You won't catch a disease, you know. I'm clean." She said as she slipped out the door, closing it behind her.

"I know. I might catch something worse," said the man to the empty room.

"One of the most beautiful qualities of true friendship is to understand and to be understood."

Lucius Annaeus Seneca

Chapter 9

"Mia, I got a call from your boss, yesterday," her husband started off first thing in the morning.

"It appears your winning personality is pissing everyone off, as usual. So here is what I want you to do. I want you to be especially nice to him. He's a school superintendent, and they are thinking of throwing the school's legal work in my direction. That would mean good things for both of us. So you're going to do your part. Do you understand what I'm telling you?"

"Yes. I'm to do whatever he says," said Mia, resigned to her fate.

"Good. How do you feel today?"

"Good," Mia winced from the pain in her butt and had to shift to take the weight off her ass.

"That's great because the welts I left all over your body last night look absolutely beautiful."

He left the house, but not before twisting her nipple viciously.

Mia had the day off since there was no call for a substitute teacher that day. She decided to write. She found herself thinking about her pen pal, wondering if he was going to reply. *I probably scared him away, unloading on him like that,* she thought. *Why did I do that?*

She didn't know why she did. It just felt good to say something to someone about what was pent up inside her. She felt like he wanted to know how she truly felt about her writing. He still hadn't written back.

Maybe he wasn't going to. He probably ran screaming away from his computer when he read it. *He doesn't care about me. It's just in your mind. Grow up! Get a grip,* she told herself.

Then the email chime sounded, and she saw he replied.

OK, I'm up to speed.

The romance genre is a tough one to crack, so don't be in a hurry. Keep doing what you're doing…reading and writing.

A word of advice…non writers never understand writers. Keep it to yourself. With spouses, the best plan is to wait until you get to the point in your writing (Like published and making money) where they ASK YOU, if they can read it. Until then, most spouses don't get it. If they aren't creative themselves it's even harder.

In terms of your writing "eating your brain," it sounds exactly like a writer. But don't expect anyone else to understand the craving though. :+)

Your question: I think my stories sound good, but I don't know if that is just because they came from my head!

That's a tough one which you'll never really figure out to your own satisfaction. (At least I haven't) That's also where a good editor will come in.

Your question: I never put myself too far out there because it is safer not to try. Does that make sense? Writing is the only thing that has made me want not to pull back. That is part of the reason why I don't want to stop.

Then don't stop. But don't over think it either. Do it for fun. Do it for therapy. Do it because the story HAS TO come out. You can

```
hire an editor to over think the details for
you. (In fact, you should)

    I hope this helps,
```

Even in pain, it brought a smile to Mia's face. Someone understood. Someone felt the same way. She wasn't alone. She started to wonder who this guy was, picturing his face, and his background. She didn't want to ask, but he had asked her background details so maybe it was okay to lob a question or two.

She was thinking these things and smiling as she walked out to the mailbox. It was a perfect late-summer day. This summer had been nice, not too hot, not too cool. She opened the box and saw a letter from another publisher. Her mood deflated. Another rejection letter probably. The thought bummed her out so much she didn't even open it. She sat back down at her computer again, looking at the email. Her smile came back. She tore the envelope open.

"It is our pleasure to inform you..."

Her novel was accepted for publication! She stared at the letter in disbelief. She thought at first it must be a mistake. The letter was for someone else. She looked at the opening, and it had her name on it. She was going to be published!

She knew instinctively her husband would not be pleased. Should she even tell him? Could she not tell him? Then she remembered her online pen pal. She started to fire off a quick email to him. She knew he would be pleased about it.

```
You're not going to believe this, but...
```

Her cell phone rang. She looked at it and it was the school. She flipped it open.

"Hello?"

"Mia? This is John Gilheart, your principal at Waterloo Elementary? I'd like you to come by my house later..."

"The power of the harasser, the abuser, the rapist depends above all on the silence of women."

Ursula K. Le Guin

Chapter 10

Mia had to hurry to Gilheart's house if she was going to get home by the time her husband got home.

She still had things to do around the house, and if she didn't do them, he'd be angry. She was nervous and apprehensive. Of course, she knew Gilheart was going to use her sexually. It was probably even going to hurt. She steeled herself. If anything, this life had taught her to accept pain in silence.

He gave her the address and directions. She got lost on the way over because she wasn't familiar with this side of town. The neighborhood was shabbier than her own. There were some teenagers hanging out on a corner in front of a store, drinking beer.

She found the number and pulled up in his driveway. His house was shabby like the neighborhood. She stepped around some dog poop on the walkway leading up to his door. She looked around the stoop. It had peeling baby-shit yellow paint and a faint, unpleasant odor. She rang the bell.

He opened the door almost immediately, like he had been standing behind it, waiting.

"Mia, it's a pleasure to see you, please come in."

The house was decayed and shabby as well. It smelled like old cabbage. There were dirty clothes lying on the chairs and half eaten supermarket deli food containers on the coffee table. He was obviously unmarried. He closed the door behind her.

"Let me put you at ease, because I know this is an uncomfortable situation for you," he said, still smiling. "I'm going to fuck you, and use you sexually, and it's probably going to hurt. Because Mia, you remind me of my ex-wife and there is nothing I would rather do than beat the shit out of her. So let's get comfortable shall we? Take off your clothes and do it now!"

Mia left herself and disappeared up into her mind to a place no one could hurt her. She mechanically took off her clothes.

"My, my, you look like you have certainly been a bad girl. Look at all those marks. Did your husband do that to you last night? Because they look fresh." Her boss trailed his fingers over her flesh. "You know, you keep yourself in very good shape, Mia. You're to be commended. A lot of women your age have already let themselves go. Do you jog?"

Mia was in her own private space and didn't realize she had been asked a question. The slap came out of nowhere, open handed, right across her face.

"You probably didn't hear me the first time and mistook my winning personality for someone who gives a shit about you. I said DO YOU JOG?"

"Yes."

"Well, exercise and healthy eating are the cornerstone of a wholesome society. Bend over and pull your cheeks apart."

Mia bent over and did as requested.

"Good now, put your face between your legs, so I can see it."

She complied.

Gilheart picked up a digital camera, rapidly zoomed on her, making sure she was completely recognizable. He quickly snapped a picture of her.

"In case, you ever think about discussing our little friendship with anyone at school, that photo will find its way to the school website, and will be posted before the rumor even stops. This entire town will know what a wanton slut you are. Those hackers are so devious. All the world will get to see it before we discover it and take it down. I'll probably have to issue a heartfelt apology to all the parents, but in a technological age, it's hard to stop these things from happening."

"I'm not going to say anything."

"That's so reassuring to hear. Stay right there and hold that pose."

Giheart left the room and returned with a whip.

"Spread those cheeks nice and wide now. That's a good girl."

Gilheart stood back, took aim, then wasted no time laying the whip into Mia's ass crack. The whip cracked. The tip entered her butt cheeks at almost the speed of subsonic sound. Mia cried out involuntarily.

"Felt good, didn't it? How do you like this whip?" Gilheart said, showing it to her between her legs. "I made it myself. Shop class is so handy. The city was even good enough to buy the leather. I got the plans off the Internet. If you're good, I'll put the metal tips on it and you can watch as I peel the skin right off your ass."

He flipped the whip around so that now he had the handle and started rubbing her pussy with it. He stuck it into her opening, pushing the handle in.

"Does that feel good, Mia? Because I certainly don't want it too."

He took the handle out and brought it up to his nose, then licked it.

"I don't think you washed thoroughly after urinating, Mia. Bad girl. But as we all know, bitches are like that. And because you're a bitch, I'm going to treat you like one. Stay there, don't move."

Gilheart went and sat in an armchair and pulled his cock out. It was long and thick. He was uncircumcised. It looked like an anteater.

"Mia, get down on all fours, like a dog. That's a good girl. Okay, come on over here girl. That's it. Come on over here and let me pat your head like a good dog."

Mia came over and he handed her a leather dog collar.

"Put it on. That's a good bitch. Would you like a bone, Mia? Here I have one you can gnaw on. Come and get it."

Mia had no choice but to give him a blow job. His uncircumcised cock stank, it tasted dirty, and made her want to retch. He held her by the hair, forcing her mouth downward on his cock. Each thrust, moving his cock further down her throat until triggering a gag reflex.

"You puke in my lap little dog and I guaran-fuckin-tee you'll lap it up."

He wasted no time and shot off a load of cum down her throat. It tasted rancid.

"Thank you, that was very good, and because you're such a sweet little dog, I'm going to reward you."

He snapped a leash onto the collar and started dragging her towards the kitchen.

"A nice big bowl of dog food, just for you..."

"Our life always expresses the result of our dominant thoughts."

Soren Kierkegaard

Chapter 11

Mia got home and her husband was already there.

For once, he didn't seem too concerned about the undone chores. He was sitting in his chair, drinking a beer, watching a game. He barely glanced up at her when she came in.

"How are you feeling today, Mia?" he asked, in a tone which was the picture of concern.

"Good. I'm fine."

"That's so good to hear. And did you have a nice afternoon?"

"Yes. I did what you said."

"That's also good to hear." He went back to his game.

It was painful to move. After having her ass brutalized by her husband the night before, then whipped by her boss, she was sore. She knew her ass was leaking blood. She could feel it seep into the back of her panties. She walked into the bathroom and started running a bath. She could smell Gilheart's house in her hair and still taste his rancid cum in the back of her throat.

She took her time brushing her teeth while the bath was running. The resulting steam and fog from the hot water enveloped her, wrapped her in its cocoon and made her feel safe. She gargled with Listerine to get the taste of his cock out of her mouth, but it still remained. She took off her clothes. She felt like burning them. Her panties, she threw away.

Mia eased into the hot water, wincing, then settled into the heat. She looked down at her legs and torso. There were red welts and scratch marks all over her. She wouldn't be wearing any dresses for a while. Long sleeve blouses were in her future. Her breasts were bruised and she knew wearing a bra would be painful. She lay in the bath, soaking a long while. Then scrubbed her hair, getting the smell out.

She finished her bath and dried herself off with a long towel. The towel was clean, fresh and felt good. She used one for her hair, wrapping it up turban style and another she draped around her thin body, tucking it in next to her breasts.

When she came out of the bathroom, her husband was gone. No word or note to tell her when he was coming back. She decided she didn't care and made herself something to eat. There was a new feeling in her today. It was a small ember of rage. Rage at her husband and rage at his abuse. She watched TV and heard other women talking and knew this wasn't the way most men acted. *Why did they act that way towards me?* She screamed silently to her mind.

She sat down at her computer and turned it on. Drying her hair with the towel as she waited for it to warm up. She opened her email and saw a message from her pen pal. She smiled to herself. She still hadn't told him she was going to be published, and she knew he would be pleased. So she started an email to him.

```
You're not going to believe this, but my nov-
el got accepted! I wanted to tell you first. I'm
so excited.

Thank you so much for everything.
Mia
```

And she hit the send button. His reply, once again, was immediate. Mia felt the connection then. He was truly happy for her. Just for her. Her excitement was his excitement. In the time it took to read his reply, she bonded with him through the ether of cyberspace. They touched. They connected in a way she had never felt before. He didn't want anything from her. He just wanted her to be happy.

```
Mia,

I am so happy to hear that. I didn't real-
ly do anything. You did it, not me. I've never
```

read your writing, but I'm sure you deserve
it. It looks like someone else besides myself
thinks so too. Go out and celebrate. Tell me
where, and I'll send flowers. I'm very happy for
you.

I hope this helps,

Once again, she felt the connection. She couldn't describe it, but
it was there. She also felt like she knew him on a more personal level.
They had never met. She didn't know what he looked like, or where
he lived, but she felt like she knew him. Like somehow they were old
friends. She also wanted to keep the conversation going. She didn't
want him to leave. She knew he must be sitting at his computer, so she
fired off another email.

If I'm bothering you just let me know because
I don't want to. But what do I do now? Are they
going to contact me? Will they just publish the
manuscript? I don't know what to expect. Can
you help me?
I don't want to bother you, so if I am, just
disregard this email.

Mia

Again the reply was immediate.

Mia,

You aren't bothering me at all. Just the opposite. I'm starting to look forward to hearing
from you. If I was in your situation, I'd want
to talk to someone too.

You'll probably get a contract by email.
You'll need to look it over very carefully.
There are a lot of details you need to be care-
ful about. I can't possibly go into them in an

email. Not because I don't want to, but without the contract in front of me, I'd forget most of them and steer you wrong and I don't want to do that. You should probably have someone look it over for you, a lawyer maybe? Or perhaps your husband. They would be a better judge of it than me.

I'm sorry I can't help more. Don't hesitate to contact me if you have questions. I'm happy to help you.

I hope this helps,

There it was. He felt the connection too, she could tell. He even invited her to talk to him. She didn't understand what got into her at that moment. She had never done anything like it before. However, before she could stop herself, she wrote back…

I don't have anyone I can show it too. Could we meet…

"Power is domination, control, and therefore a very selective form of truth which is a lie."

Wole Soyinka

Chapter 12

The lawyer slammed the door behind him and flung his briefcase onto the nearest chair. What a cunt.

Why the hell had his law firm hired that bitch anyway? She was short and fat. What was the point of having an ugly woman around? Especially one that he had to pay some sort of professional respect to.

He hated it when he was called down to the office on a weekend. If that stupid newbie bitch 'lawyer' (he used the term loosely) just out of law school hadn't screwed up, he wouldn't have had to waste most of his Saturday. He missed the Saturday football game with his friends.

His only consolation was that he spent the night with his new favorite whore. He wasn't going to fuck his wife anymore, not after whoring her out to all his friends. Now her only use was to take care of his other, more abusive needs.

"Mia! I've been home for more than a minute and there's no beer in my hand. What the fuck are you doing?"

Mia quickly turned off her computer and ran into the kitchen. She had heard her husband come in, but she was in the middle of a conversation with her new pen pal. She just couldn't tear herself away. He was so kind and understanding, something she needed desperately in her pain filled life.

After grabbing a can from the fridge, Mia lowered her head as she entered the living room. She held out the beer and was thanked with a quick smack to the back of her head.

"What the fuck were you doing?"

"Sorry. I was finishing the laundry."

The lawyer opened his beer and took a long pull from it. Mia didn't dare to move away. She knew that he was far from done with her. When he was in a mood like this, it was going to be a long night for her.

The lawyer didn't speak. He just looked upon his wife through gulps. She fucking annoyed the shit out of him but at least she knew her place. Plus, she was well trained. He never understood why other men put up with mouthy bitchy women. He finished off the beer and threw the can at Mia's feet.

"Get me another beer and when you come back, be naked."

Mia turned towards the kitchen and heard her husband undoing his belt. Maybe the beers would make him tired, she could only hope. As she stripped and grabbed another can, her mind wandered back to her computer conversation.

What would he be like as a husband? Mia immediately shut down that thought. Imagining a better life would only hurt her further, would only make her pain worse.

She reentered the living room to find her husband shirtless and holding his belt. He held out his hand for the beer and gave her a wicked smile. She could see the sick pleasure flickering in his eyes. She wasn't lucky enough. He wasn't tired at all.

After opening the second can, he took half of it in one long gulp and then set it aside. Wiping his mouth with the back of his hand, he turned his attention back on his lazy wife.

"Hands of the wall. Bend over."

Mia did as instructed. She knew exactly the position he wanted her in. She placed her hands on the wall, low enough so she could stand back and stick her ass out. The lawyer would want a good target.

He leaned over her nude back and snarled into her ear,

"If you move your hands one fucking inch, I will make this ten times worse for you. Understand?"

Mia nodded. She felt her eyes water and started to blink. If he saw tears, it would only fuel him on higher.

"And just for a little something special, no fucking noise. I don't want to hear one whimper, cry, sniffle....nothing! Now be a good girl and take what your husband has to give."

The lawyer stood back and looked at her. She did have a great body for a piece of white trash. He insisted that she run at least two miles a day. He also monitored her meals. He would not be seen with a fat wife. He loved the way her sides curved in and turned into that sweet little ass. Fuck, he was getting hard.

His belt came down onto the soft skin on her ass. Her body jerked forward, but her hands didn't move. He hit her again and saw her whole body tense. He knew just how hard it would be for her not to make a sound. It was making him even harder to think of her restraining her cries.

Another hard swat, this one was much harsher than the first two. Mia's whole body reared forward but still, her hands stayed put. The lawyer smiled to himself. What a fucking good bitch. He was going to keep this up until he broke her, though. He was going to keep beating her ass until he heard a scream or whimper.

Another smack and he got a little something for his effort. No noises but he saw her tears falling. Several tears dripped down her face and fell to the floor. Finally, he got what he wanted. A sob escaped her lips.

"Now Mia, I want to do something very special for you. I spent the night with a fantastic little whore. She was everything you are not. So I want you to come over here and suck my cock and savor what a real woman's pussy tastes like."

Fuck! How can other men live without this? the lawyer thought, as Mia got on her knees to taste another woman on her husband's cock.

"Life is a succession of lessons which must be lived
to be understood."

Helen Keller

Chapter 13

They agreed to meet for coffee at a local bakery and he would look over the contract.

No big deal. It was a chance for some fun conversation, a chance to forget the other matters of her life.

Mia was very nervous as she drove to the bakery. She had never done anything like this before. She knew there was nothing wrong with her meeting a man for coffee, and it was perfectly innocent, but still. There was a certain illicitness to it as well. At least, Mia felt there was. She realized without even meeting him, she was already starting to have feelings for the man.

Mia wondered about the man. *Was he married? Of course he was married!* She chided herself. *What did he look like? How old was he?*

He had told her where he would be sitting as well as what he was wearing. She arrived at the coffee shop, and pulled into an empty space. She did a final check in the mirror, made sure no bruises were showing and got out of her car. She walked slowly towards the front door of the bakery. She almost spun around and left, fear grabbing a hold of her. Instead, she steeled herself, opened the door and stepped in.

The smell inside the bakery was delicious and she immediately got hungry. She looked around and saw a man sitting where he said he would be. He had his head down in a book and wasn't paying any attention. It gave Mia a chance to size him up.

He was late forties or early fifties. He had brown hair. He wasn't good looking, but not bad looking either. He looked like he enjoyed eating. The man felt her eyes then and looked up at her. He had bright green/gray eyes, and they looked right into her. When he put down the book, Mia could see he wasn't wearing a wedding ring. Mia walked over to him.

"Hello, Mia, it's a pleasure to meet you," said the man, standing up.

"Hi. I'm sorry if I'm late."

"You're not late," he checked his watch, "You're right on time."

His voice was soft, calm, confident, like he had all the time in the world and was in no hurry.

"Please sit down."

"Is it okay if I get something to drink first?"

"Of course. Would you like me to get it for you?"

"No, that's OK. Thank you."

He watched her walk away and noticed her slender figure and small ass. She was a beautiful woman. *This is a woman who keeps herself in very good shape,* he thought absently. Some small feeling was pushing against his consciousness. He hadn't really meant to look into her, but it was an ingrained habit from many long years of use. While she was getting coffee, he went up inside his head and explored her.

There were walls surrounding her mind, lots of them. They were tall and black. He couldn't see over them, or through them. This is what he saw the first time during the email conversation when he sent his intention out to her. This was usually a sign of someone with something to hide, but that didn't feel quite right in this case. He probed deeper, testing and tasting the feeling. He pushed against one of the walls, and it pushed back. *She has strength, a lot of it,* he thought.

Then the certainty washed over him. Yes, she was hiding something. She was hiding her fear. She had a lot of it, mountains of it. Huge black walls of fear enclosing and encircling inside her mind. He got out of her immediately.

Mia returned with her coffee and sat down. She didn't know what to say or how to begin. The man seemed to be waiting for her to start. She looked up and he was staring straight at her.

"Mia?" he said softly.

"Yes?"

"Everything is going to be OK. You don't have to be afraid with me. Everything is going to be all right."

Mia broke down and started weeping, right there in the middle of the bakery, in front of a man she didn't know, and for reasons she couldn't explain.

As soon as she started crying, the walls broke and came crashing down. The man saw/felt with instant clarity the lifetime of abuse and it shocked him. He feared for her. His heart immediately went out to her. He wrapped her up in mental warmth, and in the confines of his mind, pulled her into his lap, and stroked her head. He saw she desperately wanted a father, a protector, someone who would always be there for her.

But she was also a grown woman, and a grown woman with needs, and desires. She wanted, no needed, a father, but also more. Someone who would help her feel good about herself. She wanted someone to take the pain away. To control her, but in a way that benefited her, and not them. She had never been taught to manage a complicated modern life. She wanted so much for someone to take the pressure away. She wanted to give her life to someone, and in return, she wanted them to give her life back to her.

"What should I call you? I don't know your name."

He looked at her without responding, waited a beat, then said,

"What would you like to call me?"

"I'd like to call you Daddy. I never had a real one. I always wanted one."

"Do you want to take a journey?"

"Where?"

"Inside yourself."

"I do if you go with me."

"Very good. Your journey is going to be based on nurturing and kindness, not indifference. So yes, call me Daddy."

"OK, Daddy," Mia said, happy, relaxed, and feeling secure for the first time in months, as the warmth and fullness invaded her body.

"When do I begin my journey?"

"Open your eyes, look within. Are you satisfied
with the life you're living?"

Bob Marley

Chapter 14

Mia left the bakery in a hurricane of conflicting feeling.

But the overriding, and most confusing feeling she had was one of
safety. She felt safe for the first time in her entire life. It was like Daddy
understood, without being told, what she wanted and needed. She
couldn't believe that. How could he possibly know?

Daddy? she thought to herself, *what a ridiculous name. Why did I
want to call him that?* Even so, it felt accurate. It felt so perfectly right
that she couldn't think of any other name that fit.

He was her Daddy. She wondered what his real name was. Then
decided she didn't care.

He was her Daddy.

There was something else. It felt like he was somehow inside her.
Not invasive, or invading her privacy, but softly, like he was caressing
her. It was like, once she dropped her defenses, he reached inside her
and took her fear away, and replaced it with strength. She could practically feel him wrapping warm arms around her, while she cried on his
shoulder. She could almost hear him gently shushing her, and stroking
her hair. And she melted into his safe, soft, warmth.

Oh, you are so full of shit! Her fear screamed at her in her mind. *He
is a man, and just like every man you have ever known, he basically told
you "take off your clothes" and do what I say. He wants to fuck you, and
use you.*

*And when he is finished with you, he will throw you away the same
as every other man has. You are such a pathetic piece of shit,* the voice

said. Then she recognized the voice. It was the voice of her husband.

FUCK YOU! She screamed silently at the voice in her head. *I don't have to listen to you! And the voice fell silent.*

Mia was shocked at the power, the venom and her rage at the voice in her mind. She was also shocked that she had controlled it. That the fear voice had listened and did what SHE said.

I do not like you. I do not want you in my mind and in my life anymore. I'm tired of your fear. He is my Daddy, because I say so. Not you. Now get out of my mind!

And the Fear Voice left. In its place was calm, peace, and the soft, gentle voice of her Daddy, telling her it was going to be ok, everything was going to be all right.

Mia walked into the house. Her husband was already home and in a foul mood.

"Mia!

"Yes."

"I never asked last night. How did you like the taste of my whore's cunt on my cock?"

"She tasted exactly like the scum bag you are." Mia was shocked the words came out of her mouth, quicker than she could take them back.

Her husband was up out of his chair in a flash, and his hand came across her face just as quick. He looked at her in disbelief. His hand closed into a fist.

"I'm going to enjoy this, Mia. I hope you don't have any plans for the holiday."

"Jeffrey Lionel Prescott, the third?" His fist stopped in mid-air at the mention of his full name. She said it the same way his mother said it, like it was the mark of nobility and privilege. "I'm only going to tell you this once. But if you ever touch me again, I'm going to cut your dick off when you sleep, and feed it to you when you wake up."

He looked at her eyes and saw she meant every word of it. He backed away, keeping his eyes on his wife like he just found a tiger in their living room. Which, in a sense, he had.

Mia turned her back on him and walked into the kitchen and picked up a knife.

"I mean it," she looked at her husband.

"You're dead, Mia. I will kill you myself."

"You already did, a long time ago. You can't kill a ghost."

Jeffery Prescott retreated to the living room in confusion. *What the fuck just happened?* he said to himself. He knew he couldn't let her insolence and defiance stand. At the same time, she carried that knife in her hand like she was willing to use it. Maybe the best thing to do is let her cool off. I can always come back later. She isn't going anywhere. She has no place to go. She can't go to her family. Her father would just beat her and send her back to me. He smiled, then picked up his jacket, and walked out the door.

As soon as the door closed, Mia deflated. *What did she just do? What came over her? Why did she say that? She knew he would come back and the beating would be worse, maybe much worse. I should go catch him, tell him I'm sorry. Beg his forgiveness. Maybe then the beating won't be so bad.* Then, she recognized the Fear Voice. It had crept back in when her defenses were down.

"GET OUT OF MY MIND," she screamed, this time aloud, to the empty house. And again, the Fear Voice retreated. *I'm going nuts,* she thought to herself, *screaming at voices in my head.*

She logged on to her computer. It hummed and whirled as it warmed up. She opened her email and saw Daddy's last email sitting in her inbox. It made her smile. *My Daddy,* she said to herself, she felt his warmth spread through her. She clicked on the reply button and wrote:

"Daddy? Are you there?" And pushed send.

The replay was immediate.

"Yes,I am."

"I want to see you again, Daddy."

"I'm glad. Because I want to see you again too. When do you want to meet?"

"How about right now?"

"Sometimes the heart sees what is invisible to the eye."

H. Jackson Brown, Jr.

Chapter 15

Daddy walked into his empty house. His footsteps echoed on the hardwood floors.

His wife left for Vietnam a week earlier, taking his son with her. He felt empty beyond words that he didn't have the usual things to do with Big Bear. If his son was here, today they would be going to the big-box home-improvement store, looking for something to build. They would create a meal plan together, then go to the supermarket and buy all the ingredients and come home and cook it together. For the past three nights, he had gone up to his son's room and just sat on his son's bed alone, looking at the little kid mess, the toys strewn haphazard around the floor. There was his packing mess as well, when he chose what clothes, what toys, what books, he wanted to bring to Vietnam.

He thought about cleaning up the room, but couldn't bring himself to. It brought him too much comfort seeing it the way his son left it.

Then his thoughts turned to Mia. Sitting there in his son's room, his actions seemed so alien. Then her last question, "When do I begin my journey?" It seemed so completely natural at the time. What had he done? Why had he opened that door? Because something in him wouldn't let him say no to her. Something in him wanted to give her what she wanted.

What is this journey? he said into his mind.

A journey you were meant to take, came back the reply.

Those days are long past, he said to himself.

Are they? said the Small Voice.

Daddy walked downstairs and went to the kitchen. He thought about making something to eat but wasn't really hungry. Besides, it was no fun cooking alone.

To Daddy, cooking was love. Cooking was about making sure the very best of everything went into his son. No store bought processed crap. No fillers, artificial sweeteners or chemicals. He made everything from scratch, so he knew exactly what went into and what was fueling his little boy.

He wasn't fanatical about it. He didn't insist on "Free Range" chickens or only organic vegetables, but he only bought the best for his son even so. Then prepared it carefully. It was a small thing that no one noticed, or even cared about. However, to Daddy, it was everything. It was his internal symbol, his wedding band, of his total devotion and love for his son.

His mind drifted back to Mia. Did he do it because he was just horny, and she was young, and beautiful, and he so missed the touch, the taste, the smell of a beautiful woman? Be honest with yourself. It was sexual once you saw her, sure. But it wasn't all sexual. Then what is it? Why is the pull so strong?

It's your journey, repeated the Small Voice.
But I don't have to take it.
No, you don't. You have free will.
I have my art. I have my son. I don't need any more than that.
Are you sure?

He walked downstairs to his office to check his email. As soon as he sat down, his computer chimed, and there was a message from Mia.

`"Daddy? Are you there?"`

The email exchange was rapid. Both sitting at their computers, firing off one email after another. He ended his by giving her his address.

Why did he do that? Why was he acting without forethought? Daddy was a careful person, never acting in haste, always with a clear plan, a direction, as well as an expected outcome. It was like he abandoned all of his principles. And there was his long-standing rule about American women. *You know this is going to be trouble,* he chided himself.

He felt her presence arrive, and he walked upstairs.

Mia parked and walked up the small path to the door. His house was in a family neighborhood in the good section of town. This was one of the newer developments, built for the expanding, upwardly mobile families that were coming into the area. It was a neighborhood of small children with an elementary school close by. His house was two-story, white, with red trim and shutters. His small, blue, Ford pickup was parked in the driveway.

Just before Mia knocked, panic started to rise up. She actually had trouble taking her next breath. Perhaps she wasn't ready for this. Maybe she couldn't do this. Mia turned and took a few steps away from the door when she heard it open behind her. She froze in her tracks.

"You aren't leaving are you?" his voice seemed to wrap itself around her. Even it made her feel warm and safe.

Mia slowly turned back to face him. "No, sorry. I'm just very nervous, Daddy."

He stepped forward and put his arm around her shoulder. "I know. Don't worry though, please. You are safe with me, always. Everything is going to be all right, Baby Doll."

Daddy led her into the house and to the living room. He turned and spoke softly. "First, know that you are not a prisoner here. You are free to leave or stay, no matter what. I will never hurt you."

He searched her face. It felt like he was trying to read her, gauge her.

"I will never force you to do anything you don't want to do. While you are here, this house is yours. You are free to use anything here. You can also stay as long as you want. There's a guest bedroom upstairs if you want it. I hope that you are comfortable and tell me if there is anything you need."

"Thank you, Daddy."

"I don't know your situation, Mia. But my gut tells me it's bad, and that you're in trouble."

"No, it isn't like that, it's…"

"Mia? There is only one rule here. Don't lie to me. It's not necessary. If I can help you, I will. If I can't, I will tell you so. All I ask is you don't lie to me."

"Oh Daddy, I'm so scared!" she cried, and rushed into his arms.

Daddy wrapped her into his arms, enveloped her in his warmth, and drove the fear from her body. He then poured his strength into her.

"Life is a dream for the wise, a game for the fool,
a comedy for the rich, a tragedy for the poor."

Sholom Aleichem

Chapter 16

Mia sat wrapped in Daddy's arms for a long time.

He didn't rush her, just sat with her rocking her back and forth.
When he thought she could talk he said,
    "Why are you scared, Mia?"
    "Daddy, I'm afraid of everything." Total honesty.
    "Okay," was all he said, and went back to rocking her and stroking
her hair.
    "Daddy?"
    "You can have me if you want, you know."
    She looked at him. He was looking at her but not saying a word. *Is
he going to reject me?* she thought. If he does I'll run out of this house.
He was still looking at her with no expression on his face. Mia started
to pull away from him, shame rushing red into her cheeks. He held
onto her, until she looked at him.
    "I want you. More than you can ever imagine. But not like this.
I don't want you in payment. I'll only accept your gift when you're
ready to give yourself to me freely."
    "I'll give myself to you freely right now, Daddy. I want you inside
me." Almost a whisper.
    He looked at her and saw it was true.
    "But Daddy? I want you to dominate me like you did at the bak-
ery. I want to do what you say, and I want to please you. I want you to
train me."
    Daddy looked at her and once again saw total honesty. More, he

saw that she needed to go back to being a little girl. She needed the acceptance and love from a father she never had.

The saw that emotionally, Mia was still a little girl. Trauma victims he knew sometimes got stuck emotionally at the age the trauma happened.

"Your body is the most beautiful thing in the world to me. Please take your clothes off."

Mia's eyes widened. This command took her off guard. Was she ready for this? She didn't move. He came close and looked into her eyes. She could see the love in them. Yes, she could do this.

As she started to slide the thin straps down her arms, she said, "Daddy, I'm scared."

"I know sweet girl. It's okay though."

With shaky hands, Mia continued to undress. Soon she was standing there in just her panties. She hesitated. Daddy was patient and calm. He spoke no harsh words nor did he hurry her along. He was letting her adjust. He was letting her get to the place of comfort herself.

"Jesus Christ, what happened to you?"

"My husband likes to beat me," she said simply.

Daddy trailed his fingers over the welts and scratches.

"He does, does he? He never will again," was all he said.

"I know, I told him so this afternoon. That was when I came to you."

"How long has this been going on?"

"All my life," was the simple, soft, reply. "My father sold me to him ten years ago. He used to beat me too."

"Why didn't leave your husband?"

"Where was I going to go? I have no friends of my own that would help me. My father sold me to him. Going home isn't an option."

Mia could see the anger coursing through Daddy. He tried to keep it under control and not show any emotion. Nevertheless, it was there. Not seen, but felt, like a storm gathering force on the horizon, thunder rolling in the distance.

When she finally got brave enough to slip out of her panties, Mia looked at Daddy's face. His expression darkened, slightly. The love was still there, but now it was mixed with anger, but she knew it wasn't at her. She nervously moved her hands to hide her bare pussy lips.

"No, that is mine to see."

His other hand moved up and took hold of a breast. Mia moaned as he squeezed it. He then took her hardened nipple between two fingers.

"Whose body is this?"

Mia wasn't really sure how to answer that. Her mind was a little foggy at the moment. Daddy tried to make her concentrate. He pinched her nipple. He moved his face closer and whispered into her neck.

"Whose body is this?"

Mia whimpered then she realized what he wanted to hear.

"Yours, Daddy. It's yours."

"Good girl. You are so beautiful."

Daddy pulled off his T-shirt he was wearing. Then he quickly un-did his belt and pants, letting them drop to his ankles.

Mia didn't hesitate this time. She dropped to her knees. She wanted what was coming next. To see her Daddy pleased, to get his praise.

Without receiving instructions to, Mia closed her mouth around his shaft. She felt him tense slightly at her sudden move. He didn't pull back, however.

She was rewarded with a long sigh of ecstasy.

"A loving heart is the beginning of all knowledge."

Thomas Carlyle

Chapter 17

Mia felt her cheeks expand and instinctively swallowed his essence automatically.

Daddy looked down at her with nothing but love in his eyes, stroking the top of her head. He started to pull out and Mia wouldn't let him go. She grabbed onto his buttocks and pulled him back into her mouth, taking the entire length of his soft cock into her mouth, running circles with her tongue around it. She wanted the taste of it. She wanted his being. At that moment, she would take his soul if she could suck it through the end of his cock. She looked up at Daddy again and saw that he was back with her. She took it out of her mouth just long enough to say,

"Whose cock is this?"

"Yours, Baby Doll. It belongs to you," Daddy whispered.

Mia smiled, and went back to her cock.

Mia didn't want to give up her cock but knew it was time. Daddy helped her to her feet with both hands, looking into her eyes the whole time. His eyes bored into her soul.

"Felt it, didn't you?"

"Daddy, I…"

"Shushh," he put a finger on her lips. "I know." His other hand went between her legs, and felt the slick warmth of her pussy. His hand came away wet. This time, Daddy got on his knees and buried his face into her pussy, dragging Mia down onto the floor, with her pussy straddling the top of Daddy's face. He lifted her off his face as he licked every drop off the inside of her thighs.

Then he started biting her inner thighs.

"Yesssss."

Mia was riding his face now. However, once again, she could feel Daddy completely with her, and almost connected to her soul through her pussy.

Mia felt herself shift to a higher plane inside her own mind. She was 100% herself in the pre-moments before a massive orgasm, but at the same time, she wasn't. She was drifting in a place of calm, peace, and utter self-acceptance.

"UUhhh, uuhhh, uuhhh," Mia was reduced to guttural sounds as she pumped up and down on Daddy's tongue. She could feel her climax building as she pushed her pussy further into his face, humping back and forth quickly….and then the release.

"Aahhhhhhh…."

Her entire being flowed out of her pussy and into Daddy's mouth. Everything she was, everything she had, her hopes and dreams, guilts and betrayals, successes and disappointments, her pain and emptiness, left her body. She was left empty, but full. Like all parts of herself had been taken out, cleansed, and replaced new.

"Whose cum is this?"

"Oh, Daddy…it's yours. It all belongs to you," Mia said, meaning it with her whole heart and being.

They both got up and moved to the couch. Daddy looked at her, got up and went into the bathroom. She heard water running, and he returned with a warm washcloth for her and handed it to her.

"I'll do it for you, if you want. There's nothing to be self-conscious of. It's a part of who you are and I love it. I love the taste, the smell, the feel of your cum. And I want it. I want all of it. Every bit of it, from now on," Daddy said, once they sat down. "I'm not a jealous man, but that is reserved for me now. No one else."

"What about my husband?"

"What about him?"

"I'm married, Daddy."

"It's mine. I'm taking it from him. He doesn't have a right to it anymore."

"Yes, Daddy."

"All truth passes through three stages. First, it is ridiculed. Second, it is violently opposed. Third, it is accepted as being self-evident."

Arthur Schopenhauer

Chapter 18

"Daddy, I don't know what just happened to me, but that was different."

Mia looked around the house. She didn't know if it was Daddy's or not. It had a large, open floor plan and was done in light oak hardwood. They were seated in the living room which could look in one direction, across the dining room to a gourmet kitchen, and in the other, to a 60-inch home theater system. There were books everywhere. There were also photos on the wall. Mostly of a little boy, from infant to about seven or eight years old, in the gradual photographic progression of time. There were also some pictures of a pretty Asian woman and many pictures of Asia, or locations within Asia. There were no pictures of Daddy.

"Okay, tell me about it. What happened?"

"I'm not sure I can explain it."

"Okay, take your time," said Daddy, patiently, letting her talk.

"It was sort of like I left my body."

"Was it a good feeling or a bad feeling?"

"It was neither. Well, I mean, you felt good. I've never cum like that before. But this feeling wasn't good or bad. This feeling just felt right. Does that make sense?"

"It does to me. As long as it felt right, what is the problem?"

"It scared me. I don't know if I want that to happen again."

"I see. So it felt good, and it felt right to you, but you aren't sure if you ever want to feel it again?"

"When you put it that way, Daddy, it doesn't make sense. It just scared me. That's all. What happened?"

"You mean something happened?" A smile playing across his lips. "Did you have an accident or something? Do you need to change your panties?"

"You know what I mean. Don't tease me!"

Daddy laughed. It was solid, honest, laughter. Not at her, but her words pleased him.

"This just happened…" And he kissed Mia on the lips. It was the first time he had truly kissed her. It was long and soft. Filled with want, but also complete acceptance and love. Mia fell into the kiss, once again swept to a place she didn't know but felt oddly familiar, and completely like home. It felt like she had been on a long journey, so long she forgot what the destination was. Then Daddy opened the door for her and said, "Welcome home. I've been waiting for you." Daddy broke the kiss, and looked at her.

"Truthfully? I don't really know any more about it than you do. I just know it exists."

"What is it?"

"It's The Truth. That's all."

"Did you learn about it in Asia?"

"Yes, and no. Like you, deep down, I always knew it was there, but I didn't know the way. Asia taught me how fucked up and sexually repressed this country is. And how that sexual repression leads to many problems found in society. As well as how it can manifest itself in the individual. It takes an especially heavy toll on the women."

"How did you know I knew it was there?"

"I just knew. It takes one to know one, maybe."

"How did you find your way there if no one showed you?"

"By following my Truth. The same as you."

"Is my truth sexual?"

"ONE of your truths is sexual, yes." Daddy said, holding up a finger.

"There's more than one?"

"Of course, Baby Doll. There is an infinite number of truths. It is a life-long journey. It may continue for many lifetimes. I don't know. I haven't found all of mine either. But I have found enough to show you how to start your own search for truth."

"That sounds like a religion. Are you like a priest?"

Daddy started laughing. "No, I'm not. Nothing of the kind. It's the opposite of religion."

"What is the opposite of religion? No religion?"

"No, The Truth."

"Daddy, why do you want to teach me?"

"Who says I want to teach you anything?"

"You keep on answering my questions with questions!"

"No, I'm not. You aren't even asking me the questions...you are asking yourself the questions. You are just 'framing' them at me."

Mia was silent, content to drift on the tide of soft warmth of feeling she got from her Daddy. And he was HER Daddy now. She felt completely possessive of him. She shrugged her way into his arms, like she belonged there, without asking for permission. She knew it was where she belonged. She leaned into him and pulled her feet up on the sofa. She wanted to sink into him, to merge her being with his as they had done during sex. She knew now it was possible to become completely one with another person in ways she never thought possible.

"Daddy? I don't know anything about you."

"Does it matter?"

"Are you married?"

"Yes, I am."

"You don't wear a ring."

"So?"

"Did this happen with your wife as well?"

"No, it didn't. She couldn't accept her own Truth. You could. Some people are trapped. They would rather be slaves to their own illusions and those of others. Some can't escape the illusions and false walls other people and society build around them. She was one of them. It wasn't her fault. It takes courage. A lot of it. Most people don't have it."

"So where does that leave us? I'm married, you're married...we have no future."

"It leaves us with right now, right here, in this moment. That is the only thing life is giving us. Let's spend it like the gift it is."

"I want *MORE* than that," Mia said, with conviction.

"Then take all you want, or you need," said Daddy, smiling at Mia, loving her.

"A true friend is someone who lets you have total freedom to be yourself - and especially to feel. Or, not feel. Whatever you happen to be feeling at the moment is fine with them. That's what real love amounts to - letting a person be what he really is."

Jim Morrison

Chapter 19

"Come on, let's go upstairs."

They walked down the hallway. The floors were the same light colored oak and up the carpeted stairs. At the top of the landing there was a bedroom with the door closed, with brightly-colored crayon pictures on the door. "Lenny's Room…do not enter," the sign said, in a child's scrawl.

Instead, they turned towards the left and walked into a huge bedroom. Mia remembered she and her husband had looked at one when they were buying a house. A "Master Suite" the realtor called it. It had an entertainment system on one wall, opposite a huge king-size bed. A desk was in another corner with a bay window overlooking the back yard. The desk had a computer monitor and books all over it. There were more pictures of the little boy in here. She could see now he was Amerasian. He was cute. He was going to be a heart-breaker when he grew up.

Still holding Mia's hand, they walked into the bathroom. It had a shower and large, oval tub with a Jacuzzi in it. Daddy started the water running in the tub.

"Do you like your water hot or warm?" asked Daddy.

"I like it hot, Daddy."

"Good…so do I."

"Here, test the water. See if it is okay for you."

Daddy stood to the rear and watched Mia in the classic pose of a beautiful woman. Her arms were held over her head tying her hair back, and she tested the water by sticking out one long, slender leg with one toe. She was in profile, her small ass and perfect breast visible. Daddy blinked, and mentally snapped a picture of her with his mind. He put the picture in a safe mental place where he could look at it later.

"It's perfect, Daddy," Mia smiled.

She got into the Jacuzzi, and Daddy followed her. There was plenty of room for them both, so Mia just moved aside as Daddy got into the tub with her. He put a leg on each side of her and sat down, facing her back. Mia dropped backward against his body and he put his arms around her. They lay together in the warmth. Neither moving or talking, just drifting in the warm water with no expectation of conversation or anything. Timeless and at complete peace with each other.

Mia thought maybe she had fallen asleep because when she became aware again, the water was getting cold. *That couldn't be*, she thought, *we just got in the tub a second ago, surely no more than five minutes.*

"Daddy, I'm getting cold."

"Oh, I'm sorry. I lost track of time." Time had stopped for him too, Mia noted. He started the hot water and added the right amount of cold to make it perfect.

"Lean forward, Baby Doll."

Daddy took the soap and started washing Mia's back and shoulders. He would drag his fingernails lightly up her back and circling them slowly around her shoulders. He'd rinse her off, soap her up again, then drag his fingernails, delicately scratching her back and shoulders.

He slipped both hands under her arms and cupped each breast, soaping them up, and rubbing her nipples. She knew Daddy liked her nipples. He would touch them and they would stand right up. His hand went between her legs and he carefully washed her pussy, making sure it was clean.

She felt his fingers exploring her folds softly, cleaning her gently. Mia just had to relax into his arms, spreading her legs, and Daddy cleaned her without a word.

"Stand up, Baby Doll. I'm going to shave you."

"You don't have to do that, Daddy."

"Yes, I do."

He got his razor, popped the blade out, and put a new one in, while Mia stood.

"Put your foot right here," Daddy said, patting his knee.

Mia knew Daddy liked her smooth, so there was no need to use shaving cream. He ran his hand up her long smooth leg and smiled at her. He just used hot water and ran the razor expertly up her leg. His razor was different than the cheap ones Mia used and got her legs even smoother. He was very careful around her thigh as he got close to her pussy. He rinsed her leg off with hot water again.

"OK, now the other one."

Same drill. Rinse and repeat. Mia stared at the look of total concentration on Daddy's face. Every movement was calculated and smooth.

"Now, I'm going to shave your pussy, Baby Doll. Put your foot on my shoulder."

She did as commanded. Her pussy was now directly in Daddy's face. With any other man, she would have died of embarrassment. With Daddy, it seemed like the most natural thing in the world to do and she didn't give it a second thought.

He then inserted one finger into her pussy so that his finger was right in back of her clit on the inside. With his other hand, he held it inside her pink lips so the skin was stretched tight, so he could shave it without cutting her. His thumb worked her clit on the outside, while his other finger worked her clit on the inside.

He finished one side of her pussy and ran his tongue over it, making sure he didn't miss any places. He then switched to the other side.

Another orgasm was steadily building in Mia. He must have felt it because he glanced up at her.

"I'm going to cum, Daddy."

"Then you know what to do."

She switched her leg and brought Daddy's face close to her pussy. His finger was still massaging her clit inside her pussy and now he started licking her clit on the outside. She felt the shudder start deep within her, radiating outward in waves. One moment before she released, she cocked her hips so Daddy could get a better angle.

After the shudders stopped, Mia's eyes became heavy.

"I'm sleepy now, Daddy. Take me to bed." All pretense gone, the little girl she truly was, but could never be, laid bare and vulnerable. Her total trust in her Daddy complete.

Daddy picked her up, and carried her to bed. He laid her on the clean sheets and she snuggled into the cool comforter, purring.

And dreamed...

"If time is not real, then the dividing line between this world and eternity, between suffering and bliss, between good and evil, is also an illusion."

Herman Hesse

Chapter 20

Daddy drifted up through several layers of sleep just enough to realize he was really horny. He was still drifting in half-sleep dreamland where he had some of the best sex dreams. His cock felt like it could reach across the room, and punch holes through the walls it was so hard. He remembered back in his early years, having his cock was such a pain in the ass. It never went down. It was such a constant pain and embarrassment. Nor did it help matters in the slightest he was over-sexed to begin with.

His teens were unbearable. He would sit in class and could swear he could smell female pheromones drifting in the air…and it drove him nuts. There were lots of cute girls in his school, many of them sexually active. Their bra less young titties bouncing and short flouncy dresses, revealing a hint of pantied ass every now and then, would send him to the "lav" to masturbate four of five times a day…just during school hours.

His twenties and thirties weren't much better. Sex was a major pre-occupation, requiring massive amounts of time and money. He couldn't stop himself from screwing any female who was interested.

It wasn't that he didn't want to be faithful; it was that he couldn't be.

He didn't make excuses; he knew he was a slut. He sincerely regretted the women he hurt. Being faithful was a complete joke. He just had to fuck anything that was female and had two legs. And women knew it. They knew he was completely helpless around them and at the whim of his dick. By his count, he lost at least a million dollars to them by the time he was thirty-five.

In Asia, it wasn't unusual to have sex five times a day. With a different woman each time. It didn't help matters at all that he found Asian women completely irresistible. Or the fact that his "habits" were not unusual, or looked down on in the slightest. Women, of course, loved him for it, and then, eventually, hated him when they couldn't keep him. They took one look at him and knew instinctively he liked them, and wanted to find out all about the secrets in their panties. Most, luckily, were willing.

His forties were better, but still no piece of cake. But at least sex didn't have the all-consuming urgency of his early years. He only needed to get off three times a day to be comfortable and not have a raging hard-on. He could gain some perspective about it. He accepted it as who he was.

He drifted up through another layer of sleep and thought about playing with his cock. It was a nice fantasy and felt very real. He would just reach down and…

He drifted up through the final layer of sleep and realized someone was already playing with his cock. He looked under the covers, and Mia was glassy-eyed rolling her tongue around the top of his cock. Some pre-cum made a long, sticky rope from her lips to his cock. She looked up at him, taking it out of her mouth and continued stroking him.

"Hi, Daddy…it's hard!" She kicked the comforter back so she was no longer underground. "You never get this stiff."

"Oh yeah, I do. If you didn't suck the cum out of it all the time, you'd find out."

"No. I like sucking the cum out of it all the time. You know what?"

"No, what, Baby Doll?"

"I made a decision."

"That's good. Does it have anything to do with coffee?"

"No. Can I make a rule, you know, about us?"

"It depends."

She stood up on her knees between his legs, one hand still grasping his cock, the other holding her finger up in the air like George Washington declaring independence, her cute titties bouncing, and said,

"From now on, you will not leave this house in the morning without me draining your balls. I'm going to do that for you, Daddy, because you need it. Besides, if I don't there are lots of little sluts out there that will and I won't let them. This is my cock now. So I'm going to drain your balls every morning and then you won't be interested in them."

"It does sound like a good plan," said Daddy, smiling at how cute she was. "I second that rule and with the power invested in my dick, hereby declare it law."

"Good. Tell me what you think of this," she got some baby oil from the bedside table, poured some on her hand and started working his cock up and down.

"I like it."

"That's not it...be quiet."

Mia got back down between his legs and taking the skin of his testicles between her teeth, started gently chewing on it, pulling the skin outward, and then running her teeth along them, all the while stroking his cock. The sensation shot through Daddy's groin like a sudden shot of electricity.

"Bite them harder, Baby Doll."

She did, looking up at him the whole time, over his balls like she was saying, "This hard? Is it hard enough?"

"No, harder."

She bit down harder and the shock was electric in its intensity. Her eyes widened when she felt the climax coming on and his cock got even harder, thickening out and getting ready to expel his juice. Mia pounced on his cock with her mouth, jerking his cock with one hand and squeezing his balls with the other.

"FFFUUUCCCK ME!" Daddy said, and erupted. Lifting his entire body off the bed in a massive orgasm as the spasms squirted multiple times into Mia's mouth as she squeezed his nuts, milking them of every drop.

Daddy felt like he needed to go back to bed. He hadn't been up ten minutes, and he was spent. Mia just looked at him. Big, round eyes, as she licked the cum off her lips and sucked at his cum hole, trying to get some more.

"Oh...my...God."

"I told you I liked your cum, Daddy."

"Yes, you did...Can I have my cock back?"

"No. It's mine. You gave it to me, remember?"

Daddy was too spent to argue.

"Did you like it Daddy?"

"Yes, it was incredible."

"Good, because you're going to get this every morning. Your cock gets you in too much trouble, Daddy. I have to do this for you. It's my job. Don't argue with me. It's a rule now."

"I'll try not to put up a fight…"

"Can we make another law?"

"You're a regular Supreme Court Justice this morning, aren't you?"

"Do you remember you said you wanted me to tell you my fantasies? Every night, I want to try a different fantasy."

"OK."

"No, Daddy, it's not that easy."

"It's not? I could have sworn that it was."

"No. We have to plan it. Some of my fantasies require things. They are detailed. Can I spend your money?"

"I don't care."

"Then you just go to work. I'll take care of everything else."

"OK."

"Am I your Baby Doll?"

"You know the answer to that already," Daddy said, smiling at her, and pulling her to his chest to kiss her. She held a finger to his lips, stopping the kiss, looking deep into his eyes.

"I love you, Daddy. Don't you ever forget that."

"The superior man understands what is right;
the inferior man understands what will sell."

Confucius

Chapter 21

Where did that little cunt go?

Jeffery Prescott stood behind his desk, phone to ear talking with a client, all the while his mind was elsewhere.

"I'm telling you Prescott, this whole land/high rise merger is slipping out of control, and it is making me nervous."

"There's no reason to be nervous, and it isn't slipping out of control," Prescott lied smoothly. "We have the planning board on our side. We should be able to break ground on schedule."

Except the planning board wasn't on their side. It seems some members were paid more than others and this was making the slighted board members cranky, and they were threatening to pull the deal.

"Yeah, you got all the right talk," continued the client, "but if it doesn't go down the way you say, you're going to be the one to walk. You can kiss that mayor's seat goodbye."

"I understand that, George. You let me take care of it. That's what you hired me for."

The line went dead without a goodbye.

"Fuck you very much too," Prescott said into the dial tone.

He had another perplexing problem. His wife disappeared. She hadn't come home last night. She didn't take any of her clothes, none of her jewelry, none of her personal items. No one at the school had seen her or heard from her. She just vanished. No one saw her leave the house, but her purse and car were gone. What did that mean? Where could she have gone? She didn't have any friends, and her family would have alerted him if she went home.

The telephone rang again.

"What?"

"Your father on line two," said his secretary.

"Okay, thank you," Prescott said into the phone, absently wondering if he should bone his secretary. He punched line two.

"Hi Dad, I'm kind of busy."

"Just got a call from George Mender. He says you're fucking up. He says you completely screwed the pooch on the planning board and they are talking about yanking the permitting. Please tell me you haven't fucked this whole thing up. I've got over ten million in this deal myself, and if you fucked the puppy on this one it's coming out of your share of the inheritance."

"He's exaggerating, Dad. I got it under control."

"How come that isn't inspiring confidence in me?"

"Really. He's blowing the whole thing out of proportion."

"Get your head out of whatever crack you're stuffing your dick into. You're in the big leagues now. Speaking of cracks, I heard your wife is missing."

Christ, the man's spies were unbelievable. His father knew things about his private life before even Prescott did.

"No. She's just blowing off a little steam."

"You got to keep those little bitches in line, Jeff, I'm telling you. A little cunt can ruin your life quicker than an IRS audit. Maybe it's time you took off the gloves. I had to put your mother in the hospital three times before she finally accepted who was boss. It isn't always pleasant but sometimes it's got to be done. Get your private life under control and get the city planning board back in your pocket. I don't want to have to step in and clean up your mess."

"I will, Dad."

His father clicked off without a goodbye either. However, his father was right. It was time Mia got taught a lesson, a hard one.

One thing bothered him though. The look in her eyes. She wasn't afraid. That looked bothered him. If she was still in the same frame of mind as the last time, he had to make sure she was too broken to fight back. That look said that she would kill him.

But still the question remained, where did she go? He couldn't beat the shit out of her until he found her.

The intercom buzzed. "Mr. Prescott?"

"Your mother on line three…"

"Thank you."

He punched the speaker phone button.

"Hi Mom. I just talked to Dad. I'm really busy."

"Jeffery Lionel Prescott! Too busy to talk to your mother?"

He rolled his eyes. He hated it when she used his full name, and she always did. It also brought back Mia's impersonation the day before. His mind flashed to a memory of his father breaking his mother's jaw when he was ten years old.

"How are things, Mom?"

"Good. I was just hoping you could come by this week. You haven't been home in a while, and Mommy misses her baby boy."

Prescott wanted to gag. He understood completely why his father broke her jaw. He felt like it too.

"Well, no promises, Mom. I've got a lot of irons in the fire and…"

"Good. I'll expect you by Friday. I've got to run, Dear. Have a good day."

The line went dead.

Why are all women such cunts? he asked himself.

His personal secretary came in after he clicked the speaker phone off and knew her boss was in a bad mood. She was twenty-two, and he had picked her personally. She had long legs and wore a short skirt. He, of course, couldn't tell her what to wear around the workplace, but he had let it be known that part of her job was to titillate him, and take his mind off of legal concerns when necessary.

She laid about a dozen legal folders on his desk, bending over far enough that her skirt rode up high so he could check out her new thong clinging to the crack of her ass. Her ass was young and round, slightly bubble-shaped, and he thought he could detect a little moisture sticking to the fold.

"Is there anything else you need?" she asked, smiling coyly.

Oh, if only she knew. I wonder if I could start training her for abuse? He thought to himself. She was on the submissive side. Thinking of wrapping his belt around her ass and raising some red welts made his cock start to distort his khakis. She glanced down and noticed his erection, mistaking the reaction as a response to her.

"No, that will be all. You've done quite enough."

She left the room, but not before pouting a little.

Maybe I'll check Mia's email. There could be a clue there, he thought, then quickly forgot it as internal fantasies and blood lust clogged his mind.

"Being deeply loved by someone gives you strength, while loving someone deeply gives you courage."

Lao Tzu

Chapter 22

Mia got up, walked over to where Daddy had thrown his dirty shirt, picked it up, smelled it, smiled, and put it on. His shirt hung down to her knees. She turned her head, smelled the collar again, and smiled again. It smelled like her Daddy. She padded back downstairs to the computer.

Daddy came home a few hours later, carry various bags from a variety of stores. He set the bags down on an empty chair and walked over and kissed Mia on the head.

"Hi Baby Doll."

"Hi Daddy," she turned to look up at him smiling. "Did you get me anything?"

"Maybe, maybe not." Daddy walked over and leaned over her shoulder, kissing the back of her neck. He looked at the sex toy page Mia was staring at.

"Get one of those, but get the smallest one,…the smallest vibrator they have."

"I already bought a bunch of them."

"Oh? Let me see." Mia clicked back to the shopping cart page.

"OK, but some of those vibrators are too big for you. They'll hurt you. Are you expecting to fit a high school marching band in there? Get the little one too."

"Very funny, Daddy," Mia giggled at the mental image of a marching band in her pussy.

"I could fit one of those big ones in my pussy if I wanted to."

"Maybe you could. But I don't want some big shlong up there ruining my perfectly tight pussy."

"Do you think I should get some nipple clamps?"

"Which ones do you like?"

"Those."

"Nah. I'll make some for you. Better than those. Do you like gold or silver?"

"You know how to make nipple clamps?"

"Maybe. Gold or silver?"

"Well, gold, of course." She looked at him like 'Don't be stupid, Daddy.'

"Of course. What else do they have?"

"I don't know what a lot of this stuff is, Daddy."

"It's your fantasy. Buy them all."

"Hey Daddy?"

"Yeah, Baby Doll."

"Today I got so horny while you were away, I went upstairs and masturbated."

"Good for you. Was it any good?"

"You're not mad?"

"Of course not. Did you save your cum in a plastic baggie for me?"

"Was I supposed to?" She looked at Daddy with alarm, eyes wide, afraid she had done something wrong. Daddy looked at her, then couldn't keep a straight face any longer and burst out laughing. Great rollicking peals of laughter rolled out of him, making his eyes tear up, holding his stomach. If anyone else had done that, Mia would have been reduced to tears and run out of the room, thinking that they were laughing at her. She didn't need to be told anymore that Daddy was just playing with her, and she pleased him to no end.

"Daddy! I swear, I'm going to…" Beating on his arms and chest with her fists in mock anger. She looked at him and saw he was enjoying himself so much, and looked so comical, she started laughing too. It was pretty funny.

"Oh, Baby Doll, I love you so much."

She looked at him suspiciously. "Daddy, you just said the 'L' word…"

"Yeah, but I probably didn't mean it."

Mia punched him again, harder this time. "You asshole, Daddy." Surprising herself that she said it out loud.

This set off another round of laughter from Daddy.

"Blake said that the body was the soul's prison unless the five senses are fully developed and open. He considered the senses the 'windows of the soul.' When sex involves all the senses intensely, it can be like a mystical experience."

Jim Morrison

Chapter 23

Daddy cooked dinner. He had been cooking a spaghetti sauce for two days in a slow cooker. It was now almost a dark-brown color and no longer red. He added the meatballs and Italian hot sausage he made himself, set the heat down low, and covered the pot.

"It'll be ready in about two more hours," he said to Mia.

Mia was already full. She had been stealing tastes out of the pot all day. She couldn't help it. The smell wafted all over the house, and she was hungry. He had told her to stir it occasionally, after all. How could you stir it and not taste it?

Daddy took a bottle of wine out of the bag, looked at the label, shrugged, and started opening it with a cork screw.

"Want a glass?"

"No thanks, Daddy. I thought you didn't drink?"

"I don't."

"Wine is alcohol."

"Is it? Nobody ever told me."

He poured himself a glass of Merlot, swirled it around and took a sip.

"Not bad."

He took some fresh French bread out of another bag, cut it in half lengthwise, and started buttering up both sides with some melted butter and garlic, he had sautéed moments before. He quickly mixed a tossed salad, and made his own dressing with balsamic vinegar, honey, and olive oil. He threw some sunflower seeds into the dressing for good luck.

"We have a couple of hours before this is ready. Would you like me to give you a bath?"

"Would you?"

"Of course, come on."

They walked up the stairs to the bedroom. Mia was swinging her arms holding Daddy's hand. They walked to the bathroom and Daddy started the bath. Mia watched him as he waited for the hot water, then adjusted the cold water. Once he got it the way he wanted it, he sort of looked sidelong at her, silently added a little bit more hot. Mia shrugged herself out of Daddy's shirt and it fell to the floor. She stood before him completely naked and totally at ease with her body for the first time in her life. She didn't cover her pussy with her hand. In the back of her mind, she noted that it was the first time it happened with any man.

"Let me help you take your clothes off, Daddy." She unbuttoned his shirt and pulled it free of his pants, then undid his belt, released the button and unzipped the zipper. His pants fell in a heap and he stepped out of them. They worked together now silently, completely in sync with each other. It had only been a couple of days and it was like they were merging with each other as one, Mia thought. Each knew what the other was thinking and words were unnecessary. She got the rest of Daddy's clothes off and stepped into the tub first. Daddy followed her, and they lay back together in the heat and warmth and drifted off, completely at peace and comfortable with each other.

Again, one second passed and the water was cold again. Daddy didn't seem to notice. Mia let some of the cold water out of the tub, and added more hot water.

Suddenly, she understood. She was a Goddess to her man. She felt the power again. He would do anything for her. The power she felt was undeniable, and very, very, real. For the first time in her life, she mattered to someone. She more than mattered. She was his EVERY-THING.

"Oh, Daddy, that felt good."

"Tasted good, too,"

Mia sat back down in the tub, facing Daddy. Her shave forgotten, her hands on both of his shoulders.

"What does my pussy taste like?"

"Like nectar from the Gods."

"No, really," she said, totally serious, looking him in the eye.

"I was being totally serious."

Daddy grabbed her face and forced his tongue into her mouth, rolling it around the inside of her mouth.

"Like that."

Mia smacked her lips together and her tongue licked her lips, tasting.

"You're right…I do taste pretty good."

Daddy smiled, forcing the power of his love for her out of his eyes, and showering it all over her like a hurricane of feeling.

His love hit her like a solid, tangible force. Mia gasped, fell back on her ass, staring at him, open-eyed, then started crying softly in the perfectness of the feeling.

"The higher mental development of woman, the less possible it is for her to meet a congenial male who will see in her, not only sex, but also the human being, the friend, the comrade and strong individuality, who cannot and ought not lose a single trait of her character."

Emma Goldman

Chapter 24

There was a subtle change in Mia. Nothing she could really put her finger on, and it was very slight. But it wasn't something she noticed, but rather, something she could feel. The sex games between her and Daddy were growing more intense. However, that wasn't it. Sometimes, she felt like there was a train far off in the distance, growing closer. She felt a power and fury sweeping towards her, but it was totally unlike any power or fury she had ever felt before. This power and fury was HER, and at the same time; it felt cosmic, that was the only word she could think of to describe it. She giggled to herself at the absurdity of the word.

Secondly, she wasn't afraid of it in the slightest. Yes, it was power, and yes, it was fury, but unlike any other, it was a part of her. She could no more be afraid of it, than she could fear her own hand.

Daddy sat on the bed, just looking at her. He would sit there now, he could sit there for hours, just looking at her, a small smile on his lips. It used to infuriate her. Now it was like she moved into it. She liked it. She felt like she was a beautiful flower, and he was opening her petals, so he could look at more of her beauty. There was nothing invasive about it. She could feel his pure joy, at this beautiful flower, he could touch, smell, and look at.

"Lay back, my Goddess, and put your arms over your head the way I like."

He loved it when she did this. It was a gesture of total surrender. She opened herself completely up to him. She knew it also lifted her breasts, and made her nipples stand up. He liked that. She could almost feel the pleasure course through him, through his eyes.

"You are the most beautiful woman I have ever seen in my life. You are a Goddess," he whispered, then bit her earlobe.

The contrast between his softness, then the sudden pleasure/pain of his biting made her pussy jump, then run with liquid.

"You belong to me. You are mine. I chose you, and you chose me. Who am I?"

"You're my Daddy," Mia whispered. Mia had long since forgotten her pussy. She knew the bed under her was soaked.

"And your Daddy loves you, more than he can say," he whispered.

Daddy took a large red candle off the night stand, and brought it into her line of vision. It was large, and thick, like the kind you saw in church.

"What are you going to do with that, Daddy?" Fear started to creep into her gut.

"Wait and see," he said as he lit it in front of her eyes.

"I'm not sure I like this, Daddy." That was the thing about Daddy, you never knew what he was going to do. That thought, the uncertainty, made her wet too.

He paid no attention to her. He just watched the candle burn. Next he tipped the candle, and the hot wax ran down the inside of her arms. It was hot, and hurt, afterwards it went instantly cold. Again, the shock of pleasure/pain made another gush of cum come out of her pussy and soak the bed.

"Who am I?"

"You're my Daddy," Mia gasped, as much from the shock as the pleasure. She was squirming in her own pussy juices now. Daddy poured more hot wax right into her armpit.

Daddy looked into her eyes, then poured more into her other armpit. Daddy put the candle down on the night table and ran his hands over her body. He brushed the dried wax off of her. Kissing her, shushing her softly. Running his hands again down her arms, lightly, softly, like a butterfly's wings.

Her armpits were slightly burning. It wasn't uncomfortable, but there was a trace of heat. Mia came off the bed when Daddy picked up an ice cube, and ran it into the burns of both armpits.

Mia wasn't sure where she was. She had just been hit with bolt after bolt of pleasure/pain. First soft caresses, then biting, next hot, after that cold. She felt a sensation of leaving her body, watching Daddy from above, then slid back into herself. Daddy moved himself so he was right between her legs, pushing them apart with his knees.

"Look at the mess you made between your legs, Mia. The entire bed is soaked. Did you pee yourself again? Bad girl."

Daddy picked up the candle and quickly, before she could move, poured hot wax into her navel. Then just as rapidly, as the wax dried, scooped it out, and stuck an ice cube in there.

"Oh Daddy, Oh Daddy, Oh Daddy…" was all she could say. He then took one leg, lifted it, and put it inside her arms, behind her tied wrist. He took the other leg and did the same. She was now stretched in a "U" shape. Her pussy and her ass were completely exposed to him.

"Maybe I should pour some hot wax on your clit. Would you like that, little girl?"

"Noooooo…."

He still hadn't touched her pussy.

"No? A bad girl like you? Doesn't want to be punished? Look at you.

"Daddddddyyyyy…NOOOOO…"

"I'll take that as a yes."

"No Daddy, No daddy, No Daddy…." She knew he was going to do it. He was going to pour hot wax on the softest, most sensitive, most private part of her body. She tensed for the shock of the heat.

Daddy slipped the vibrator tip into her pussy. The vibrator tingled and hummed. Mia felt something, once again. She had never felt before. It felt GOOD. Daddy slipped it in a little further. Mia was long past any kind of words. She left her body again, and saw herself trussed up like a Christmas turkey with Daddy running the vibrator in and out of her ass. She slammed back into her body.

Her pussy was fully distended now, a round, dark tunnel, as Daddy slipped the vibrator in and out in a quicker and quicker tempo. Then he slipped it out, and stuck his tongue into her pussy. His tongue moved along the walls of her pussy, licking and sucking the juice. Occasionally, his tongue ran across an unfamiliar part, and her ass, pussy, and entire body came alive. He never stayed there long and kept licking, eating, sucking her pussy. Then he zeroed in on her internal g-spot and jammed his tongue directly on it. Mia's cum shot from her body with such force it completely drenched Daddy's face.

Mia more than left her body this time. Her spirit completely disappeared into another time and space. On which was timeless, perfect, utterly loving. It was like drifting in a warm bath of soft, golden, love. Just when she decided that she never wanted to leave, she slammed back into her body again, breathless. Daddy released all her bonds, then curled up beside her. Loving the wetness of the sheets and bed. He reached down to her pussy, scooped up some of her honey and rubbed it all over himself. He took her in his arms, smoothed her sweaty forehead, and kissed her lovingly.

"Daddy, Daddy…"

"Yes, Baby Doll?"

"What happened? Who am I?"

"You're a Goddess, Baby Doll. You just became a Goddess. You claimed your birthright."

Time passed, or maybe it stood still. Neither knew, nor cared.

"Follow your bliss and the universe will open doors where there were only walls."

Joseph Campbell

Chapter 25

They lay together on the cum soaked sheets. Daddy still hadn't gotten off, and didn't seem to care. Mia reached down, but his cock was limp.

"Do you want me to get you off, Daddy?"

"I did, through you. I got off when you did."

Mia giggled. "Daddy, you are so weird, sometimes."

"Am I?"

"Yes. Definitely."

Long silence. Total peace. They lay all over each other. Mia wrapped herself around him, entwining herself around his legs, holding him tight.

"Daddy? I went somewhere."

"I know."

"Where was it?"

"I don't know."

"What do you know?"

"Like I said, just that it exists. Isn't that enough?"

"WHAT is it?"

"I don't know for sure. However, I think it is where you came from. It is your origin. It is the place of your creation, before birth. It is the truth of everything. I think it also might be where you go when you die. But I don't know."

"It's beautiful. It's beyond words."

"Ohhhhhh, yeah. I can also tell you, you will be forever changed. You will spend the rest of your life, searching, trying to find a way back to it."

"Can I go back?"

"Yes, some people live there. Buddha called it 'bliss' or the State of Nirvana. Other religions call it other things. All religions speak of it. I think maybe sex is a pathway to it, or a road of some sort. But through the extreme pleasure of sex, you can touch it, or glimpse it."

"How do you find it?"

"Again, I don't know. I'm looking for my way back myself. What I know is that it has something to do with living your life completely in truth. That your entire life, and maybe hundreds of lives, are designed to lead you to this truth. Understanding that this IS YOU, you are a part of it, it is a part of you. It is infinite love and creation. This is what your soul, in perfection, looks like. I think also, that if you do find your way back to it, and you're able to stay there, you will vanish out of this world."

"You mean die?"

"No, I don't think so. I don't think there IS such a thing as death. Only more creation in another form. I think maybe you are allowed to create art in a universal form, because you really are, a creator. Or maybe, you are the art you create."

"You mean like God."

"No. I don't like the word. It is so misleading. God is some old guy with a white beard, sitting upon a throne, scowling in judgment, throwing lightning bolts at sinners and casting them into hell for eternity because they masturbate. As you can see, it's not like that."

"Well, when you put it like that…it does seem sort of silly."

"It's worse than silly…it's a lie. It leads you away from the truth, not towards it."

"We're adulterers, Daddy."

"Yes, we are."

"I'm married, so are you."

"Does it feel like you betrayed anyone?"

No answer. Long silence, total peace, then…

"I'm tired Daddy. Will you hold me really tight, and never let me go?"

"I'm gonna try, Baby Doll. I'm gonna try."

Mia's head was resting on Daddy's chest. One of her legs was wrapped around his.

"Daddy?"

"Yes sweetie?"

"Why do you say you love me?"

"What do you mean?"

Mia lifted her head to look up at Daddy. Her eyes were very serious, but she could tell that he was looking at her with humor.

"Daddy, you barely know me. You don't even know all the bad things I have done before I met you. How can you love me?"

"I don't need to know your past. I know your soul. You are good. You are mine."

Mia rubbed her nose through his chest hair. "Maybe you are making a mistake."

Daddy grabbed Mia's chin and lifted her face. "Never say that to me again."

His face was so stern, Mia felt a little scared.

"Daddy," she whispered.

"No, Mia. I love you for you. Never question that and never call it a mistake."

Tears filled her eyes. She roughly pulled her face away from Daddy and laid it back down on his chest. She was confused, worried, and happy all at the same time. How could she believe him? His words were strong, but she still worried. What had she done to deserve his love?

Daddy lay back. Feeling exhausted at the enormity of the journey he'd chosen. How could he make her see what he saw? How could he explain to her that there were no mistakes in life? That there were only actions and the results from those actions, freely chosen. And that she had freewill and free choice in choosing what those actions and results were? How could he explain to her, after a lifetime of brainwashing and cultural conditioning, that everything she knew was wrong, and designed to control her? And as a woman, for the most part, it was designed to control her sexuality.

That yes, there was right and wrong, good and evil. However, they existed to balance each other. Not to punish her. There would be no such thing as good, if there wasn't evil. The same as there would be no such things as light without dark, or hot without cold. That didn't make hot "bad" and cold "good." That all of her actions, the good ones and the bad ones, were designed to bring her to a state of bliss and self-acceptance that she truly was an image of her universal creator. She was a Goddess, and Goddesses can do nothing wrong.

All of her actions, the good ones and the bad ones, were nothing more than a lesson to be learned in a universal classroom. There was no retribution for past sins. The same as she would never punish a child for an unintentional accident. The universe wasn't concerned in punishing her. The universe wasn't interested in revenge, or controlling her.

But she could find hell if she wanted. It was right here on earth. It was right in her own mind. It was her constant companion in life until she learned to reject it herself from her truth, and instead, live in truth. The same as heaven is.

Daddy understood clearly he could not show her what he saw in her. He didn't have that ability, or any answers on that scale. She would only understand once she saw it for herself. And she would see it when she truly, honestly, wanted to, when she was at the point that truly opening her heart and soul were the only paths left open. Because she exhausted all the fake ones. He pitied, and loved her at the same time. Pitied because he had walked the same path, once upon a time, and understood too well the pain, the confusion, not being able to believe in the perfectness of herself as she already was. He loved her, for the courage it took to even BEGIN such a journey of self discovery. Most people couldn't, he knew that. Instead content to live in their own private hell of illusion. He could not explain it to her. It was so far, far, beyond the words he had, and the answers were only available by feeling the truth for herself. He could just open the door and invite her in.

She would have to take her own journey towards the truth.

So instead, he said, "Baby Doll, we are all flawless imperfections. We are all absolutely perfect mistakes, every single minute of our lives. That's why I love you. If I am making a mistake, it is a mistake I freely choose, and choose to learn from. You are in my life for a reason, and I am in your life for the same. I freely choose to make the mistake of loving you. And I freely accept the results of that decision. Now go to sleep."

"Group conformity scares the pants off me because it's so often a
prelude to cruelty towards anyone who doesn't want to
- or can't - join the Big Parade."

Bette Midler

Chapter 26

Prescott was starting to get curious about the whereabouts of his
wife.

She had been gone for two days. There was no sign that she had
returned to the house. Her clothes and jewelry were still there. Only
her purse, and her car were gone. He sat in his chair in the living room,
twisted off the cap and reflected that was the first time in ten years he
had gotten his own beer.

He replayed the events in his head. Yes, he had beaten her, but it
was nothing unusual. He had beat her harder in the past. What he
didn't understand in the slightest was the look of pure hatred in her
eyes. He wasn't prepared for that. He hadn't been prepared for her
picking up a knife either. Somehow, in the space of only a few hours,
she had either grown a set of balls, or found a new fountain of strength.

He adjusted the crotch of his pants, unzipped his fly and pulled
his cock out. All these thoughts of beating Mia made him horny. He
stroked his cock, with one hand, and drank his beer with the other,
thinking about what he was going to do to her when she returned.
There was no doubt she would return. He ejaculated on the floor and
didn't bother cleaning it up. He'd make Mia clean it with her tongue.

Another question that entered his mind right then was, *where had
she been staying?* Maybe she was at a homeless shelter downtown, or
one of those pathetic halfway houses for abused women. He made a
mental note to check both. That gave him an idea. He pulled out his cell
phone and called the office.

His secretary answered.

"Layla, I need a list of all the homeless shelters around the city along with all the spousal abuse halfway houses. Can you get me those in a hurry?"

"The homeless shelters are no problem. But not the halfway houses."

"Why not?"

"They're secret. Only law enforcement knows where they are."

"You've got to be kidding me."

"No, why do you need those?" her curiosity peaked.

"A new case I'm working on. A man's wife disappeared, and he wants to make sure she didn't get amnesia and wander off the street."

"I didn't see any new cases come in…"

"Will you just do it Layla? Save me your pithy comments."

"Yes, sir."

Prescott drove the homeless shelters, showing a picture of his wife. The bums of course, wouldn't talk without a financial inducement, usually consisting of a ten or twenty spot and he soon ran out of cash. So he went and bought a case of rotgut wine and passed that out instead. The people running the homeless shelters weren't much help either.

Most said they gave up looking at the lodgers a long time ago and Elvis could come in holding hands with Marilyn Monroe, and they wouldn't notice. Prescott tilted his head towards an Elvis impersonator nodding off in the corner.

"See? What did I tell you?" the woman said.

So Prescott sat in his Lexus, in the poor part of town getting stink-eyed by gang bangers, and called a cop buddy.

"Flynn, you fucktard. It's Prescott."

"The King of the West-Side Weenies. Did you cry when the economy tanked your trust fund?"

"Very funny. Did you cry when your girlfriend came home dreamy-eyed and my cock on her breath?"

"Look, Prescott, I'd love to shoot the breeze all day, but you know, I do have citizens I need to beat the shit out of. Maybe taser a couple of grannies to keep them in line, so…"

"I need to know the addresses of the spousal abuse shelters."

"Yeah, well, good luck."

"You can do it. I'll make it worth your while."

"Why? Did you lose your wife into one of them?"

Oh, that stung. Flynn always was quick on the uptake, the bastard.

"It's for a client, so it goes on the expense account."

"Let me get back to you."

The line went dead.

His cell phone beeped a couple of hours later and some addresses rolled up on the screen. Flynn came though. Now he wondered what it was going to cost him. He cruised over to the first one, drove past slowly checking it out, then pulled in up the street, so he could watch it in his rear-view mirror. Within minutes, the cops arrived. Luckily, it was Flynn. He hit the siren, and kept the blue lights flashing.

"You aren't too bright, are you Prescott?"

"I was just checking it out. I thought citizens had a right to be on city streets."

"Not since the Patriot Act. Citizens are tax paying terrorists now. Didn't anyone tell you? So move your ass off this street before I taze you along with Granny."

"Thanks Flynn, I owe you."

"Oh yeah, you do, buddy. I'm going to collect too."

Prescott pulled away wondering what his next move was. He drove around town about an hour or so and called the office.

"Layla, do we have any investigators on the payroll? Who are we using now?"

"We got a couple of ex-cops we use from time to time, but no one permanent."

"Gimme their numbers would you?"

She read them off her Rolodex.

"You know if you need me to work late, and help you relieve some stress, I could. You sound like you're under an awful lot of pressure," she inquired helpfully.

Actually, the stress was building up in Prescott, and he wanted to see if Miss Layla might be the new and improved version of Mia.

"You know, Layla, there is an awful lot you can help me catch up on. Of course, I'll be working out of my home office. I hope that doesn't make you uncomfortable."

"Not at all, Mr. Prescott. Should I bring some takeout?"

"An excellent idea, Layla." Thoughts of Layla's cute round ass raging through his head triggered his blood lust, and he started rubbing his cock in anticipation.

"In matters of truth and justice, there is no difference between large and small problems, for issues concerning the treatment of people are all the same."

Albert Einstein

Chapter 27

Daddy sat down at his desk and got his thoughts in order. After hearing Mia tell him of her treatment by Gilheart, he had made his decision.

He was going to break Gilheart in two.

Since Mia's rape at Gilheart's house, a slow ember of rage started to burn. Daddy couldn't remain passive. He sent Mia shopping to buy some baby-doll underwear and a few other props for tonight's sex games. Since opening Mia up, she had come into her own sexually and all she wanted to do now was create inventive ways to have sex. Not that Daddy minded. He was sporting a permanent erection that hadn't gone down in days.

He sat in his office and thought about the best way to handle Gilheart.

Daddy had learned a long time ago that it was wise not to confront adversaries head on, if at all possible. It was best to stay in the background if possible, unknown and unseen. They could be confronted indirectly much easier. You just had to apply the right kind of pressure. Daddy, of course, didn't have any leverage. So he had to create some.

A truism of modern American life was that everyone was afraid of someone. No matter if you were big or small, powerful or weak, you feared somebody. The more powerful you were, the more people you had to fear, because there were more people you had stepped on and more people who wanted to step on you.

Daddy knew, the easiest way to bend someone to your will was to get someone who they were afraid of to do it for you.

Daddy picked up the phone, and dialed the number of the school.

"How may I direct your call?"

"John Gilheart, please."

"Transferring." The line clicked and buzzed. Gilheart picked up on the second ring.

"Gilheart."

"Yes, Mr. Gilheart, this is David Frieling, at the State Board of Education. How are you today, sir?"

"I'm doing well. How can I help the State Board, today?"

"Well, it's my unpleasant duty to inform you that a complaint has been opened against your school."

Gilheart wasn't too perturbed. Half the parents in the district wanted to sue the school, and the other half already had.

"Oh? What is it now? Not enough blueberries in the pancakes at breakfast?"

"I wish it were. This one is of a more serious nature."

"Okay."

"There have been allegations of sexual abuse."

Gilheart's morning had just got more interesting, but he still wasn't too perturbed. After all, sexual abuse was the charge de jour for any disgruntled parent with an ax to grind, or any child who got sacked from the cheer leading squad.

"Well, what can I do to help?"

"Well at this point I'm just collecting information prior to deciding how to proceed."

"Well, I've got to say, this is the first I've heard of it. So you're going to have to orientate me as to which direction you'd like to proceed."

"Well as I'm sure you can appreciate, due to the sensitivity of the subject, we must remain circumspect in our handling of the matter."

"I can certainly understand the sensitivity of the subject. But, pardon me, I have no idea what you're talking about," Gilheart said.

"An underaged student has accused one of the staff at your school of rape."

"And due to the sensitivity of the subject, you're not going to let me have any details of the allegations? Then I don't see how I can help you."

"Well, as you know, we have to take allegations of sexual abuse very seriously, especially when they involve an underage female."

"Then, once again, I don't see how I can help. Without any information to go on and without having heard any mention of this incident before this phone call, I'm at a loss as to what information you're looking for, or what I can provide."

"You are the one who has been accused of rape, Mr. Gilheart. I'm simply calling to get your side of the story before deciding how to proceed."

Giheart blew his coffee all over the papers in front of him, completely taken by surprise.

"What?"

"Yes, sir. A female has come forward and said that she was invited into your office and unwanted sexual advances were made. When she refused, she claims you forced yourself on her. Penetration was made both vaginally and anally. It was reported to the police, and a rape kit was conducted. Motile sperm was recovered in situ on the girl's body and DNA testing has begun. No charges have been filed pending investigation. I wanted to get your reaction, for the record, prior to removing you from your position."

Gilheart started sputtering, his world upended in the space of a verbal paragraph.

"I can assure you, no such…"

"Can I take that as a denial?"

"You're God damned right you can take it as a denial. I'd like to know who leveled these charges."

"Well, once again, as you can appreciate, that has to remain confidential, and I'm not at liberty to disclose that. I would, however, like to ask some questions."

Gilheart got himself under control. This was complete bullshit, so there was no reason to get worked up. However, even the taint of such a thing could ruin his career, and he knew it. He was three years shy from his pension and after sucking ass in the school department for seventeen years, the thought of losing it was almost too much to bear.

"Of course. Please proceed. Do I need a lawyer?"

"That's up to you, and the teacher's union is under obligation to provide one for you. May I proceed?"

"Yes, of course."

"Are you circumcised, Mr. Gilheart?"

"Excuse me?" Gilheart said, wanting to vomit. He was starting to shake. This entire conversation just took a surreal turn.

"I believe the question was clear, sir."

"No, I am not."

"Do you now, or have you ever, engaged in sex games involving a dog collar and a leash?"

Gilheart was floored. He didn't know how to respond. He couldn't admit to such a thing on an open line, and refusal to answer would make him look guilty.

"I'm not sure…"

"Did you make a whip using school department materials in the shop class?"

"Who the fuck do you think you…"

"Then let me give you a word of advice," continued Daddy, his voice low and soft, and full of violence. "You ever so much as touch Mia Prescott again, I will personally reign hell down on your world to such an extent you will look forward to Armageddon. Do you understand, Mr. Gilheart?"

"Who is this?"

"Someone you never want to meet," said Daddy, hanging up the phone.

Daddy sat back in his chair, then leaned forward, tapping on his computer keyboard. Daddy knew it was only a matter of time before Mia's husband tried to find her. He'd start the search with her email. He attached a virus to Mia's email account. If someone tried to hack, or open her email without a special password, they'd get a little taste of Daddy's magic.

Fuck 'em, if they can't take a joke, he thought.

"The moral arc of the universe bends at the elbow of justice."

Martin Luther King, Jr.

Chapter 28

No sooner had Prescott finished putting out all the telephone fires of his day, Gilheart called.

"Mr. Prescott? A John Gilheart on line two."

Christ, what did he want?

"Gilheart, I thought you were smart enough not to call me at work."

"I don't know what game you're playing Prescott, but I won't go down easy."

"What the fuck are you talking about?"

"Don't play innocent with me. If you and your bitch think you're going to shake me down for more money or try a little blackmail, just remember, you can get hurt too."

Prescott was completely mystified.

"Gilheart, I have no idea what you're talking about."

"You didn't have the State Board goon call me up?"

"What State Board goon? You want to try making sense so we can have a conversation?"

Silence while Gilheart reexamined the situation from the light of new information. Prescott's voice had the ring of truth.

"I got a call a little while ago, from a David Freiling, an investigator, for the Education Department. He seemed to know a bit too many details he could have only gotten from either you, or Mia. Since your wife isn't that smart, you were left as the only man without a chair. What gives?"

Now it was Prescott's turn to be silent, processing this new development.

"What was his name, again?"

"David Frieling. Don't bother, I already tried running him down. There is no investigator there by that name. Which leaves you."

"Have you seen my wife? Has she been in to work?"

"Hey, I have an idea. How about we stay on my topic for a change?"

"Okay, here's what I know. Mia left a few days ago. I haven't seen her. I don't know where she is. I'm looking for her too. So, if you could get your head out of your ass long enough, we might be able to get to the bottom of this."

"You were supposed to have her under control, Prescott. That was your end of the deal. So she's swinging you around by the dick too, is that what you're telling me?"

"I need time to think. I'll call you back."

"I'll give you an hour. After that, I'm going to put some wheels in motion. I didn't walk into this without some protection. Don't think you're dealing with a hayseed. If I go down, you go down too."

"Okay, an hour."

Prescott sat back in his chair, rubbing his temples. Mia's got an ally he doesn't know about? How could she? She doesn't fuckin' *DO anything*. She goes to work, and she goes home. Maybe one of the teachers at school took pity on her? A guidance counselor noticed the bruising and asked too many questions and she broke down?

What about her writing? She had been on the computer a lot lately. Prescott got up from his desk and punched the intercom.

"Yes, sir?"

"I'm going out, probably home. I don't feel well and will very likely take the rest of the afternoon off. Hold all my calls."

"Yes, sir."

He grabbed up his jacket and went out the back way down to the parking garage. He had meant to check her email the other day and then had completely forgotten.

He got home and could tell immediately the house was empty. She hadn't been there. No clothes were gone, which meant maybe her laptop was still here. He walked into the other room, his five hundred dollar Gucci wing tips slapping the linoleum. Her laptop was where she left it.

Prescott flipped open the cover and powered it up. He came up with a login password screen. That little bitch passworded her computer off? When had she done that? Now he knew there was something she was hiding. He tried to think of what she might use as a password. He didn't think she would get that imaginative. He tried her birthday. No luck. Various combinations of her name. Nothing. He tried names of some of the characters in her book. Nada.

She was starting to piss him off.

He tried her name with her birth year in back of it. Nope. He next tried her name with 19 in front of her name, and her birth year in back.

And the login worked.

The desktop popped up in front of him and he started scanning for her email program. It occurred to him he could have accessed her email online and he could have done it from his office. He was too rattled by Gilheart's call to think straight.

As soon as the Internet connection was made, the screen went dark. Then ghostly, cackling laughter started coming from the speakers. A small icon appeared, tiny in the blackness of the screen, growing larger as it came closer, and into focus. It stopped when it took up the entire screen. It was a fist.

Then it slowly moved backward, and the middle finger extended.

Prescott had an enemy, and he didn't know who it was.

Prescott picked up the laptop and threw it against the wall, shattering it. It fell to the floor in three pieces. He started screaming and trashing the house.

Battle lines were being drawn.

"Fear is the parent of cruelty."

James Anthony Froude

Chapter 29

"So have you found your bitch yet?" said Gilheart to Prescott, getting more and more disgusted with him by the moment.

They met at a local cafe to discuss the problem and share a coffee.

"No. She's disappeared."

"Well, isn't that nice for you. Tell me Prescott, have you ever heard of a telephone trap?"

"Yes, of course."

"What is it?"

"It records a telephone conversation along with a time/date stamp. Usually used in legal proceedings," rattled off Prescott, knowing already where this was going.

"That's right. And if someone wanted to make sure there was a record of his calls, after all, you never know who might be wanting to sue the school principle, he might tape all his calls. It makes one wonder what the City Council, not to mention the voters, might think of someone who sells his wife to get beaten."

"Don't threaten me, Gilheart. So far, we're on the same side, with the same interest. Don't mess with that equation, or you might find you'll have some pretty impressive problems of your own."

"Oh, I think we're both looking at felonies. How many more 'impressive problems' do you think you have up your sleeve?"

"Look, don't panic. If this 'David Frieling' isn't with the Education Department, and he isn't with me, you have no problems."

"So who is he, then?"

"I don't know yet. But I'm working on it."

"Okay, then let's sum up our situation, shall we? Mia is missing, and you don't know where she is. She has a 'friend,' who you don't know, who isn't above making threatening phone calls and computer hacking. Who obviously knows way too much. Between them both, we're looking at multiple felony counts. How am I doing so far?"

"I think you're blowing it out of proportion. Let's try my version. Mia wrapped some dipshit around her finger, gave him your number and said 'go get em, tiger'. A random computer hacker got into her computer and started screwing with her."

"Do you really believe the bullshit that comes out of your mouth? Or is glib idiocy automatic with lawyers?"

"Well, then how about I offer you a freebie? Call her in to work. Let's she if she comes in. If she does, then we have her where we want her. You just give me a call, and I'll do the rest. We'll find out who's right. I bet I know my wife better than you do."

"I still don't see the freebie in this for me."

"If she comes in to work, do whatever you want with her. Make it hurt. Make it hurt bad. Then hand her over to me. I'll make her hurt even worse."

Mia and Daddy were having breakfast. Daddy, deciding to clog all his arteries with cholesterol, made eggs, home fries, and bacon for breakfast. Of course not being contented with a normal breakfast, the home fries also had onions, jalapeno peppers, and were dripping with Swiss cheese. They sat at the breakfast counter, drinking fresh ground Columbian Supremo coffee.

Mia was wearing another of Daddy's shirts. Daddy could catch occasional glimpses of her breasts and panties, and it was already driving him nuts. Seven a.m. and after having his balls drained once this morning, his erection was starting again. He was looking at her smiling and contemplating whether there was enough room on the breakfast counter for a quickie.

Her cell phone rang and Mia looked at the display.

"It's work. I should get this," she said. She hadn't been to work in almost a week, not that it mattered. There were plenty of substitutes, but she didn't want them to start not calling.

"Hello?"

"Hi Mia, John Gilheart. One of our teachers took sick. I thought I'd see if you're interested." Clipped, no nonsense, professional. No mention or indication of their encounter before.

"What class?"

"She had a light day, but there was also some teacher's conference scheduled later in the afternoon. Are you interested?"

"Yes, what time is the class?"

"Eleven a.m. to four p.m. Miss Harriman's room, 206. Teacher's conference scheduled at five p.m. Go to the gym."

"What about…"

Gilheart clicked off without a goodbye.

"I've got to go in to work," Mia said to Daddy.

"You sure that's wise?"

"I can't hide out here with you for the rest of my life."

"Why not?" Daddy said, smiling. "I was just thinking of my favorite 'over-the-counter' fantasy I wanted to practice."

"That's because you're a pervert Daddy," said Mia, giggling.

"I'm a pervert?" Daddy grabbed her around the waist, and lifted her up on the counter, plates crashing to the floor, and glassware scattering. "Let me show you perversion."

"Daddy!" Mia giggled and struggled to get free, as Daddy easily pinned her arms over her head, and then they slipped around his neck. "You know I want to stay here, Daddy. But I shouldn't."

"It could be dangerous," said Daddy, stroking her face.

"I don't think so. There are always lots of people around. Besides, there was no hint in his voice. He just wanted a substitute to fill his role."

"All the same, you be careful."

"Of course, Daddy. I'm not stupid."

Mia went upstairs to get dressed. Daddy had bought her all new clothes, so she wouldn't have to go back to her house. He could hear giggles upstairs as she tried on one, then the other.

Something doesn't feel right about this whole thing, thought Daddy. He cast his intention out, but nothing came back. *Gilheart would be a fool to try anything after being warned off.*

In Daddy's old world, one warning was all you got. And most of the time, you didn't even get that.

Mia came back downstairs, twirling her dress, modeling it in front of Daddy.

"What do you think?"

"Can I study in your class?"

"No. We don't allow old perverts like you on school property," said Mia, smiling.

"Well then, how about I just sit on a park bench and look up your dress?"

Mia giggled. "I'd let you look up my dress any day, sailor."

"All cruelty springs from weakness."

Lucius Annaeus Seneca

Chapter 30

Mia, luckily, didn't see Gilheart all day.

The kids were being their usual unruly selves with a substitute. Some days, they just loved to learn. Other days, they just loved to burn. She went through her classes thinking about Daddy and what he was doing. She had lunch to herself and sat daydreaming about Daddy. She knew he'd have some surprise waiting for her. She finished grading the papers from the class before in the teacher's lounge. When it was time for the teacher's conference, she walked towards the gym.

The gym was set off from the main building by a little ways and she had to walk down a long hallway to get to it. Her pumps slapped a beat against the tile floor, echoing her progress. She could see the lights of the gym up ahead through the double doors.

As soon as she stepped through the doors, Gilheart came up behind her, put a hand over her mouth, and lifted her off the floor. She knew it was Gilheart instantly by his smell, and she started fighting. With her legs off the floor, she could get no leverage, and couldn't fight back.

Daddy help me, she screamed into her mind.

Gilheart slammed her against the cinder-block wall. His breath was coming in quick bursts, hitting Mia's neck. She tried not to make a face at the smell. It smelled of coffee and bad cheese. He had her pressed up against the wall, his chest pressed to her back. The principal was kissing and licking her neck. It took everything Mia had not to pull away from him.

As he continued sliding his disgusting lips and tongue over her jaw,

Gilheart moved his hands up to Mia's breasts. Roughly he squeezed them through her shirt.

"You know, I normally go for bigger tits, but I guess these will do."

He grabbed her dress and tore it open. Mia heard several buttons fly across the hardwood floor of the gym. Gilheart made grunting noises as he continued to fondle her. She could feel his erection digging into her lower back. Just the thought of that filthy thing had bile rising.

Suddenly, he released her and stepped back.

"Strip."

When Mia hesitated, Gilheart slapped her. The sound of the whack echoed around the empty gym. Mia took a deep breath and turned around to face the pig.

"No."

"You don't do it, I guarantee it will hurt worse."

With no emotion, she robotically obeyed and removed all of her clothing. She watched the repulsive glee spread over his face. Mia then tried to retreat to the steel cage in her mind. She had been beaten and taken against her will so many times that it was usually very easy for her to hide in her mind. For some reason, that wasn't true this time. It was like she had nowhere to go. Mia was in the moment, she was living this all the way.

Gilheart closed the gap between them and grabbed her breasts. He then leaned down and licked a nipple. Mia again got a whiff of his nauseating breath. This time she couldn't stop the grimace on her face. He must have noticed because at that moment he bit the side of Mia's breast, hard. She gasped loudly and tried to pull away, which only made the pain worse.

When he finally took his teeth out of her skin, Mia looked down. His teeth marks were clearly visible.

"Oh, I like that," he sneered.

Gilheart moved over to the other tit and bit the top. Mia cried out as she felt a couple of his teeth break the skin. When he pulled back, she saw small trickles of her blood on his teeth. There was a piece of her breast stuck between them. She wanted to gag. Why did this have to be the one time she couldn't mentally retreat?

"Very nice. I want you to remember our little meeting. Those should do." His eyes were gleaming with sick pride.

Without warning, he turned and bent Mia over. Pressing her

onto her back. Tears were now streaming uncontrollably down her face. Her breasts still throbbed from the bites. Her ass cheeks were on fire, and now her rectum was torn. All this and she was here, in the moment; raw.

Gilheart pulled out of her ass when his orgasm finally stopped. He let go of Mia and stepped back.

"Now, lick my dick clean, cunt. It has your blood and shit on it and I don't want it smelling of your shit."

Mia slowly came up off the wall and started to turn and kneel.

"And don't stop those tears. They make it that much better."

Mia lay on the floor, blood once again, pouring out of her violated ass. Gilheart looked at her in disgust and pulled out his cell phone. He speed-dialed Prescott.

"Your bitch is here. Come get this piece of shit out of my school."

"Wickedness is its own punishment."

Francis Quarles

Chapter 31

Daddy heard Mia's mental cry for help and was out of his chair and moving toward the door.

Wait. Stop. Think. What was going on, he thought. *First, where was she? She had to be at the school. Second, who was he going up against? Gilheart, more than likely. What's the plan?*

He thought he could figure that out as he moved.

He went into the garage and picked up some three-pronged tire spikes he had made earlier. At the time, he didn't know why he made them. They were made to instantly disable a moving car by flattening their tires as soon as they rolled over them.

He looked at his Mossberg 500, a Tactical Pump Shotgun, but decided against it. It was too much firepower. Moreover, things could go south real quick as soon as firearms were introduced. Besides, with Gilheart he didn't think he'd needed it. He knew, without even meeting him, he was going to be a coward. He picked up two rolls of quarters instead and put them in his pocket.

Next, he tested some military issue telescoping combat batons. The slide of their casing was like lightning greased with butter. He put one up each sleeve, and backed his pickup out of the driveway. He was on his way in less than five minutes.

He parked on a side street next to the school, not in the lot, and walked through some woods surrounding the school. He arrived at the parameter of the school and looked at it. Most of the lights were off except in what he assumed was the gym. It had large double doors leading to the football field. He stayed on the edge of the woods completely invisible.

He remembered an acronym from his bad 'ol days. S.T.O.P

Stop.

Think.

Observe.

Plan.

It was time to think, observe and plan.

He contemplated moving closer to the gym and maybe seeing what was inside, but just then a car turned into the parking lot. It was a late model Lexus. It pulled into a space close to the gym door, idled, then shut down with the lights going off.

Daddy heard the door chime going off, then the interior light came on, and a man stepped out of the car.

This must be hubby, Daddy thought. Red rage started growing from the base of his spine, wanting to move up his backbone, but he quashed it down. *This is no time for emotion.*

How does this change the equation? It was now two against one. Daddy, however, had the element of surprise, weapons, and tactical knowledge of attack. He knew perfectly well with those advantages on his side, the odds could be four to one and they still wouldn't stand a chance against him. He didn't feel the slightest pity towards them, nor would he have any mercy.

After all, Gilheart had been warned.

Prescott stepped out of the car, shot his cuffs, adjusted his coat, and started walking towards the gym door unaware he was being tracked from the shadows. As Prescott went towards the school, Daddy moved in the opposite direction, always keeping behind him, out of his line of vision. Prescott tested the door, then walked in.

Daddy jogged towards the Lexus and wedged a number of spikes under his wheels. If this went south and Prescott wanted to give chase, his car wasn't going to be of any help. That done, he stood up, and sprinted towards the school. Planting himself flat against the wall, solid black, in a solid dark shadow.

Daddy chanced a look through the door. He could see Mia, standing between two men. The dress she has been so proud of hours before in tatters, ripped down the front. There was blood leaking down her leg.

Once again, red rage coursed up his spine, blood lust threatened to take over his mind. He pushed it down again. Daddy looked once more and mentally snapped a picture of each man's face, and put it in a safe place to study later.

Now I know what you look like, he thought.

Prescott walked into the gym and studied the scene before him.

"Hi there, Trailer Trash, remember me, your loving husband? You really didn't think you'd be able to go on holiday without me, did you?" Then directing his conversation at Gilheart said,

"How was she? As tight as you remembered?"

"Actually, I think she was getting lazy on vacation and didn't bother doing her Kegle exercises. She's getting a little loose down there."

"Well, if they don't have a strong man around to point them in the right direction, they do get lazy real quick."

"Ain't that the truth."

"Mia, you do look a little worse for wear. Sort of like a homecoming queen after she's been gang-banged by the varsity football team. I know you're having fun at the prom and all, but it's time to go home. Don't worry Mia, there is still lots of fun to go. Wait until you see what's at home waiting for you. A brand new present."

"Do you mind if I come with and watch?" Gilheart said hopefully.

"Sure John, the more the merrier. You can take over when I get tired. Say, John, I've been meaning to ask you, do you offer any advanced courses in anal cattle prods?"

"Funny you should say that. Just this week I was thinking of adding it to the curriculum. I didn't because I figured I should study the subject more first."

"Well, tonight's your lucky night because Mia here has volunteered to advance your education."

"Well, she is very giving in that way. A true educator."

"Let's go, Mia. Time's a wasting," said Prescott.

Daddy stood flat against the wall. A solid black form in a dark shadow. The gym door opened and he could see Prescott leading the way, with Mia in between, followed by Gilheart bringing up the rear.

They never saw him coming, and they never had a chance.

As soon as the door closed, Daddy stepped behind Gilheart swinging his body in a complete 360-degree turn, snapping the baton out at the last second and catching Gilheart in back of the kneecap. The centrifugal force of the blow was so great it forced his kneecap out the front side of his leg, crippling him for life. Still moving in the same circle, he brought the pointed tip of other baton handle down right at the edge of his face where the eye socket meets the temple. The force of that blow caved in his temple and extruded the eyeball out of his head. It fell on his cheek, dangling at the end of the optic nerve.

Daddy completed the spin, then started another. Prescott heard the crack of bone and sensed something was wrong. He turned back to see what the problem was. Daddy, this time stepped over Gilheart and in front of Mia, dropping the baton. He grabbed Prescott just under the chin, where his jaw meets his face, his fingers like talons digging into the soft area at the base of the jaw, ripped his head viciously around in a circle. Prescott was unconscious before he hit the pavement. Both men were down in less than two seconds.

Mia didn't know what happened. All she saw was a swirling black shape and then both men crumpled at her feet.

"Come on, Baby Doll, we can send get-well cards later," said Daddy, taking her hand and running for the woods to his pickup.

The pain hit Gilheart just then, and he started screaming, holding his hands to his face.

"Pray that your loneliness may spur you into finding something to
live for, great enough to die for."

Dag Hammarskjold

Chapter 32

Once they got to Daddy's truck, he put a blanket around Mia, and
helped her into the truck.

"Daddy?"

"Shush, Baby Doll, don't talk."

Mia stayed quiet and Daddy drove her back to the house in silence.

"Come on, let's go inside. Careful, now."

Daddy led Mia into the house and upstairs to the bathroom. He
started the bath.

"Baby, I'm going to have to do things now. They aren't pleasant,
but I have to do them even so."

"What kinds of things, Daddy?"

"I have to collect evidence."

"Are we going to the police?"

"They won't help."

"Then why collect evidence?"

"Just in case."

"In case of what, Daddy?"

"Mia? Please be quiet and let me take care of you, okay?"

Mia stayed quiet and Daddy worked silently, completely focused on
what he was doing.

First, he took pictures. He took photos of the bite marks on her
breasts from many different angles. He took full-frontal pictures of her
and another from the back. He took more photographs of her from
each side with her arms raised. He then photographed the bruising on

the inside of her thighs.

"Baby Doll? I know this sucks, but I have to do more. I need to photograph the damage around your ass. I need you to bend over."

"Daddy, is this necessary?"

"Yes! Don't play with me right now, Mia. I'm in no mood for games."

Mia had never heard anger in Daddy's voice before. She had been around angry men her entire life, but she had never heard anger so deep-seated and full of latent violence.

"Okay Daddy, I didn't mean to make you angry."

"You didn't, Baby Doll." His regular voice was back. Soft and patient.

Mia bent over and Daddy quietly reset the flash and took multiple photos of the injury to her ass.

"Okay, that part is done. Now, I have to take trace evidence."

"What does that mean?"

"I have to collect saliva and sperm."

"Jesus Christ Daddy! Do we have to?"

"Yes, we do. I'm doing this to protect you. Turn off the water, please."

He swabbed her breast bite with a Q-Tip then put the Q-Tip in a plastic baggy. He also swabbed her vagina and anus, and put them in separate baggies, labeled, and dated them. He then put them side by side, and photographed them. He left then and came back a short while later with all the photos printed out. He took all the trace evidence and photos, put them in a manila envelope, dated it with the time, and sealed it with candle wax so the envelope couldn't be tampered with.

"Okay, all done. Now the last part. This part is the most unpleasant. I have to clean your wounds now. It's going to hurt."

"Daddy? What did you do to them back there?"

"Only what they had coming."

"Mr. Gilheart had his eye laying on his cheek."

"Yes, he did. Do you feel sorry for him?"

Mia thought for a moment. "No."

"Good. He is a miserable excuse for a human being."

"Did you kill my husband?"

"No, I don't think so. Not because I didn't want to. I couldn't get my grip right. He got off lucky this time."

"Where did you learn how to do that stuff?"

"Did anyone ever tell you, you talk too much?" Daddy said, but he had a smile. "Hold on Baby, this is going to hurt."

"I can handle pain, Daddy."

He used hydrogen peroxide and cleaned and disinfected her cuts. He bandaged them and then sat back.

"Okay, that's the easy part. I'm going to tell you what's coming next so I don't shock you. Before you ask, yes, it is necessary. I'm not doing any of this because I'm having fun."

"Okay, Daddy."

"I'm going to have to douche you with a disinfectant, to make sure he didn't leave any germs behind. It's probably not going to be pleasant."

"I can do that, Daddy. You don't have…."

"I'm not finished."

"Oh."

"Then I'm going to have to give you an enema with the same disinfectant. I've got to make sure your gastric tract is completely clean. I can see the tearing. That means there's a good possibility of infection. It's going to hurt. I do have some painkillers, though. I can deaden the pain."

"Oh no, Daddy! You go too far!"

"Either I can do it, or you're going to the hospital, and a stranger can do it. One way or another, it's in your future."

Mia started weeping. "Do I have to?"

Daddy got down on his knees, and pushed his finger beneath her chin until Mia was looking right into his eyes.

"You have nothing you need to hide from me, and nothing you need to be ashamed of. Do you understand me? I never should have let you go to school today. You are my responsibility, and I let you down. I'm going to make it right. But first, I have to take care of you. So let's just get this over with."

After he was finished, he eased Mia down in the bath, poured some Epsom salt into the water and told her to soak. She was mentally, emotionally, and physically wiped out by her ordeal and didn't put up a fight. She winced as the salt hit her wounds, then sank into the healing hot water. Daddy stayed outside the tub, pouring hot water over her shoulders, and gently washing her hair.

"Come, Baby Doll, it's time for bed."

"It's warm Daddy. I don't want to leave the bath."

"I know, but the bed's warm too. You're safe."

He stood her up and dried her off, then carried her to the bed. He wrapped her up in the comforter and went downstairs to his study. He stared at the walls in silence, trying to connect the dots.

He looked at the sign over his desk, "*Face your fear and just do it.*"

He took the pictures of Gilheart and Prescott out from the photo album in his mind and examined their faces. Gilheart wasn't going to be any trouble for a while. But he would still keep tabs on him just in case.

Prescott however, was another story. He had a bad feeling about this journey then. He looked at the feeling, tasted it, and decided he didn't care. He was tired of this life anyway. But he didn't want to leave Mia or his son behind.

A random lyric came to his head from Rock and Roll's early years:

The New York Times said God is dead
And the war's begun...

Part Two
Mia

"Intense love does not measure, it just gives."

Mother Teresa

"I felt like the news business was a little rough for me and a little sleazy. So I glided right over into acting."

Emily Procter

Chapter 33

"Coming up at eleven, prominent city attorney and school principal brutally beaten outside Waterloo Elementary School. Film at eleven…"

Daddy and Mia were sitting in the living room. Mia had woken up, and not seeing Daddy in bed with her had come downstairs. She was still sore and it hurt to walk. Daddy was sitting on the couch by himself, clicking through the channels.

Mia came into the living room silently, shrugged her way into his arms, and curled up next to him dragging her blanket around them.

"Hi, Baby. You should be upstairs asleep."

"Then you come upstairs too, Daddy. I want to sleep with you."

"In a while. I want to see what the news has to say."

"Thanks, Dan…" The news anchor was a pretty blond woman with over sprayed hair and sporting a serious expression. She was standing in front of a fire department ambulance amid sweeping blue police lights. "We're live outside Waterloo Elementary School where a brutal beating took place earlier tonight. Police aren't releasing many details, but this is what we've gathered so far.

"A prominent city attorney and the school principal here were working late on a project for disadvantaged children. When they left they were brutally attacked by a gang that left one in critical condition. We have also learned…"

"What! Daddy that is such bullshit! They are lying. They are…"

"Be quiet, Baby. Just listen…"

"Cassandra…can you tell us who was attacked?" This coming from back in the newsroom, the camera went to split screen, and an equally serious male anchor with his hand to his ear, was acting as though his opinion actually mattered.

"Dan, details are sketchy at this time. However, Jeffery Prescott, one of the victims, has agreed to talk with us."

The camera angle shifted, widened, and Prescott was sitting in the ambulance in a white neck brace.

"Mr. Prescott, what can you tell us?"

"Well, John and I came here tonight for the 'Children Without Hunger' campaign, a cause we both believe in and are very active in. We came out after we finished and were immediately attacked by some vicious thugs. They must have been laying in wait for us to leave. John, that is, Mr. Gilheart, suffered serious injuries. My heart goes out to his family. I just hope the police catch who was responsible."

"Thank you, Mr. Prescott, and I just want to say…"

The anchorwomen droned on.

"That is such complete and total bullshit, Daddy! That makes me so mad. They were raping and beating me! They sit there and make it sound like they are humanitarians?" Mia was almost shouting.

"Calm down, Baby Doll. So what do you want to do about it?"

"Can you stop them?"

"Why would I want to do that?"

"They are lying about you. About us."

"So? We have physical evidence of your attack. We can prove Gilheart attacked you with his DNA. We cannot prove your husband had anything to do with it. Do you want to go in front of that camera and tell the world your side of the story?"

"Well, no…"

"Okay then. I'll ask again, why do we want to do that? What will it change?"

"It will make me feel better."

"Yes, but it won't solve your problem."

Mia was quiet and folded herself into Daddy's warmth.

"What do you think we should do about it?"

"Beat them at their own game," said Daddy, quietly.

Much later.

"Daddy? I'm never going home am I?"

"That's right. Your life with Prescott is over."

"How can that be? You can't just say 'Your life with Prescott is over,' and Poof! It's gone."

"Why not?"

"Because I'm legally married to him. He owns me."

"He doesn't 'own' you. People get divorced all the time. Didn't someone just say 'You're married' and Poof! You were married?"

"But that was legal."

"Who says it was? Just because the government gave you a marriage license makes it real?"

"Well, yeah, Daddy. Duh!"

"It takes more than a marriage license to make a marriage real. The government doesn't sleep in your bed. The government didn't get beat up every night. Who are they to say what happens in either place? If they are going to grant the license, they should share in the responsibility of their decision. But they don't. If you make a decision, you are responsible for it. If they make the same decision, they aren't, and suffer no ill effects from it."

"So what are you trying to say?"

"I'm saying learn to take responsibility for your own decisions and don't give ANYONE the power to make that decision for you. If you want to be divorced from Prescott, then take responsibility and go get a divorce. No one will do it for you. The government won't help you. But yes, you can just say 'I'm divorced' and Poof! you'll be divorced. It is in your mind only. The same as the marriage was. The government is just acting more powerful than it actually is."

"You are very strange, Daddy."

"I know."

Silence. The clock chimes the hours, and they slip past. No words were spoken. Daddy thought Mia had finally fallen asleep until she said,

"You're right Daddy. No one can tell me who to love, or who to give my body to. I want a divorce!"

"That's my Baby," said Daddy smiling.

"Daddy? I don't want you to suffer because of me. None of this is your fault. You're getting dragged into something you had no part of."

"Daddy's a big boy. He can also make his own decisions."

"My husband will kill you, you know, if he finds you."

"I know."

"You don't care?"

"It's not that I don't care, but this isn't my first rodeo."

"What are you going to do?"

"I'm going to help you. That's all. I'll let the rest work itself out."

"You'd really do that for me, wouldn't you? You don't even know me. But you'd die for me."

"Well, it's a big step from helping you to dying. Let's just take it one small step at a time."

"Daddy?"

"Baby, you're tired. You're still in shock. You should be sleeping." He started to lightly stroke her hair.

"I will, Daddy but I need to ask you something first."

"Shoot."

"Why are you helping me? You know this shit storm is mine, not yours."

"You are mine now, which means that any storm you have to weather, I have to weather. I wouldn't have it any other way."

Slow tears started to drip from Mia's eyes. How could she deserve anyone this good? Why would he want such a damaged girl? She started to cry harder.

Daddy stopped stroking Mia's head and pulled her up onto his lap. "Don't cry. I will make this better. Everything is going to be all right." He left a trail of soft kisses over her head and cheek, taking some of her tears.

"Daddy, you would be better off without me, you know."

"Never say that or think that. You have given me more than you will ever know. Now go to sleep. Daddy will be here."

"Disease is an experience of a so-called mortal mind. It is fear made manifest on the body."

Mary Baker Eddy

Chapter 34

Prescott was sitting up in his hospital bed when Flynn walked in.

"Gee Prescott, I bet that neck brace makes it hard to tie a bow tie on your tux when dressing for your charity fund raisers, like 'Children Without Hunger.'"

"Fuck you, Flynn. I'm not in the mood. What do I owe the displeasure?"

"Well, you know me, always nosy. That was quite the crime scene last night. I caught you on the news too. It was a real tearjerker."

"Now all you need to do is catch those bastards, and you'll be earning your tax dollars."

"What makes you think it was plural?"

"Huh?"

"You said, 'bastards,' plural form of 'bastard.' Didn't they teach you English grammar at that prep school you went to?"

"Well, there had to be at least two, maybe three."

"What makes you think so? Did you see that many?"

"I didn't see anything but black."

Flynn stood looking at Prescott. He shifted his six foot four frame, and adjusted his utility belt. Prescott looked at his service automatic.

"Is that the Glock 17 I gave you when you passed the Sergeant's exam?" Prescott asked.

"Yes, it is. That's right, Prescott, we go back. I wouldn't have made it through the law classes without you. I know that. I'm a beat cop. A flat foot. I don't have your connections. I know I owe you. You don't have to rub it in."

"I was doing nothing of the kind. I was just..."

"What's this?" Flynn threw one of the tire spikes on the bed next to him.

"I have absolutely no idea."

"It's a tire spike. They're used to disable cars and make it impossible to give chase. I found four of them under the wheels of your car."

"I don't understand what that means."

"Why don't you tell me about the pool of blood I found inside the gym?"

"Once again, I don't know what you mean."

"That's strange. I found your footprint in it. Well, you were attacked outside, right?"

"That's right, as soon as we left the building."

"Then why was blood found INSIDE the gym? Pooled on the floor as well as on the wall?"

"I don't know, maybe..."

"Look, Prescott, you stupid shit. Follow the bouncing ball, Okay? Are you up to that in your delicate condition? One, you had your tires spiked. That was a contingency plan. Two, I found footprints over by the tree line where someone had been waiting. That means someone was expecting you, or watching you. Three, there was unknown blood found, away and removed, from the crime scene. Four, gang bangers don't use homemade tire spikes. Five, gang bangers don't recon their targets. Are you following me?"

"Flynn, you lost me around number one."

"You weren't attacked by gang bangers. You were attacked by a professional, or professionals. Which leaves us with the question, just what the fuck are you into? Is this about your wife?"

Prescott was saved from answering that question when both his parents walked in. Elder Prescott looked Sergeant Flynn up and down like the cheese smelled bad.

"Sergeant Flynn. It's very good to see you. I hope you're here to tell us you've caught Jeffery's attackers."

"Mr. Prescott, good to see you too. We're hot on their tail, with Jeffery's help." He added sarcastically, with enough venom so that only Junior Prescott would feel the sting.

"Jeffery! What have those hooligans done to you!" Momma Prescott came rushing to her son's bedside.

Elder Prescott stepped aside, to let his wife in, so she could suffocate the occasion.

"Sergeant Flynn was just leaving Dad. He's got enough information to go on now, I think."

"Jeffery, I knew working late at night in those dangerous places, this was going to happen. I told you so, didn't I?"

"It was an elementary school, Mom. It doesn't get much less dangerous than that."

"Well, you say that now…"

"Sergeant Flynn, could I have a word with you?" This coming from Elder Prescott, grabbing Flynn's elbow and steering him out of earshot.

"Can you tell me what happened?"

"He got attacked by a pro. He's lucky. He should be dead is my guess."

"I see. Have you made any inroads on finding his wife?"

"I didn't know I was looking for his wife, Sir. Has she gone missing?" Flynn said, all innocence.

"I think you might want to concentrate your investigation in that direction."

"Thanks for the tip." Flynn pulled out his cell phone and speed-dialed.

"Sally? Why don't we blood type the blood we found at Waterloo Elementary with Mrs. Mia Prescott's and see if we can get a match? Could you do that and get back to me? Thanks."

"Was that actually necessary, Officer Flynn?"

"I think it was, yes. Just trying to do my job as a public servant," Flynn said, looking Elder Prescott dead in the eye, disliking his phony upper crust accent.

The private hospital room was starting to get pretty cramped when the doctor walked in, squeezing past the men.

"You're a lucky man, Mr. Prescott," the Doctor said.

"How so?"

"Am I free to talk around everyone present? HIPPA requirements and all, state that I have to ask."

"Get on with it." The Elder Prescott waved the formality away with his hand.

The doctor ignored him, and directed the question at Jeffery.

"Yes, of course, go ahead."

"X-rays reveal mild concussion from when your head hit the pavement. I wouldn't expect any problems from that unless you start vomiting. Your neck muscles have been sprained on the right side and there is a laceration under your jaw. Basically, you've got a scratch and whiplash. You'll be wearing the neck brace for a while, but other than that, I'll discharge you today."

"I can go now?"

"I don't see why not," answered the Doctor.

His mother was already pulling his clothes out of the closet, and laying them out.

"Well, you'll just have to come back to the manor…"

"Thank you, Doctor."

True to his word, within minutes an orderly and a wheelchair showed up to take Prescott downstairs and back out into the cold, cruel world. Prescott got seated and the orderly put his feet up on the platforms, then moved behind to grab onto the handles in back of the chair.

"I'll take it," said Flynn, and started pushing Prescott, who was feeling like an invalid and an idiot, out into the hallway.

Flynn stopped halfway down the hall. "What about Gilheart?"

"Fuck em," Prescott said. "He's no use to anyone anymore."

"It is not death or pain that is to be dreaded,
but the fear of pain or death."

Epictetus

Chapter 35

The Doctor continued walking down the hall, checking a door chart, here and there, making his rounds.

The Doctor came to Gilheart's room in the orthopedic ward and pushed through the door. There were no "get-well" cards on the window sill, no flowers on the table. *This is a man who had no one who cared,* thought the Doctor.

"Mr. Gilheart, my name is Dr. Peters. I'll be responsible for your recovery. Has anyone informed you of the extent of your injuries yet?"

Gilheart was lying flat on his back. His leg was encased in plaster from toes to groin and suspended in the air with ropes and pulleys. There was a metal brace around his knee with four long screws going into the plaster helping to maintain immobility of the kneecap. His head was also wrapped with bandages with the left side completely covered down to his nose. He had a stainless steel trapeze handle to pull himself up with. Only his right eye tracked Dr. Peters' movement.

"I've been told some, nothing substantial," Gilheart said.

"I don't need to tell you your injuries are grave. The good news is, you only suffered minor brain damage when your skull was crushed. We were able to get all the shards of bone from your brain. You will probably suffer some memory loss.

"We were able to replace your kneecap with a synthetic. You're looking at a year getting your leg working, then several years of re-habilitation to ever walk again. In fact, you may never walk again, at least with the use of that leg.

"The bad news is, your eye is another story. We couldn't save it. I'm sorry Mr. Gilheart, you're going to be blind in that eye for the rest of your life."

Gilheart took this news without emotion. He had a morphine self-medicator, and the only sign of emotion was his thumb pushing the red button.

"So what happens, now?" Gilheart asked.

"You're going to get used to hospital food, I'm afraid. You're going to be in here for a while. We'll continually monitor your brain function to make sure there is no swelling, as well as your kneecap as you recover to make sure it heals properly in place."

"What if it doesn't?"

"Then a team of surgeons we have on call is going to go in and make sure it does."

"I'm fucked, aren't I, Doc?"

"Well, I wouldn't go so far as to…"

"Don't sugar-coat. I'm fucked, aren't I?"

"Yeah, pretty much," the doctor sighed.

The doctor left and Gilheart remained on his back staring up at the ceiling. A watermark from the floor above spiraled itself into the face of Christ, or at least so he thought from the morphine induced haze. He was still trying to put the pieces together in his mind of the attack. He didn't remember the attack at all and had been no help to the police investigators.

Prescott…the name seemed to have significance. Then out of the drug fog came the huge bow of the Good Ship Memory. Mia Prescott! He had been raping Mia Prescott right before the attack. He could see it in his mind. He could see the blood leaking down her leg from his phantom eye, or maybe it was his mind's eye, or possibly they were the same now.

He smiled at the memory. Maybe Jeffery Prescott attacked him. He wouldn't put it past the slimy little shit. Or at the very least arranged it. He remembered Prescott saying, what was it, yesterday morning? That he could have some "impressive problems of his own" if Gilheart didn't play ball. This certainly qualified as an impressive problem.

The morphine fog was closing in. He knew he was going to be out soon, but he wanted to hang on to this thought, it seemed important.

Now he remembered. Mia Prescott was Jeffery Prescott's wife. Jeffery Prescott pimped his wife to him.

And he had a recording of the conversation.

With that, the Good Ship Memory went bow down into the black waters of his mind, and sank beneath the waves of consciousness.

"You were born to win, but to be a winner, you must plan to win, prepare to win, and expect to win."

Zig Ziglar

Chapter 36

Let's start off with what we know, thought Daddy, trying to put the pieces together and connect the various dots.

We know Prescott is probably psychotic. Could that be used as an advantage? We know that either the need to control Mia, or some other external factor is fueling his desire to find her. We know he has money, power, privilege, and connections as his advantages. We know that...

"Hi Daddy, what are you doing in here all by yourself?" Mia said, poking her head in through the door of his study.

"Just thinking."

"You spend a lot of time thinking. Let's have some fun. I was thinking today I could be Nurse Naughty and you could be Dr. McNasty." Mia opened the door wider, and Daddy could see she was wearing a see-through nurse's outfit. She was smiling wickedly, tapping a large vibrator in her palm.

Daddy smiled. "I think Dr. McNasty could come up with a few places to put that."

"Oh no, this is Nurse Naughty's toy. You go find your own."

"I think Nurse Naughty has been dipping into the pharmaceutical supply cabinet once too often if she thinks she has a 'medical procedure' for Dr. McNasty with that toy."

"Oh, come on, Daddy, it will be fun."

"Oh, it will, will it? Since it will be so much fun, I think I'll use it first on Nurse Naughty."

"You are absolutely no fun, Daddy." She harrumphed, then a pout, next she stuck out her tongue, a head toss, and then she disappeared.

Daddy went back to his thought process.

We know that Gilheart and Prescott were working together. Was that by accident, or plan?

OK, what are my advantages? They don't know who I am…yet. They don't know where Mia is. They are looking in the wrong direction, so far, looking for gang bangers. But most of all, they aren't trained in this world. Don't fool yourself. They can hire trained operatives if push came to shove. Lastly, we can use the DNA advantage against them and flush them out.

OK, then. What's the plan?

We now have the tactical advantage. So we push that advantage. First, create a plan for divorce and be the first to file and pollute the legal proceeding in Mia's favor.

Next, go after Gilheart and completely destroy him, in order to put pressure on Prescott to cave in on the divorce, and agree to our terms.

OK, you've got a plan. So now, what could go wrong…?

"All right Daddy, how about this?" Mia was standing in the doorway in her "Baby Doll" outfit. Pig tails, white knee socks, and short, oh so very short, plaid school uniform skirt.

"Well, that is one of my favorites…Come here, you."

Mia giggled and jumped into Daddy's lap.

"You aren't healed yet. It's too soon for fun and games," Daddy said softly.

"Those painkillers you have are pretty good. I don't feel a thing."

"No kidding? Yeah, I can tell," Daddy said, dryly. "It's just masking the pain. The damage is still there, and it hasn't healed. No more sex games for you, at least involving your vagina or ass, for a couple of weeks."

"Daddy! That's way too long. What are you going to do? You'll be sniffing after every pussy on the block. Oh, no. No way. I can still take care of you with my mouth then."

"I won't refuse, Baby Doll," said Daddy smiling.

"Then come to bed, I'll take care of you now."

"Later, as soon as I finish."

"But Daddy, you're not doing anything. You're just sitting there."

Daddy gave her a look that said 'don't mess with me,' she sighed, then she jumped out of his lap, tossing her hair as she left, and vanished.

OK, where was I?

Oh yeah, what are the problems I can see that I can plan for? Gilheart is out of commission. He is a sitting duck. No problems there. I would be surprised if Prescott was hurt that badly. Probably his pride was hurt more than anything else. Don't underestimate the pride of a wounded psychotic.

What is his next move? What would I do?

I would pull out all the stops and try to find out who I am, in his position. He can't make a move until he knows who he is dealing with.

Okay, let's follow that line of thought.

HOW is he going to do that?

He's probably got police on his payroll. His law office has investigators. Which means it is only a matter of time until they figure it out.

What happens when he figures it out?

He'll come at me with everything he's got. Not only to get Mia back, but to destroy me. Or, he'll try to kill us both.

Are we safe here?

Only for the time being. Which means we need a safe house, or an alternate fall back location, not in my name or Mia's.

Is it possible I've completely underestimated Prescott, and he has forces far greater than I'm expecting?

Anything is possible. Even so, he does have a powerful family who may not want their little boy to go down in flames.

Is that an advantage that can be used, or a disadvantage?

It depends on how dirty they are.

What are the unknowns involved?

One, who is working with Prescott?

Two, how close are they to finding out who I am?

Three, how quickly before they do, and the shit hits the fan?

OK, what is the plan of attack?

One, find a safe location.

Two, get the divorce proceedings in motion.

Three, go after Gilheart and destroy him.

Four, flush Prescott out and get him to back off Mia forever or if that doesn't work, destroy him as well.

Five, hope like hell I've covered everything and not overlooked something obvious.

"It was a wealthy family, and they heard me talk about movies, and they told me I should go into movies. That's the benefit of hanging out with rich people; they have no sense of what is or isn't possible."

Michael Patrick Jann

Chapter 37

Flynn and Prescott were seated at Prescott's home, looking at each other and saying nothing.

Prescott had his neck brace on and found turning his head painful. Flynn still had his uniform on and found looking at Prescott painful, for different reasons.

"So what do we know?" Prescott asked.

"'We,' and I'm using the term loosely, know nothing. How did this become a 'we' situation? I think you're using the wrong pronoun. So let me rephrase. *YOU* know nothing."

"I need you to find some information for me."

"I need you to come clean about what you're into."

"Look, I knocked Mia around a little, OK?"

"That blood in the gym wasn't a bloody nose. The lab found fecal matter in it. Which suggests anal rape, vicious enough to injure."

"Well, Gilheart may have gotten carried away."

"Oh, I see. Now it's Gilheart?"

"Look, I don't see what this has to do with the guy we're looking for," Prescott said, pissed off that he was getting backed into a verbal corner by a cop. Who was the lawyer here?

"It has everything to do with it. I want to know what I'm getting myself into. I might owe you Prescott, but I don't owe you my life, or my career."

"Okay, here's the situation. Mia and I like rough sex, okay? And it got a little carried away. She got scared, and she split. I got Gilheart, her boss, to call her in to work so we could talk. Gilheart must have gotten carried away too. Are you satisfied?"

Flynn laughed without the slightest bit of humor.

"Not even remotely. Sounds like a whole lot of people getting carried away beating on little 'ol Mia, to me."

"Can you help, or not? I can make it worth your while."

"Here's what I can tell you. This guy got in, and got out, without a trace. He left nothing behind. He took both of you out like warm butter. He set it up, so even if he failed, you still wouldn't have caught him. While I know you like to pride yourself on beating up little girls and being the Great White Hunter, in this situation, you are the game. You are the mouse to his cat. It is YOU being hunted. And I personally, don't want this guy hunting me. So you're going to have to do a whole lot better than 'I can make it worth your while.'"

Flynn continued, "Have you looked at this from his point of view, yet? He didn't go looking for this fight. You brought it to him. He's just trying to protect his woman from getting raped and beaten. So what happens? He warns you off, via Gilheart, and what do you do? You give her to Gilheart to get raped and beaten some more. So tell me, Prescott, you fuckin' Einstein, does that sound like a smart move on your part given the circumstances?"

Prescott sighed. Flynn did have a point. Not that it mattered any.

"Yeah, well, all that's water under the bridge now. Besides, Mia isn't his woman to protect."

"Oh, right. She's just your woman to rape and beat as you please. There goes Einstein talking again. $E=MC^2$, uh, buddy?"

Both men looked at each other. Prescott knew he was going to have to show his father some progress. He still hadn't dealt with the planning board. He hadn't been to work in days. So far, the office was covering for him, but that wouldn't last long.

"What would happen if I put out a missing person report on Mia?"

"The city would look for her. We would check the hospitals and the morgue. If she is spotted on a city street, she might be detained and questioned. If she says she left of her own freewill, then that's it. She'll be released. It's not against the law to get away from an abusive asshole. But if she is injured, I doubt that she's out looking for a new pair of shoes. She's holed up. Her mystery guy is keeping her low.

Which would make finding her next to impossible."

"Well then, Officer Flynn, I guess it's time I filed a missing person's report. Tell me, Flynn, if we catch this guy can we have him charged with kidnapping?"

"Not if Mia says she went willingly."

"Let me worry about Mia. You worry about setting this guy up with evidence suggesting abduction and forcible rape. Can you do that?"

"If this plan of yours goes to shit, don't expect me to carry your water. You're on your own. I don't like this, Prescott. I'm not your very own personal dirty cop."

"Also, do you have anyone who's good with computers?"

At that same moment, Mia and Daddy were across town, sitting in Daddy's kitchen. Daddy took his time, grinding the coffee beans just right. Not too fine, not too coarse. He added some salt to the beans as well as some semi-sweet chocolate shavings, which would melt, then drip down through the coffee, smoothing the acidic taste of the coffee beans.

Mia watched him. Daddy was always so focused on whatever he was doing. He didn't just 'make' coffee. It was a painstaking and elaborate ritual, he carefully carried out. He did it just right, every single time. It fascinated her, but she didn't understand it. Why not pour hot water over the beans and be done with it?

"You're weird sometimes, Daddy."

He looked up at her. "I know."

"Why not just use instant coffee? It's a lot quicker."

Daddy looked like she slapped him. "Instant coffee? Tell me you just didn't say 'instant coffee' in my kitchen. Now look what you've done. My coffee beans are crying."

Mia rolled her eyes.

"I need you to tell me everything you can think of about your husband. I need to know everything. Where he works, where he eats for lunch, his friends, his TV shows, magazines he reads, where he works out, everything."

"Why do you need to know all that?"

"Just because I'm nosy. Start talking." Daddy took out a notebook and started making notes while the coffee brewed. Two hours later, after multiple cups of coffee and asking every question he could think of, and Mia getting surly, he had enough information to begin.

"Here's the first thing I want you to do. I'm going out today and I'll probably be gone all day. I want you to stay here and don't open the door for anyone. Just pretend no one is home if the doorbell rings. Sleep, read, watch TV, do whatever you want, but don't go out. Don't answer the phone. Okay?"

"Okay."

Daddy went downstairs to his office, spun the lock on one of his safes, and chose an ID from the dozen or so he had stashed there. He emptied his wallet of anything that could identify him, and added the fresh ID instead. "James Peniwinkle" the new driver's license said. He thought that name had a certain, non-threatening sound which was perfect for what he wanted to do today. Landlords like non-threatening types. He also chose some distinctive eyeglasses with clear lenses, which would call attention to themselves and not his face.

I look like Elton John, he thought, *or Bono.* He next helped himself to some cash.

Next, he went to the garage and changed the plates on his truck to match the ID. This would pass any cursory, roadside inspection by law enforcement, but not an in-depth one, so he better not get hauled in.

He kissed Mia on the head as he headed out the door.

"To my real estate agent, Chernobyl is a fixer-upper."

Yakov Smirnoff

Chapter 38

Daddy was looking for a certain kind of landlord. One that was more concerned with cash, than credentials.

He chose to start his search on the South side of town. These were mostly working-class neighborhoods with a steady transient population. He checked the Internet listings and came up with about a dozen which looked good. He called them, introduced himself as James Peniwinkle, put on an unassuming, 'I'm afraid of my own shadow' tone into his voice and made appointments.

A couple of them were large apartment complexes, which might work if nothing else panned out, but it wasn't what he was looking for. He was looking for a landlord who owned a few units as rental income. One who was more concerned with making his bank payments and getting tenants renting rather than checking ID's and signing hundreds of disclaimers.

He found one on the sixth try. It had its own driveway and covered entrance. He could drive in and not be seen until he drove back out again.

The landlord met him at the door with a handful of keys on a ring. He took a moment to size up his would-be tenant, and he wasn't very impressed. The guy had a threadbare overcoat on and ridiculous glasses. He looked like a broke cheapskate who didn't realize Liberace had died. None of the keys seemed to work in the lock in front of him. So instead the landlord kept up a steady patter of conversation which was designed to put him at ease, but in reality was probing questions about his character. Daddy, of course, acted too stupid to guess this tricky maneuver.

"So do you work around here, Mr. Peniwinkle, did I say your name right?"

"You certainly did, sir. Yes, I work over at Wells Fargo as an accountant." Daddy honked his nose into a well-used handkerchief he had just bought at Goodwill.

"Well, that's a very good job. A lot of my tenants haven't been that lucky, you know, the economy and all."

"Well, you keep your eyes down and your nose to the grindstone, I always say. It's worked for me."

"Ah! Here we go." The door finally opened. Daddy could see the door had been forced open at some point in its recent history, probably with a crowbar. "As you can see, it's a one bedroom, heat and hot water included. You even have your own thermostat."

"Well, that does make a difference," Daddy added helpfully, pushing his glasses up his nose.

"Are you married, Mr. Peniwinkle?"

"Oh, call me James. Well, I have a couple of friends I see from time to time. And they do stay over occasionally. Is that a problem?"

"I'd say it might be a bigger problem if they didn't," the landlord winked conspiratorially, as though it was a secret just between us guys.

Which means he's probably gay, thought the landlord.

"It has a large living room and a big kitchen, as you can see. I replaced the appliances last year so you shouldn't have any problems with them. The bathroom and bedroom are here. When were you thinking about moving in James?" They were old buddies on a first-name basis now. The sudden friendship warmed Daddy's heart.

Okay, we got past the suspicion and were now talking money. Good, thought Daddy.

"Well, I have to be out of where I'm at the first of the month. Of course, I'd be willing to give you first, last, and a security deposit now if I'm going to take it."

"Well, do you see any reason why you wouldn't want to?" The landlord was starting to see his fish slip away. He moved into used car salesmen mode to nip that idea in the bud. "I can negotiate on the rent if you want."

"Oh no, that won't be necessary. I think it's more than fair." Time to close the deal, and land this kahuna into the boat. "I'll tell you what. I don't have a lot of time. I'm on my lunch break and all. But what do you say I give you first, last, and a security deposit and then three months rent in advance. I like being out ahead of my bills. I have cash, of course."

The landlord was floored. His lucky day. Cash, no less, no taxes. "I can certainly understand that, you being an accountant and all." The sound of ass sucking was loud and clear now. "I'll tell you what. If you want to sign the papers right now we can dispense with all the rigmarole. I think you're an honest guy, and I'll just hand you the keys now."

"I was hoping you'd say that, because I really need to get back to work," said Daddy as he pulled out a wad of cash and blew his nose into the handkerchief again.

"Why do you need a computer hacker," asked Flynn, back out at Prescott's house.

"Well, he hacked into Mia's computer, remember? Can't you guys do a back trace or something like that to the point of origination?"

"You've been watching too many Bruce Willis movies. Technically speaking, yes it can be done. Practically speaking, you're going to spend a bundle and the computer Gods would need to be smiling."

"Can you do it or not?"

"I can give you a number. After that, you're on your own. I don't want to be your go-between, or know anything."

"How soon can you get it?"

Flynn scrolled through his cell phone, pulled out his notebook and wrote down a number.

"Is that soon enough for you?"

Prescott picked up the number and was dialing. Flynn just sighed.

"Hi. My name is Jeffery Prescott, and I got your name from Sergeant Flynn at the Urbandale PD? I was wondering if you were available for a little freelance work?"

Prescott listened in the earpiece for a minute or so, then said,

"Excellent. If you can meet me over at my house, I'll give you the address. I can tell you what I want done."

Flynn could hear an indistinct buzz over Prescott's cell phone.

"Well, then let me give you the address, and…"

"Courage and conviction are powerful weapons against an enemy who depends only on fists or guns. Animals know when you are afraid; a coward knows when you are not."

David Seabury

Chapter 39

Daddy returned home after finding the new apartment and found Mia watching TV.

"Hi Daddy."
"Hi Baby."
"Did you do what you wanted to do?"
"Yes, I did. Did anyone come by the house?"
"No, everything was quiet. What did you do?"
"I got us a new apartment, in case we needed it."
"Are we going to need one?"
"I don't know. I still have more to do and need some time to think."
"Okay."

Daddy went to his study, emptied his ID out of his wallet and put it back into the safe. *Now, for the next part of this plan,* thought Daddy, sitting down in the chair.

I need to get into the hospital and get some of Gilheart's DNA. Hospitals are open and active twenty-four hours a day. The easiest way to move around a busy hospital is either as a patient, or as a doctor or staff. Doctors and staff however, have to wear ID. Patients don't. Daddy sat back and considered his options. He could make an ID if he had something to copy. Then, he had another idea.

"Baby, I have to go out again. I probably won't be back tonight."

"Why Daddy? I don't want to stay here alone without you."

"It's necessary. Come here, I want to show you something."

Mia walked into Daddy's study. He was sitting there with a pump shotgun on one side of his desk, and a handgun on the other.

"Do you know anything about guns?"

"No, Daddy. You're scaring me."

"Don't be. Come on in."

Mia came in and stood next to him.

"I'm going to give you two guns while I'm gone. This one," he said, pointing to the handgun, "you'll keep with you. It's small, it's light. You need to keep it always close to your hand. The other, the shotgun, I'm going to put upstairs, in the walk-in closet off the bedroom."

"Why Daddy? I don't understand why I'm going to need them."

"You probably won't. They are 'just in case.'"

"In case of what?"

"In case the world goes to shit. Now quit asking questions and just listen to me, please!"

"Okay, Daddy."

Daddy picked up the handgun. "This is called a Smith and Wesson Model 60. It used to be the handgun of cops. It's a revolver, so it is very simple to use. You simply point it, and pull the trigger. It holds six shots. Come on over here and hold it."

Mia came forward hesitantly, looked at it, fascinated in spite of herself.

"Go ahead, pick it up. It's not going to hurt you."

She reached out and picked up the revolver. It felt heavy, and oily. It felt solid. It had a certain amount of silent, deadly, power sitting in her hand.

"Okay, let me show you how to use it. Never put your finger on the trigger when you're handling a gun. Your finger only goes on the trigger if you intend to fire it. Instead, let your index finger rest right here." Daddy moved her index finger to the correct location.

"Is it loaded?" asked Mia, mesmerized by the sight and power represented by the gun.

"No, it isn't. So right now, it is perfectly safe."

"How do I load it?"

"See that button next to your thumb? Push it."

Mia pushed the button with her thumb, and the cylinder popped open.

"Awesome. Are you going to teach me to shoot?"

"Yes, but not today. This gun I want you to keep with you. Chances are almost ninety-nine percent you won't have to use it. But if your husband should find you and come for you while I'm gone, I want you to have something. Your husband is a coward. If he sees you with a gun, he'll back down. Even so, you need to get used to this gun, having guns around, and being comfortable around guns."

"What happens if I squeeze the trigger?"

"Nothing will happen. Well, it will 'dry-fire'. Go ahead. Do it."

Mia squeezed the trigger. Nothing happened.

"Pull it harder."

This time the hammer came back and came down suddenly with a dry sounding click. Mia put the revolver down on the desk, and unconsciously wiped her hand on her jeans.

"If you ever have to shoot it, aim at the center of their chest, and just keep pulling the trigger. Don't try to aim. Just line it up and let it go. Understand me?"

"Okay, cool," Mia said, interested despite herself. "What about that one?" she asked pointing at the shotgun.

"This one is my baby…"

"I thought I was your baby."

"You are. This one is my other baby. Be quiet and listen. This one I'm going to put upstairs. This is your game plan. If you're downstairs and need to use a gun, you'll use it to get to the stairs, then go upstairs to the closet. Just run there and close the door. If someone gets in your way, shoot them and keep running. If someone comes during the night, then just run into the walk-in closet. This one is a bit different, but still very easy to use. The thing to remember is, if you're going to shoot it, you have to click this button off…see it?"

"What will happen if I don't?"

"The gun won't work. The second thing you'll need to do is called 'Racking the shotgun'. You do it like this," Daddy racked the hand slide. The unmistakable sound of a quality pump shotgun being racked, echoed throughout the room. "Now here's the thing. If you're in the closet and someone hears that sound, and everyone knows what that sound is, and what it means. Only the most insane will try to fuck with you. The sound alone almost guarantees your safety. So, click that button, then rack the shotgun. Got it?"

"Can I try it?"

"Yes, go ahead."

Mia picked up the shotgun. It felt heavier, and oozed destructive power.

"Hold it like this," Daddy showed her how to hold it properly. Mia, even a small girl, could hold it easily. She looked at Daddy, and with her left hand slid the slide down and back up again.

Chuk-chuk.

"What do I do then?" Mia asked, clearly pleased and impressed.

"If they come through the closet door, same drill, aim for the chest and let them have it. They won't make a second attempt. Once you're safe, or in the closet, call 9-1-1. Wait for the police to arrive. Like I said, chances are it will never get this far. But I want you prepared in any case. This is called 'Plan B.'"

"What's 'Plan A'?"

"Lay low, keep your head down, and hope for the best. Now I got to go…"

"Nothing inspires forgiveness quite like revenge."

Scott Adams

Chapter 40

Daddy stood near the intersection, watching the cars. When the right one came along, going the right speed, he stepped in front of it.

Daddy bounced off the hood of the car, did a stunt roll, as it came to a screeching halt. He lay on the ground moaning, completely unhurt, as the occupants got out, worried they had killed someone. *I'm getting too old for this cowboy shit,* thought Daddy.

"God damn it, Bill. I told you, you were going too fast! Didn't I tell you that?" said an older woman, blue-haired, in her sixties.

"He stepped right in front of me! Didn't you see it?"

"You didn't see a damned thing, you old fool. That's the problem."

"Hey Mister, you okay?" asked the older man as he reached Daddy. "Jesus, I'm sorry."

"My hip, my hip." Daddy gasped, in mock pain. "I think it's broken."

"Of course he isn't okay!" the woman said. "You just ran over him. Where's your cell phone you old fool?"

"I don't have it. I never carry it. Don't you have yours?"

"Of course not, only the grand babies call me on it..."

For Christ sake, I had to choose Ma and Pa Kettle to run me over? thought Daddy.

"An ambulance is on its way!" said a bystander.

The EMT's arrived a few minutes later, saving Daddy from listening to Ma and Pa fighting over who ought to be 'in charge of that cell phone technological thingie'.

The EMT's were brisk and professional. They quickly took his vitals, did a fast visual exam, probing with their fingers and a 'does it hurt here? Or here?' Then they loaded him on a gurney. They made it to the hospital in less than ten minutes.

Once inside, they admitted him, and placed a hospital identification strap around his wrist from the fake ID he was carrying. They wheeled him into an emergency room set aside and shut off by circular curtains. Once he had his privacy, he slid off the gurney, took off his clothes, put on a backless hospital gown, making sure his ass was exposed to the breeze. He quickly put on a professional bald skull cap used in movies and theater. Checking himself in the stainless steel reflection of a bed pan. Only if someone got up close would they see the skull cap was a fake. He now appeared exactly like what he wanted to look like...an aging terminal cancer patient.

Daddy slipped out the emergency curtain, and with his ass flapping in the wind and his clothes folded under the hospital gown, went in search of a wheelchair, which he found immediately. He settled himself into it, putting his clothes under him, and started pushing himself out of the emergency room by his arms. If anyone looked like they wanted to ask him questions, or get friendly, he just let his legs splay apart.

Is there anything more pathetic than an aging terminal patient with his cock and balls hanging out? Daddy thought, ruefully. It stopped two nurses cold in their tracks.

Daddy had already "socially engineered" the room number where Gilheart was, so he pushed himself into the elevator. Everyone in the elevator was overly polite and studiously avoided looking at him.

Daddy got out on the proper floor, and wheeled himself past the nurse's station.

"This isn't Oncology," one of the nurses said, "would you like me to get one of the orderlies to help you?"

Daddy let his legs slide open again and said, "No thanks. I'm just getting some air." Which ended that conversation and he rolled right past them. He got to Gilheart's room and pushed through the doors and into the room. No one paid any attention to him.

Gilheart was laying in bed on his back. Asleep, dozing with the morphine maidens. He wheeled himself to his bed, and sat looking at him.

Gilheart woke and there was a dying cancer patient in his room staring at him. He figured it was part of a hallucination until the apparition spoke.

"You're a fuckin' mess," Daddy said, quietly, and calmly.

"Look who's talking," said Gilheart.

"Yeah, but the difference is, you didn't put me in this condition. I put you in that hospital bed."

Gilheart's eyes flew open. He wasn't sure if he was hallucinating or not, but this dream just took a turn for the nasty.

"What did you just say?"

"I think you heard me."

"Come to finish the job?"

"Oh, hell no. I like you just the way you are."

"So what do you want?"

"I want to know if you can help me."

"Why would I do that?"

"I can think of a number of reasons. One, the choice I prefer, is to screw Prescott, because you know he is going to fuck you over now that you're no longer any use to him. Two, if that doesn't work, because I can hurt you even more than you already are."

Gilheart looked at Daddy and realized two things. This wasn't a hallucination and two, the apparition meant every word.

"So which is it going to be? Door number one, or door number two?"

"I got a recording."

"A recording of what?"

"Prescott selling his wife to me to beat up and rape."

"Do ya now? Where is it?"

"I don't remember."

"Knee complications suck," Daddy continued like he was conversing with an old friend. "Very tricky. Some people have to go in for multiple surgeries you know. And guess what? They aren't going to give you morphine forever. In fact, they won't after the second surgery. Risk of addiction and all that. I wouldn't be surprised if they don't start downgrading you to demerol very soon. So all I have to do is tighten one of those screws here, and loosen a screw there, and you'll be right back in hell's very own cutting room in no time. Without your girlfriend morphine to keep you company. "

"It's in my house somewhere. You caved my skull in, remember? I have memory loss."

"Awww, poor boy. And you ass raped my Baby Girl. Maybe even left her with some permanent damage. And that was after I warned you off. You got off easy, buddy."

"Then kill me. It'll be better than living like this."

"Have you ever read 'The Count of Monte Cristo' by Dumas?"

"Of course."

"Then you know, the Count's preferred method of revenge was to completely destroy the life of the people who did him wrong. He destroyed them, mentally, physically, emotionally, and financially. That is your future, Gilheart. I'm going to completely, and without mercy, destroy every aspect of your life for what you did to Mia. Not only will you have the problems you have now, but the black cloud of bad Karma is about to visit your life. I warned you I was someone you never wanted to meet. You didn't listen. In the end, when I'm finished, you'll take your own life in despair," Daddy said quietly, without emotion.

"Please…"

Daddy reached out and grabbed a chunk of Gilheart's hair and pulled it out, roots and all. Gilheart winced, but felt nothing, thanks to the morphine.

"I need this for a science project I'm working on. Fuck you very much, Gilheart," said Daddy, as he turned his chair, and wheeled himself out of the room.

"A Hospital is no place to be sick."

Samuel Goldwyn

Chapter 41

Daddy slipped into a bathroom, put his street clothes back on, took the skull cap off, and left the hospital.

He walked to an all-night cafe and ordered a coffee to sit down and think. So now he knew there was an incriminating recording of Prescott selling his wife to be raped and beaten for the sick pleasure of other men. His heart went out to Mia. He couldn't fathom the years of horror and abuse she had to live through. His rage at Prescott threatened to boil over, and he forcefully calmed himself down, as he gripped the coffee cup.

"Would you like me to warm that up for you?" a pretty young waitress asked.

"I'm sorry?"

"You looked like you were out of coffee."

"Yes, please."

"Is everything okay, mister?"

"Yeah, just one of those nights."

Daddy liked her smile, so he left her a twenty dollar tip for a $1.50 cup of coffee. He went back to the house and was very careful calling out Mia's name when he entered and whistling in the prearranged fashion.

"Mia! It's me. If you're awake, put down the gun."

Mia came out of the bedroom, rubbing her eyes. She was wearing white panties and nothing else.

"Hi Daddy. I was sleeping. Is everything okay?"

"Everything is fine. Maybe even better than fine."

"What do you mean?"

"It seems Gilheart was smart enough to make a recording of your husband selling you to him."

"Why would he do that?"

"Protection would be my guess."

She looked at him, uncomprehendingly.

"We live in a sick world, baby," he said softly.

"So what are you going to do now?"

"I'm going to go find it."

"I don't understand. How does that help us?"

"We have evidence to nail Gilheart with his DNA left by your rape. But we didn't have evidence linking your husband to the rape. Now we do. At least, we will once I find the recording. Where is Gilheart's house?"

"It's a dump over on Margold street."

"Do you know the number?"

"426."

Daddy parked on a parallel block, cut through a backyard, coming at Gilheart's house from the back. Mia was right; it was a dump. He checked a cellar window, found it unlocked, and squeezed inside, feet first. He turned his flashlight on, found the stairs, and turned it back off again. From there, he made his way in the dark to the stairs and climbed them.

The cellar opened up into the kitchen, and it stank. In fact, the whole-house stank. Opened boxes of deli food, had been left out for days. They had rotted and contributed to the entire overall stink.

Worse, Daddy was going to have to wait here in the stink until daybreak because he wasn't going to risk his flashlight being seen in a darkened house. He found a place on the floor, he wasn't going to use one of Gilheart's chairs, and cleaned it the best he could. He sat down on the floor cross-legged, and waited for the sun to rise.

Daddy stilled his mind, stilled his breathing, and went into a meditative state. Hours passed like minutes, and when he became aware, the sun was coming through the thin, unwashed curtains.

If I was Gilheart, where would I hide a recording? thought Daddy. He didn't relish the idea of searching this house. The whole place made him feel like bugs were crawling on him.

He looked about the room he was in without getting up. He saw sex toys and porn DVD's. He picked some up. *Satan's Slave, Tied up and Tortured, BDSM Hotel,* were a few of the titles. Daddy was no prude, but Christ, this place reeked of small dicks and inferiority complexes. His psychology suggested he would stick it INTO something. He was a penetrator.

Okay, if I was a little dick with an inferiority complex, where would I hide a recording? thought Daddy. *Well, I have to assume it is a mini, or micro cassette which doesn't make my job any easier. Let's narrow down the rooms then. Would I hide it in the living room, kitchen, or bedroom?* Still sitting on the floor, he looked around the living room. *In the couch? No. Seat cushions? No. Inside the TV? Maybe.*

Daddy got up, walked to the TV and using a Leatherman Tool, opened the back of the TV. Nope. *What about inside the wall sockets?* Daddy spent half an hour opening up all the wall sockets. Wrong again. He walked around looking at the central cooling grates. None appeared to have been unscrewed lately.

He walked in the bedroom, and the smell got worse. It smelled of desperate dreams, shit, and old cum. He was glad he was wearing gloves because he certainly didn't want to touch anything with his hands. Drawers revealed shabby clothes and more sex toys. Usually of the restraining variety. Another TV and more sex, bondage, and torture tapes. *Oh, and lookee here, a fake snuff film. Well, that certainly fits.*

On the bed were more sex toys. These, however, were vibrators and dildos of different sizes. He picked up one that was heavy and easily twelve inches long, and turned it on. It hummed and vibrated in his hand. Gilheart hadn't bothered to clean it so there were dark specks and streaks on it. *Did he use it on himself?* Daddy threw it down in disgust.

Daddy picked up another one. This one was lighter than he thought it should be and made from some sort of realistic-looking latex. It had thick, exaggerated veins, and what looked like bumps all over it. He turned it on, and it didn't work. He shook it, and tried it again. No joy. Then he realized the lightness was due to not having any batteries.

He unscrewed and opened the bottom of the vibrator, and a micro cassette tape fell out of the bottom.

"I'm still a hacker. I get paid for it now. The main difference in what I do now compared to what I did then is that I now do it with authorization."

Kevin Mitnick

Chapter 42

"What I want you to do is a back trace. I think someone is hacking me, and I want to find out who it is," Prescott explained to the police computer tech. "Is that possible?"

"It's possible given a certain set of circumstances, but it's not possible in every situation," replied the computer tech.

"What are the circumstances in which it is possible?"

"When a computer is attacked, it's often possible to obtain an IP address that's close to the attacker's location. However, it is usually not an exact location. Why don't you let me take a look at the computer and I can tell you more."

Prescott sheepishly handed him Mia's laptop, which was now in three different pieces. The keyboard, screen and drive were separate parts. The police tech gave him a sidelong glance.

"I got pissed. What can I say?"

"No problem. All I need is the hard drive anyway."

He went to work unscrewing the back and extracting parts. He laid the hard drive out on the table, then hooked his computer into it and started tapping commands into a DOS screen.

"How do you know the computer was hacked?"

"As soon as I connected to the Internet the screen went blank, and a message appeared."

"What was the message?"

"Well, there was no message. It was just a graphic with a middle finger."

"Okay, so we have a trojan more than likely. Did the computer freeze up?"

"I don't remember…"

"That was when you broke the computer into three pieces?"

"Well, sort of, yeah."

"Let me go back into your data logs and see what happened."

The computer tech worked quickly and quietly, his hands flying over the keyboard. Multiple black-and-white DOS screens opened up on the computer, then shut down as he finished with them.

"Okay, I isolated the intrusion."

"What does that mean?" asked Prescott.

"I can see when, and where it happened. That's the good news. The bad news is I can't trace it back to its point of origin."

"Why not?"

"Because the hacker cloaked it. In other words, he knew what he was doing. How badly do you want to catch this guy? The problem was only isolated to this computer, so any other computers you have in the house are unaffected. If that is your worry."

"Can we catch him?"

"Sure. Well, with luck. What were you doing, or trying to do, when the hacker entered your system?"

"I was trying to get into a Gmail account."

"What I could do is attach a bug to the Gmail account. If someone tries to log in to read their email, I'll be able to track their approximate location."

"Okay, do it."

Mia was bored. Daddy still hadn't come back from Gilheart's house, and it was now ten-thirty in the morning. She flipped through the morning shows, but they bored her too. Her injuries had been healing nicely, according to Daddy, who checked her every single day. He continued to give her douches and enemas everyday, not taking any chances. Now she thought, he just did it to piss her off.

Her bruising had faded to a dull yellow. There were no more deep purple colorations on her skin. Daddy checked those too. It was like having her own personal physician, but more intimate. He still wouldn't allow any sex games though, which also contributed to her bad mood.

She was thinking about going upstairs and playing with herself when the door opened. Mia grabbed the gun, pulled back the hammer, but kept her finger off the trigger as Daddy had taught her. She heard a whistle, their prearranged signal, so she wouldn't shoot Daddy in fright.

"Mia, it's me. Put the gun down, Baby." He still took no chances.

She put the gun down.

"It's okay, Daddy."

"Hi baby. Did you sleep well?" He walked over to kiss her head.

She drew back in horror, eyes wide.

"You smell like Gilheart! Go take a shower. You stink! Burn your clothes."

"Okay, baby, I forgot, sorry." He backed away and headed up the stairs.

"Did you find the tape?"

Daddy just smiled from the stairs. *Does a raccoon defecate in the woods? Is the Catholic Church filled with pedophiles?* His grin said.

Mia sat there, still bored, then decided to check her email. She hadn't checked it since this whole ordeal began and figured now was as good a time as any. She put in the secret by-pass password just as Daddy taught her.

"You are not going to believe this," said the computer tech.

"What?"

"Someone is checking her email right now."

"Can you trace it?"

"I can try."

His hands flew over the keyboard. Occasional fits of swearing were interspersed with bursts of laughter, more swearing, and awe.

"Oh, you tricky bastard…"

Then occasionally, "Oh yeah? Fuck you, too." or "Take that, ass-hole, you think you're better than me? Huh? Do ya?"

Prescott was ready to start beating the computer tech over the head with what was left of Mia's laptop, when he said,

"I got him."

He hit a button, and a long string of numbers printed off his portable printer.

"That's your hacker."

"These numbers?"

"Yep."

"Well, what am I supposed to do with this? This isn't a location."

"Sure it is. See that string right there? That means he's on the West side of town. Probably North West Urbandale."

"So are one hundred thousand other people."

"That's true. I told you, you wouldn't get an exact location."

"So what am I supposed to do with this?" Prescott repeated.

"You go before a judge, and get a warrant and force the telecommunication provider to provide you with the exact location of that string of numbers there," said the computer tech, pointing to a string of numbers.

"How long does that take?"

"How should I know? You're the lawyer. I just tap and trace. By the way, that'll be a thousand dollars."

"Government is an association of men who do
violence to the rest of us."

Leo Tolstoy

Chapter 43

"First up at eleven, Jeffery Prescott reveals a shocking plot to kid-
nap his wife. Film at eleven!"

Daddy and Mia were curled up on the couch, as Daddy flipped
through the channels. Both came awake when they heard the news
blurb.

"It sounds like your husband is starting to up his game," said
Daddy.

"Why would he do that when he knows it's a lie?"

"Could be a lot of reasons. First, we'll need to see what the news
has to say."

The blond news anchor with the over-sprayed hair appeared shortly
outside Police Plaza, holding an oversized microphone in her hand.

"Dan, we're outside Police Plaza where Jeffery Prescott, who you
may remember was attacked last month in a brutal beating outside
Waterloo Elementary school. He has just revealed his wife, Mia
Prescott, has disappeared."

The news show went to split screen.

"Cassandra? Cassandra?" the talking head back in the studio with
his hand pressed to his ear again said. "What can you tell us?"

"Details are sketchy at this time. What we can tell you, is that Mia
Prescott disappeared at the same time as the beating."

"Cassandra, are you saying that Mia Prescott was kidnapped?"

"As I said Dan, police aren't releasing much information…"

The screen filled with a recent photo of Mia taken during a school function.

"…However, it's fair to say that a Missing Person's report has been filed, and police are looking for a Person of Interest in the case."

"Cassandra what is the condition of the other man who was beaten with Prescott?"

"He still remains at the hospital in serious condition. He lost one of his eyes, and hospital officials report he may never walk again."

"Good," said Mia, "I hope he hobbles off a cliff. That's a horrible picture of me, though."

"Quiet, Baby."

"So Cassandra, let me summarize. Jeffery Prescott has released information tonight that during a gang-related attack last month, which left his colleague seriously injured, his wife was kidnapped, and police are looking for the suspects. Is that right, Cassandra?"

"Yes, Dan, that is correct."

"Have Police said anything about a ransom demand?"

"No, they haven't, Dan. However, sources close to the investigation have said, off the record, that the attack may have been politically motivated…"

With those words, the doors behind Cassandra at Police Plaza opened and Jeffery Prescott himself, stepped out. Leaning on a cane, with his neck brace still on, Prescott stepped into the lights.

"Mr. Prescott! What can you tell us?"

Prescott was looking surprisingly resolute for an injured man who had been "brutally beaten" in his best Burberry top coat, and red Windsor power tie. There was a little eye leakage, which he quickly dabbed away before stepping up to the mic.

"First of all, I'd like to wish my good friend and colleague John Gilheart a rapid recovery, and a speedy return to our charity 'Children Without Hunger'. I would also like to say, to the person, or persons that kidnapped my wife, just return her safely, and without harm, and I'll do everything in my power to show leniency."

"Mr. Prescott, what motive would the perpetrators have for kidnapping your wife?"

"We believe it was politically motivated, Cassandra, in order to derail announcing my candidacy for mayor."

Both anchors went momentarily silent as they absorbed this new bombshell. Then the screen split with a picture of Prescott and Mia at a charity function. The camera zoomed in on Mia's face.

"Mr. Prescott are you saying your wife was kidnapped in order to intimidate you into not running for mayor?"

"That's exactly what I'm saying. But as you can tell, I don't shy away from tough decisions. I don't give in to demands of terrorists. I'm still intending to run for Mayor of this great city. However, I miss my wife very much and want my wife to be returned unharmed. So if the people responsible are listening to this, please know, if you return her uninjured, I'm prepared to show mercy. If you do not, you will be hunted down to the ends of the earth. Thank you very much."

Prescott walked away from the camera, and the camera followed him to a waiting car. He opened the back door, turned, gave a final wave to his future voters before getting in, and closing the door.

"There you have it, Dan. Shocking details have emerged tonight concerning Jeffery Prescott. Not only did he reveal his intentions for political office, but delivered a second bombshell concerning his wife, Mia Prescott."

Mia's picture once again flashed up on the screen with a scrolling number of a tip hotline under it.

"I was just handed this from the police, Dan. If anyone sees Mia Prescott, they are urged to do the right thing and call this number on the bottom of the screen. Do not try to apprehend, or rescue this young lady yourself. Her abductors could be armed and dangerous. Police are urging the good citizens of this city to get involved and help them solve this case."

"Thank you, Cassandra."

"Back to you, Dan.

"There you have it. Mia Prescott is missing and presumed kidnapped. Jeffery Prescott has announced his bid for Mayor."

"Excuse me, Dan," this coming from the co-anchor. "Coming from the political cynics among us, is it possible this is a political stunt to kick his campaign off?"

"Well, I certainly hope not, for Mia Prescott's sake. However, Jeffery Prescott does come from a wealthy, well connected family. Ransom is a real possibility. I wouldn't be surprised if the Governor didn't get involved. His father, William Prescott is a known campaign contributor."

"What do you think the odds are that Mia Prescott will be found alive?"

"I wouldn't want to speculate. Now, a word from our sponsors..."

Daddy leaned back on the couch and started laughing. Mia looked at him like he had gone off his rocker.

"What's so funny? They're going to charge you with kidnapping, Daddy."

"Yes, it looks like they are going to try."

"So why are you laughing?"

"I'm thanking the Gods for giving me stupid enemies."

"Law-abiding citizens value privacy. Terrorists require invisibility. The two are not the same, and they should not be confused."

Richard Perle

Chapter 44

"Your Honor, I have every reason to believe my wife is being held against her will at this location. For that reason, I'm requesting that you grant this order requesting the telecom company to release this information immediately."

The judge looked at Prescott. After almost twenty-five years on the bench he'd seen up-and-comers of all shapes and stripes. Jeffery Prescott looked like the latest variety. Slick, blow-dried hair, power tie, good clothes, rich family, and a faint whiff of 'metro-sexual' clinging to the whole ensemble. He'd caught the news the night before, actually it was hard to miss. The entire community was talking about it, and it made him slightly sick. What passed for politics in this country today made him wish for a revolution.

"How did you come by this information?"

"Excuse me, your Honor?"

"The question was plain enough, Prescott. My question is, why are you presenting this to me instead of the District Attorney's Office?"

Now Prescott had a problem. He couldn't admit he came across the information illegally, that he hacked it from Mia's computer without her knowledge and misappropriated police resources. At the same time, he was in the lion's den and had to say something.

"It was delivered anonymously, your Honor."

"Then how do you know it has anything to do with the where-abouts of Mia Prescott?"

"The donor assured me it did."

"I thought you just said it came anonymously?"

"I did. I meant that the paper that came with the IP address identifier said so."

"I see. May I see that, please?" continued the judge, already smelling the stench of corruption and family favors.

"Well….that was given over to the police as evidence. I'm afraid I no longer have it. I didn't know you would have need of it," said Prescott, easily lying through his teeth.

"So, then, I am to understand this correctly, you have no evidence subsequently to support the invasion of this person's privacy, is that correct?"

"Well sir, I believe the law states that if there is a 'Clear and Present Danger' you are free to grant the petition." *Fuck, why is this judge busting my balls?* thought Prescott.

"I'm aware of what the law states, as well as my responsibilities under it, *young* Prescott," the judge said dangerously. "It's also my responsibility to uphold the constitution of this state. Which says a person has a right to privacy, and you're asking me to violate that. In addition, you're asking me to do so, without any direct evidence, on your word only. Petition denied!"

"But sir, my wife's life could hang in the balance. Surely, you can see this is an extenuating circumstance."

"Mr. Prescott, I know your wife. I've met her on several social occasions. Personally, I like her a lot more than I like you. I'm inclined to grant the motion for her sake only. However, that would be against the law. To do so you are asking me to go out on a limb for you personally, that is what it sounds like to me."

The judge continued. "While the implication is unsaid, it sounds like you would like me to grant this in return for future favors once you are elected to office…."

"Oh no, oh no, your Honor, you misinterpret…" Prescott was scrambling now. The judge had seen through his charade like he had x-ray vision. "I was just trying to explain…"

"Shut up, Prescott. I'll grant the order for Mia, not you. But if you ever pull this shit again in my court, I'll bury you long before you get to the mayor's chair." The judge signed the order, and dismissed Jeffery Prescott.

Once presented with the proper court order, the telecom company handed over the name and address of the account holder without any problems at all. It was almost anticlimactic. He looked at the name and at the address. It meant nothing to him. It rang no bells. He didn't know this person nor had he ever heard of him.

It was time to gather the troops, mount an attack on this individual, and rescue Mia.

He called Flynn.

"What do you mean 'mount an attack'? What do you think this is, the Battle of Gettysburg?" said Flynn, incredulously. "Let's see that." He pulled the papers out of Prescott's hand. He also read the name and address.

They met over at Prescott's house later for a beer. Flynn was still in uniform. He sat down at the kitchen counter, popped a beer, and shifted the weight of his belt onto a chair and not his back.

"Can you run that name and address through the police system, so we can see who we're dealing with?" asked Prescott, never being one to run out of asking favors from people who are risking their careers to help him.

"Not without a good reason, I can't. I just can't call them up like in the movies. I need a reason."

"What would be a good reason?"

"If I saw her, or him, I could pull them over if I see them violating any traffic rules, then I would have a reason."

"So what you're telling me is, if I could come up with the information when they were leaving the house, you could pull them over on a technicality and run the name that way, right?"

"I'm not telling you anything, Prescott. I simply answered your question. If a citizen were to see them and call the tip hotline, then I would be obligated to respond. And in responding, I would be derelict in my duty if I didn't thoroughly check the background of any person with her." Flynn looked at Prescott with no expression on his face whatsoever.

Prescott looked at Flynn, then pulled out his cell phone reaching into his other pocket for a slip of paper. He punched in the numbers, continuing to look at Flynn.

"Allied Research and Recovery."

"Art Williams, please.

"Please hold while I transfer you."

Muzac played in the background while Prescott rolled his eyes.

"Williams."

"Hi Art? Jeffery Prescott. I got your name from my law office. I'd like to hire you to do a twenty-four hour surveillance on an individual in connection with the kidnapping of my wife. Is that something your office can handle?"

Prescott listened for an extended period as the voice outlined the various expectations, and the usual private investigative disclaimers. Flynn thought the other party's conversational tone sounded leery with a hint of curiosity.

"Yes. Yes, I understand. I understand the daily rate, yes."

More conversational buzzing.

"Excellent. When can you start? Very good. I'll want daily written updates as well as verbal news immediately if you spot them. Good. I'll also want you to do a background check on an individual in relation to this investigation. Is that a problem?"

More cell phone chattering and buzzing. However, the tone was friendly as befitted a promising "in the news" investigation.

"Excellent. Start tonight and let me give you the name and address…" said Prescott, wrapping up the conversation.

"The best revenge is to live on and prove yourself."

Eddie Vedder

Chapter 45

Daddy took the hairs from Gilheart and sealed them in a small Ziplock baggy.

The forensic trace evidence was brought out of the safe and together he sent them to the laboratory. He asked, and paid for, an "expedited order." Even then, he knew it would be a minimum of four days before he received a reply.

He received the reply and the paperwork five days later. It conclusively proved Gilheart was the donor of the sperm and saliva found on Mia's breasts, vagina, and anal cavities. Of course, there had never been any doubt, but faced with unassailable DNA evidence, it made his hands literally shake as he read the report.

He thought back to his last conversation with Gilheart. There was no remorse for his actions. If there was pity, it was self-pity that he couldn't talk his way out of his present circumstances. His "then kill me now" statement reeked of not wanting to bear the true cost of his actions.

He thought carefully about how he wanted to proceed.

What is justice? he asked himself.

"Hey, Mia? Come in here, please."

"Yes, Daddy?" she was once again, clad only in a teddy and panties. She had healed, and looked beautiful. There had been no complications of infections, and her tearing had mended perfectly.

"I have a question for you, and I want you to think carefully before answering it. Please don't answer emotionally. I know it will be hard. But try to think about what is the fair solution."

"What is your question, Daddy?" Daddy noted the strength of character in her, he hadn't noticed before. Before she would have been fearful when confronted with that preamble. Now, there was simply curiosity and confidence. He smiled at her. Her mind was healing as well as her body. Soon, she wouldn't need him anymore.

"You have the means to make Gilheart pay for what he did to you. What is a just punishment?"

Her look darkened at the mention of his name. She opened her mouth to speak, then shut it without saying a word, and considered his question.

"First, I would like to be assured that he will never, ever, do it to another person."

"Agreed."

"Second, I want him to pay for the rest of his life. I have to pay for his actions, I want that not one day goes by that he is not reminded of what he did to me, and what he paid in return."

"How would you do that?"

"I don't know, Daddy. Why don't you decide?"

"I'm trying to…with your help. Do you want him to go to jail? You can do that, or at least, try to. Even so, the outcome, even with conclusive evidence is not guaranteed. He could get off on a technicality."

"What do you suggest, Daddy?" Mia sat down in his lap and put her arms around his shoulder. She started rubbing his cock unconsciously with her other hand and biting his ear.

"I think we should destroy him completely. Take away his health insurance so they kick him out of the hospital. Next go after his pension, and take away his money. Then go after his name, and destroy that too. Once we have taken those, hand the evidence over to the police. If they prosecute, good. If they don't, it won't make much difference."

Mia stopped her teasing and looked at him. "I never want to get on the bad side of you, Daddy."

"You never would." Daddy kissed her back, then started nibbling at her ear, instead. "I think you've earned a sex game."

"Really? Anything I want?"

"Anything you want, Baby Doll."

What followed was a completely sperm draining two-hour sex

marathon, which included Nurse Naughty and Dr. McNasty. It made him appreciate what women had to go through every year at the OB-GYN's.

"You're just lucky you don't have a pussy," Mia said smiling.

"Don't I get credit for being an excellent battlefield doctor?"

"Ha! Amputation would have been preferable. Speaking of amputation, maybe we should get rid of a couple of inches of this," she said holding Daddy's cock. "It really is a tad too big you know."

"No, no, no, no, Nurse Naughty, you stick to known procedures."

"We could call it a circumcision." Mia added helpfully.

"I'm already circumcised."

"Awww...Come on, Daddy. It's just a 'nip and a tuck," she added gleefully. "If you wanted me to get bigger breasts, I'd do it for you."

"I don't want you to get bigger breasts. I like your breasts just the way they are. But I would like it if you made them smaller. Would you go under the knife to make them tinier?"

"What? No one goes to have their breasts smaller!"

"Oh...and you think men are just lined up to have their dicks made shorter?"

"Okay, I will if you will," said Mia, grinning.

"You are evil, Nurse Naughty."

Daddy returned downstairs having a hard time walking upright without a limp. He made an effort at completely draining her sexually. He counted five orgasms, but then lost track having problems controlling his own until she was finished. She was back to being herself, an absolute sexual hell-cat in bed.

She was sleeping soundly. He never got tired of watching her sleep. So far, he hadn't seen any symptoms of PTSD, which he thought was a minor miracle. No night sweats, no nightmares, no anxiety or panic attacks.

He made copies of all the photographs, the chain of custody, as well as the DNA conclusions. He included a signed, notarized statement where Mia described what happened in detail, where and when it took place, along with details leading up to the attack. On Daddy's advice, she left out any mention of Jeffery Prescott's involvement. That would come later. He mailed one set to the State Education Board, another set to KTTO Channel Nine News, and another set to the District Attorney's Office.

He used gloves when handling all the documents as to not leave any fingerprints. Instead of licking the envelopes, he used a wet sponge so no trace evidence was left behind.

The last set he addressed to William Prescott, and mailed it to his parent's house. He wanted them to see what their darling little boy had done to his own wife. Of course, when he sent a copy of the tape recording, it would become clear what a monster he was. However, that would be later. Until then, they could look upon the horror that was inflicted on their daughter-in-law. He included a note, printed out on his computer in simple Times New Roman font. It said simply,

"Tell Jeffery, I'm coming."

"When you're in the news business, you always
expect the unexpected."

Helen Thomas

Chapter 46

Twenty-four hours later Daddy and Mia were drinking coffee at the breakfast bar when the news came on with the local TV news station on.

"Breaking news in the ongoing drama surrounding Jeffery Prescott." The anchor, looking serious as befitted his station in life, stared at the camera. "Our attorneys have informed us to tell you that due to the nature and content of this report, it may be disturbing to some viewers and is not intended for children.

"KTTO has learned, and confirmed, that John Gilheart, who you may remember was with Jeffery Prescott when they were attacked outside Waterloo Elementary School, was possibly involved in the rape and abduction of Mia Prescott. We received a tip from an anonymous source yesterday…"

"Oh Daddy, what did you do?" asked Mia, looking at him horrified.

"What we discussed, Baby."

"Can you describe for us the nature of that tip, Dan?"

"Yes, it consisted of a sworn affidavit from Mia Prescott herself, along with DNA evidence and some very vivid photographs showing the extent of her injuries. Because of the graphic nature and privacy of the people involved, we can only show a small portion of the photos."

A number of the more tame photos with eyes black-barred out and private parts blurred, appeared on the screen.

"Daddy! You sent them the photos?"

"I sure did."

"But I was naked! So now the whole world gets to see me naked?"

"I don't think anyone is going to see your body. They will see the injuries though."

"You could have discussed that with me."

"I did discuss it with you."

"Yeah, but you didn't tell…"

A number of pictures flashed up on the screen. Mia's face and body parts blurred in each one. The wounds, however, were in Technicolor.

"Dan, are you saying that John Gilheart, the man wounded during the attack is guilty of this horrific crime?"

"No. We are sharing an anonymous tip which has been vetted by our legal team. In no way are we suggesting guilt, or accusing anyone. That is the job of a judge and jury. However, we felt as journalists, we had an obligation to our viewers as well as the community."

"How has Jeffery Prescott responded?"

"So far, our calls have not been returned."

"Is there any word on where Mia Prescott is now?"

"No. So far, she has not surfaced to confirm or deny these allegations. We have an obligation to share what we know with the police and we have done so. They have promised to 'vigorously pursue' this investigation. However, sources close to the investigation have revealed they received the same evidence as we did, at the same time."

"What does this mean to the Prescott campaign for mayor?"

"So far, there has been no comment from the Prescott campaign. This is Dan Anderson, at KTTO news."

"The proverbial shit, has just hit the proverbial fan," said Daddy.

"What does that mean?"

"That means it could get dangerous for us both very quickly."

"What do we do now, Daddy?"

"Time to visit some lawyers."

Daddy spotted the surveillance team as soon as he walked out of the house. Two guys sitting alone in a parked car on a suburban street stand out like a flasher in a trench coat in July at an elementary school.

Fuckin' amateurs. Daddy thought, *Good. My luck is still with me. Which means these guys are private, not police. But I've been found. Not that that will do them any good.*

Daddy brought Mia to the truck and opened the door for her. He started up his pickup, backed out of the driveway, didn't pay any attention to the tail, and drove to the end of the street. He stopped at the sign, signaled left, turned out of view of the tail car, and immediately pulled over to the curb. He heard the tail start their car and within seconds, they blew through the stop sign after him. Realizing their mistake too late, they had no choice but to continue past Daddy.

Daddy banged an immediate U-turn and went in the opposite direction, making a series of left and right turns, and reverse track-backs designed to hopelessly confuse the situation. He lost the tail inside of five minutes.

Daddy had a list of ten lawyers, and he stopped in front of the office of the first one.

"Okay, here's what I want you to do," Daddy said, turning around in the seat to face Mia. "I want you to walk in there, tell them your name, and ask for an appointment with the lawyer listed. Don't accept anyone else. If he's in a 'meeting', or 'on a call' then say you'll be back later. Trust me, he'll find time for you. When you get into his office, don't even let him get a word in, just sit down and immediately start telling your side of the story. Don't embellish, don't lie. Then leave the packet of information I just gave you."

"What will happen then?"

"The lawyer will more than likely be floored. He won't want to accept the case and go against the Prescott family, but his curiosity will also get the better of him. So he'll make a show of listening to you, and examining the evidence."

"He's going to be looking at pictures of me?"

"Yes, he is."

"Okay, then what?"

"Tell him you want to start a divorce action against your husband."

"What will he do?"

"He'll more than likely beg off, busy schedule, conflicting court dates, that sort of thing. But he really just doesn't have the balls to go against Prescott."

"What if they really aren't in?"

"Leave the packet with the receptionist."

"What if he says he wants to?"

"Ask how much, and what his retainer is, etc. Then it is your turn to say you'll consider it."

"If you're not going to hire them, why are we doing this?"

"For two reasons; one, these are the best divorce attorneys in town. Now that they are familiar with our case, they can't take Jeffery's side because of conflict of interest, which deprives your husband of the best attorneys. He'll have to go out of town to find one, which gives us an advantage if it ever goes to court. Two, no one, I mean no one, gossips more than attorneys. Which means Jeffery's dirty laundry is going to be aired all over legal and political communities by the end of lunch. This is a sensitive time for him, with the campaign and all. He's again, at a disadvantage and on the defensive. His venerability plays into our hands."

"So this is what you meant by 'thank the Gods for stupid enemies'?"

"It is exactly what I meant by it."

"We're going to win this, aren't we, Daddy? I'm going to be free of him."

"There is still a long way to go. Don't pack your suitcases yet."

"Thank you, Daddy," Mia said softly, meaning it, looking straight into Daddy's eyes.

"You're very welcome, Baby Doll."

Mia got out of the car, her back straight, eyes directly ahead. She walked without fear towards her freedom.

They could get to seven of the ten lawyers on the list that day. They were on their way home when Officer Flynn spotted Mia, he hit the lights and siren, and pulled them over.

"It is to be regretted that the rich and powerful too often bend the acts of government to their own selfish purposes."

Andrew Jackson

Chapter 47

"Just what the fuck do you think you're doing?" Elder Prescott shouted, and threw the pictures of battered Mia into Jeffery Prescott's face.

"Look, I didn't know they were going to take a bunch of pictures and spread them all over the news," Jeffery Prescott said defensively.

"Really? No shit? That wasn't a part of your master plan? Well, that makes it so much better," Elder Prescott said sarcastically.

"Look, Dad, I think this can be contained."

"How are you going to do that?"

"Well, so far he has implicated Gilheart, not me. Obviously, we'll have to hang Gilheart out to dry, but I see no reason to panic, and…"

"Tell me, Jeff, look at the last line of that letter, what does it say?"

"It says 'I'm coming.'"

"Does that suggest to you, this person, whoever he is, is going to let sleeping dogs lie?"

Prescott the junior stayed silent.

"Here's what it suggests to me," continued Elder Prescott, as though his son's opinion didn't matter. "He's coming at you full throttle. Which means you have a dangerous adversary on the loose. Worse, you have an adversary who knows how to use the system. He is systematically destroying Gilheart, then you. He's not going to be happy until he pulls down this entire family. He's going for your jugular, you stupid shit! What do you know about him?"

"We know his name. We know where he lives. Mia, or him, hasn't been seen for the last several days. We're tracking down his various business interests. We know his credit history and criminal record."

"What are those?"

"He has perfect credit. He has no criminal record. Not even a speeding ticket. He pays cash for medical care, so there is no insurance documentation on health conditions. He owns several guns, legally purchased and has a permit to carry a concealed weapon. He has no educational affiliations, nor any background whatsoever before 2008."

"What do you mean he has no background before 2008?"

"I mean exactly that. He has a Hong Kong birth certificate and an American passport. No entries prior to 2008."

Elder Prescott just looked at Junior, disbelief in his eyes.

"What kind of hornet's nest have you kicked over?"

At that moment, Momma Prescott popped into the room carrying a tea service. "I have some coffee and some scones if you boys would…"

Elder Prescott turned on her in an instant and punched her with a closed fist right in the face. Dropping her and the fine china all over the floor. When all the china finished breaking, Elder Prescott said, "Get the fuck out of here. We'll let you know if we want coffee. Until then, stay the fuck out."

Both men instantly dismissed her without looking at her as she scuttled out of the room holding her face.

"Dad, you're overreacting and…"

That earned Jeffery Prescott the same fist to the side of his face as his mother.

"You stupid fuck, you don't even know what you've done, do you?"

Officer Flynn stepped out of his cruiser, undid the safety strap on his Glock 17 and walked in the blind spot up on Daddy's left. Daddy's window was down, and his hands were on the wheel. He remained silent.

"Did you know you failed to use a turn signal?"

"Did I?"

Flynn looked at Daddy. Daddy mentally snapped a picture of his face, and looked at his identification badge.

"Mia? Could you get out of the car please? Sir, please stay inside the vehicle and keep your hands where I can see them."

Mia looked at Daddy.

"It's okay, Baby. Everything is going to be okay," Daddy said softly, "just answer the way I told you."

Mia got out of the truck.

"Please come to the other side, on the curb."

Flynn walked to the front of the truck, watching Daddy the whole time, and stepped up on the curb to where Mia was.

"Is everything okay, Ma'am?" he asked.

"Yes, of course. Why wouldn't it be?"

"You have a missing person's report filed on you as a possible abduction. If you're in any danger, you aren't now. You can come with me. I'll make sure you're safe."

"I'm not in any danger, and I don't want to go with you," Mia said calmly.

"I see. You know it's not uncommon for women to identify with their captors, even to the point of willingly staying with them."

"Except I wasn't abducted. Therefore, how could I be a captive? I left of my own freewill."

She had Flynn there.

"I just wanted to make sure you're safe."

"I am, Officer, thank you."

Flynn walked back over to the driver's side of the truck.

"License, registration and proof of insurance, please?"

Daddy already had them handy and held in such a way, by the edges, that he wouldn't be able to get fingerprints from them.

"Yes, hand them to me, please."

"I am. Take them, please. I'm not resisting."

Flynn had no choice but to take them in the same fashion. Both men looked at each other. Each understanding the game of the other.

"I'll be back in a moment. Please stay here."

Flynn walked back to his patrol car and punched the info into his laptop dashboard computer. Daddy noticed the dashboard cam. So there was also video being taken as well. Good. If it goes to court that video will need to be subpoenaed.

No wants or warrants were out in Daddy's name, according to the computer. So he couldn't hold him on anything. He had broken no laws, and Mia wasn't going to leave with him. Flynn also noticed no history at all prior to 2008.

That's strange, he said to himself.

While he had the chance, he reached into his console and took out some black fingerprint powder and quickly dusted the plastic on the license. He detected a print, got some fingerprint tape, and lifted it off the license. He blew off the powder and got out of the police cruiser. He walked back to Daddy's pickup, always staying in the blind spot.

"Here you are, Sir." Handing his paperwork back with the license on the top, so he would have to use his thumb to grab it. Once again, Daddy didn't. He took the paperwork, tilted it up, and let the license slide into his palm. That was when Daddy noticed the black fingerprint powder that sprinkled into his hand.

"I'll be letting you off with a warning this time. Remember to use your turn signal the next time."

"Thank you, Officer Flynn, I'll do that." Both men looked each other in the eye and took the measure of the other.

"Privacy and security are those things you give up when you show the world what makes you extraordinary."

Margaret Cho

Chapter 48

Flynn took the tape with Daddy's fingerprint on it and transferred it to a slide, then digitally reproduced it on the computer. At that point, the fingerprint tech walked in.

"Okay, what are we looking at?"

"I got this off a driver's license. The perp has no history prior to 2008, and it made me curious. I want to send it off to the Hong Kong police as well as Interpol and see what they come up with on him."

The fingerprint tech made a number of copies, transferred them digitally to the proper forms, and sent it off.

"You ought to have a reply in twenty-four hours or less. Anything else?"

"Can you also run it through our own AFIS system and see if we get any returns?"

"You want to run it through the FBI?"

"Why not. I might as well touch all bases."

Within twenty-four hours, Flynn did have his replies. However, he still had no answers. The answers he had, made no sense.

Born in Hong Kong in 1962, father an American diplomat. Mother was an Army brat. Both died in a car accident when he was ten. Poor kid. Alone at ten, that's got to fuck you up a little, Flynn thought. *Tested extremely high in mathematics and languages. Then he drops off the face of the earth.*

He resurfaces once more, in 1981 in Burma of all places, or at least his prints do. Then he disappears, and comes up for air once again in 1991 during the Thai insurgency as a military attaché. That's what the military call you when they don't want anyone to know what you do. Then he disappears again, and the prints don't show up until 2008, when he was fingerprinted prior to coming into the USA at LAX.

That meant, Flynn's next stop had to be Army and/or Navy Intelligence. He made the call.

He was expecting the usual disclaimers and bullshit the military put out whenever the police asked a question they didn't want to answer, which was always.

What he wasn't expecting was the phone call an hour later from a Colonel Littier, from the 3rd. Recon Battalion, stationed at Camp Schwab, Okinawa, Japan.

Third Recon? thought Flynn, *that's Marines.*

"Sergeant Flynn can you tell me what this is in regards to?"

"He's a person of interest in an ongoing case," Flynn replied carefully.

"I see. Can you tell me what the nature of the case is?"

"It has to do with a possible abduction and/or kidnapping."

"Sergeant Flynn, in all due respect, I sincerely doubt it. Would you like to try again?"

Okay, the bullshit isn't going to fly, thought Flynn.

"He's an ex-Recon Marine?"

"I can neither confirm, nor deny that. Does this have anything to do with the Mia Prescott case?"

"You're very well informed, Sir."

"Well, it is what we do. Let's try my version. You found his prints and checked him out and found he had no prior history before 2008. This got you curious and you started digging and pretty soon you and me are talking on the telephone. How am I doing so far?"

"What can you tell me?"

"Here's what I can tell you, Sergeant. He wouldn't have anything to do with what you're describing. He lives by a strict code. He wouldn't violate that code, no matter how many years after he left the service, if he was ever in the service. You have no understanding of the person you're dealing with. The very best thing you could do for yourself is to lose those fingerprints and cross him off your suspect list, then leave him alone."

"You're not giving me many answers."

"Oh, but I am. A wise man once said, 'silence can answer many questions'. Good day, Sergeant Flynn."

Flynn sat back in his chair after hanging up the phone, staring off into space. He tried putting the pieces together.

What do I know? Well, for openers, the name he gave was a fake. A fake backed up with original US documents. That means his background is also fake. Which means, he probably has more identities I don't know about. Which means he can disappear at will. That means, I have absolutely no idea who I'm dealing with. A colonel with Marine Recon was alerted in response to my inquiries. I was warned off.

What does Marine Recon do? They go into Indian territory before anyone else, and scout the way. They watch, and they listen. They are trained in escape and evasion, and who knows what else. He's an old warrior that still has some teeth left.

So what does it all mean? It means I'm dealing with a retired deep cover operative who's been buried so far underground I couldn't get at him if I found him standing over a body with a smoking gun in his hand.

"Hey Flynn? Captain wants to see you," said one of the detectives from Robbery/Homicide.

"I hear you're making a name for yourself, Sergeant," said the Captain of his division when he walked into his office.

"I don't know what that means, Sir."

"It means I just got a call from on high. That means my boss got a call from his on high, and THAT means whatever the fuck you're doing, you better stop. The fact that you're two years from your pension was brought into the conversation twice. Is there any part of what I just said that isn't clear?"

"No, Sir. It is quite clear."

"Excellent Sergeant, is there anything else? Then carry on, McDuff."

"Opportunities multiply as they are seized."

Sun Tzu

Chapter 49

"I'm sorry, Baby, but we can't go back to the house."

They were driving down Grand Ave, away from the legal district. Flynn had pulled them over and just let them go. Daddy made sure he used his turn signals, kept within the speed limit, and obeyed every law. He was also on the look-out for any surveillance, but hadn't spotted any yet.

If they were good, and knew their business, I wouldn't spot them anyway, thought Daddy.

"So we're never going back to your house?" Mia asked.

"We can go back after this is finished."

"How come we can't go back to your house. I like your house, Daddy."

"It's no longer safe."

"Where are we going to live?"

"I got us an apartment over on the South side of town."

"Gilheart lived on the South side of town."

"Yes, he did."

"What are we going to do?"

"I'm going to make sure you're safe, then I'm going back to the house to get the necessary things we'll need."

Daddy knew that a professional tail would be up ahead of him, behind him, as well as on parallel blocks on each side. They would be in contact with each other and constantly switching positions so he couldn't detect a pattern in the cars.

They could also have put a GPS tracking device on the pickup and then they wouldn't need a four to eight man surveillance team.

So the first thing he would need to do is look under the car for a tracking device. Then try and detect any parallel surveillance. That would be the easiest. If nothing was detected, then his luck was still holding and he would get Mia to the safe house. He pulled off the road before crossing an intersection, and then watched the cars behind him. None showed any interest.

He got out of the car and checked the underside of the truck. It sat higher off the ground than most cars. With a high intensity LED flashlight he kept in the glove box, it didn't take him long to spot the tracking device hidden inside the back bumper. It was held on with a powerful magnet.

In his haste, he didn't spot the second one hidden above the gas tank.

Daddy pried the tracking device off the frame and examined it. It looked commercial, not military. Which meant he was still dealing with the yahoos from this morning.

At least they still aren't a threat. It also means, there was probably no other surveillance. They stood back and let the GPS do the dirty work after he slipped them. Give them points for having a back-up plan, though, thought Daddy.

Daddy got back in the car, and drove to a gas/convenience store by the freeway. As he walked in to pay for the gas, he chose a minivan with out of state plates and a yellow "Baby on Board" sticker. He attached the tracking device to its bumper.

"Where are we going now?" Mia asked, once Daddy returned from paying for the gas.

"I'm going to show you your new palace."

"Does it stink?"

"Maybe a little," said Daddy smiling.

Prescott Senior looked at his son holding his face, then looked at the spilled coffee all over the floor. *What a fucking mess, both literally and figuratively,* he thought. He didn't feel the slightest shred of pity for either his son, or his wife. They were simply tools to be used as he saw fit. If his wife didn't have political uses, he would have killed her a long time ago.

He walked over to his desk and pressed the intercom button.

"Momma? Get in here and clean up your mess."

Momma came in immediately. Her face was already swelling, and blood was still leaking out of her nose. She started cleaning up 'her' mess silently, picking up the shards of the china as she wiped the hardwood floor.

"Look Dad…"

"Shut up, Jeff. Let me think."

Elder Prescott sat down at his desk and started rubbing his temples.

"Where are we with the planning board?"

"With all that his been going on with Mia's abduction…"

"You haven't done a fucking thing about the planning board, is that what you're trying to say?"

"I got it handled. They just want…"

"You're going to go 'handle' it right now. Don't come back until every single one of them is back in your pocket. Do you understand?"

"Yes, sir."

"Also, who do you know in the police department you can trust?"

"I know a guy or two."

"No, I mean, can you *trust* them?"

"Yes, we've owned him for years."

"Reach out to him and tell him to give me a call."

"Want to tell me what this is about?"

"I'm cleaning up this mess. You have only two things to do. Deal with the planning board and keep that fucking wife of yours in line as soon as I get her back. Do you think you can handle it?"

"Yes, sir."

"Then get out of here."

After Jeffery and Momma Prescott left, he dialed the Police Commissioner.

"Jack? William Prescott. I haven't seen you around the links lately."

"Hi, Bill. No time for golf. Gotta keep the city safe, and all. By the way, I was getting ready to call you. Your name just came up in a conversation not too long ago. You might want to tell Jeffery he's humping against the wrong dog."

"Oh? I could never tell with Jeff if he was humping another dog, or a fire hydrant. What can you tell me?"

"Let's just say I no longer want this feud on my city streets."

"You seem to be much more informed than I am. Perhaps, you'd care to share?" Elder Prescott said, trying again.

"Nope. Not really. Not with the size of the dogs you're playing with."

"Okay. Thanks Jack."

"As a public servant I'm here to help. Been great touching base, Bill." And he rang off.

William Prescott sat back in his chair, reached forward, selected a Costa Rican cigar, snipped off the end, then leisurely lit it up.

So what have we here, he thought, *what has that little slut wife of his stumbled into? I can only assume by the police commissioner's lack of help, it goes way over his head. Who's over his head? Well, the mayor, but he's a lame duck now that Jeffery is running for office. No, it has to go higher.*

The governor? If he is involved, it means he is getting pressure from Washington. Could the shit be that deep?

Elder Prescott, deep in thought, blew a smoke ring towards the ceiling.

At that moment, his private cell phone rang.

"Hello?"

"Sir, my name is Flynn. I'm with the Urbandale PD. Jeffery left me a message to get in touch with you."

"Hello Sergeant Flynn. I was hoping our paths would cross again. Could we meet somewhere in plain clothes?"

"Well, I'd really like to know why we're meeting."

"I think you already know."

> "I didn't attend the funeral, but I sent a nice letter
> saying I approved of it."
>
> Mark Twain

Chapter 50

"I'm sorry, Mr. Gilheart. There's really nothing we can do pending the outcome of this investigation. That was the decision of the Educational Board." The Teacher's Union Representative was apologetic.

The Teacher's Union Rep. was a lawyer, of course. He had on the slick clothes and the good shoes. His business card was embossed and glossy. It even had his picture on it. His hair was blow-dried. He was about thirty-five. He was still young enough to think he'd get ahead in this life.

Gilheart was starting to feel the pain. Daddy had been right, the next day they downgraded his painkillers from morphine to Demerol, and it wasn't the same. Rolling waves of pain radiated up from his knee. It seemed timed to his pulse, causing his head to throb with the power of a migraine with each heartbeat.

"It was the decision of the board to suspend your health insurance as well as your pay until this matter is concluded. Criminal charges are expected as well. As your representative, I came here to tell you we will of course do what we can, but until you're cleared of criminal charges, our hands are tied."

"What about my medical care?"

"Well, that is kind of a sticky issue. The medical insurance policy clearly states that medical injuries resulting from the commission of a felony are not covered by the policy."

"I haven't been convicted of anything."

"That's absolutely true and exactly what I told the Insurance Commission. However, their position was, that until there is a trial deciding the issue, they have to withhold payment. Of course, if you're acquitted, then they would pay your medical bills in full."

"So, I have no medical insurance?"

"That's what I'm trying to tell you, yes."

"What happens to me now?"

"You'll have to leave this hospital, unless you can get them to agree to your care pro bono."

"And if I can't?"

"You'll go to St. Mary's downtown. So there is really nothing to worry about."

"Isn't St. Mary's for the homeless and destitute?"

"Well, I wouldn't characterize it like that…"

Gilheart found himself unconsciously pumping the button on the automatic drug injection device. Unfortunately, that no longer worked. He had to wait for the nurse to bring a syringe. One thing about pain, it cleared his mind wonderfully, when he could grab a thought.

"The Union will be handling my legal expenses, then?"

"Well, no, actually. Your union contract also becomes null and void in the event of a felony. But I have lined up an excellent public defender for you."

"You've got to be shitting me. So I have no health insurance and no access to legal counsel, is that what you're telling me?" Gilheart asked.

"That's it, in a nutshell, yes."

"Then I am absolutely fucked."

"I think you should concentrate on the positive side of this…"

Gilheart waited until after the Union Rep. left and considered his options. According to the news, they had DNA evidence. Which meant he was probably going to get convicted of rape of that little pig Mia Prescott. That also meant the police would be in anytime to cuff him to the bed. It probably meant his leg would never heal properly, and he wouldn't get the physical therapy and rehabilitation it would need. He'd be a one-eyed rapist who couldn't walk, when he joined general population in prison.

He thought there had to be a joke in there someplace, but he couldn't find it.

If, no, *when* he was convicted, they would move him to a prison hospital. Until then, he would be in the lock up wing at St. Mary's. It meant his house was gone. His pension was gone. Everything was gone. His wife and kids deserted him a long time ago, and they certainly weren't going to have anything to do with him now. His conviction might even be enough to kill his mother and father.

Gilheart recalled Daddy's last conversation with him, *"I'm going to completely, and without mercy, destroy every aspect of your life,"* he had said.

Well, good work. You certainly did that.

"Good morning, Mr. Gilheart," said the nurse walking in. "I'm sorry you had to wait for this shot, but we're busy getting you ready for transfer. This should make you more comfortable."

The nurse put the needle in his ass and pressed the plunger. She put the syringe down by the bedside and said,

"Let me see if I can make your bed for you. That way, the covers won't be bunched under you."

In the course of making the bed, she forgot about the syringe she had laid on the table. Gilheart palmed it as he rolled over as she made one side of the bed, then the other, trying to keep his leg steady.

"There. I'll get you some more ice water, and you'll be all set," she said.

The Demerol was working now and the pain dialed back a notch or two.

The nurse returned with the ice water and set it down where he could reach it.

"It'll only be an hour or two more before they're ready to transfer you. If I don't get to see you again, I want to wish you the best."

Gilheart said nothing as she left. As soon as he was alone, he took the syringe and filled it with air. He carefully inserted the needle into the vein at his elbow and drew the plunger up, watching the blood swirl into the syringe.

He recalled Daddy's last words, *"In the end, when I'm finished, you'll take your own life in despair."*

Gilheart pushed the plunger down, injecting the air bubble into his vein. The air embolism stopped his heart five minutes later.

"The skilful employer of men will employ the wise man, the brave
man, the covetous man, and the stupid man."

Sun Tzu

Chapter 51

Daddy pulled into the safe house driveway. The first thing he did
was change out the plates on his truck. He made sure it was registered
to James Peniwinkle. He wouldn't be using his old identity anymore.

He led Mia upstairs to the apartment, let her in, and gave her a key.
He had the apartment furnished so there was a minimum of comforts.
The kitchen, and refrigerator were well stocked. Mia walked in, looked
around, and stood staring at Daddy.

"This sucks, Daddy."

"It's temporary."

"Does it at least have a nice, big bed?"

"Check it out."

Mia walked down the hall towards the bedroom. She peered into
the bathroom, wrinkled her nose, and continued walking. She went
into the bedroom and stood looking at the bed.

"It's a queen size."

"I know what it is."

"I want all my toys. You have to go back and get them."

"How about if we buy new ones?"

"No. I want those."

"Hey look, we got to talk."

"About what, Daddy?" she asked with no fear. A month ago that
question would have brought on the 'deer stuck in headlight' eyes.
The 'what did I do wrong' look. Now, she just looked at him with
curiosity. She trusted him completely to make the right decisions.

"My name is now James Peniwinkle. I work at Wells Fargo as an accountant."

"You don't look like a James Peniwinkle."

Daddy stood up, got his overcoat from the closet, slipped his Elton John glasses on, and slumped his shoulders. Using his best mousy voice, said,

"How about now?"

"You look completely stupid, Daddy."

"Thank you, dear."

"Is that the best you've got?"

"Well, James Peniwinkle will still let you dress up in the baby-doll panties."

"Really? I knew I liked Jim for a reason. Can we start now?" Mia said, unbuttoning her blouse.

"I think so, yes." Daddy said, smiling.

Daddy suddenly dived on top of her. Mia, giggling, wriggled and fought to free herself, until finally surrendering with her arms around Daddy's neck.

"I love you, Daddy."

"I love you too, Baby."

They made slow, passionate love into the early hours of the morning.

Daddy got up and set up his laptop. He had broadband connected to the apartment so he'd have an internet connection. The first thing he did was check his email while the coffee brewed. He couldn't access his email from this new connection.

Strange.

Next, he tried going to his website and accessing the email through his C-panel of his web host. He couldn't access that either.

Next, he tried his bank accounts. They were sealed, and he was told to contact his bank.

He tried his Pay-Pal account as well. It was discontinued.

Once is a mistake, twice is coincidence, three times is enemy action, thought Daddy.

Daddy got up, went and made a cup of coffee and sat back down in front of the laptop.

Daddy studied the chessboard in his mind. *It was a good move, freezing his assets,* thought Daddy. *One which seems oddly out of place for Jeffery Prescott. Jeffery doesn't think with that kind of finesse. Is it pos-*

sible we have a new player on board?

"Good morning, Daddy," said Mia, looking fresh and smiling like she always did after good sex. She was wearing her baby-doll panties and one of his shirts, tied high under her breasts, with the buttons open. She looked young, happy, and absolutely stunning in the morning light. He snapped a mental picture of her for his memory collection.

"Hello Baby, you look beautiful."

Mia stretched with her arms over her head in the morning light like a cat. Her shirt rode up on her breast revealing a small, stiff nipple before she pulled it back down again.

"What are we going to do today? Go see more lawyers? That was getting kind of fun. You should have seen them clawing up that packet and slobbering all over the photos. I didn't even mind they were looking at me. A couple of them let me know they were 'available' after the divorce. They're jerks."

"Yes, they are. I'm not surprised. I'm sorry if it humiliated you. I couldn't think of any other way to quickly do what we had to do."

"I'm just glad we're not hiring any of them."

"Today, you're going to stay here. I have to go and get us some stuff. It's safer if you don't come with me."

Mia just looked at Daddy and said, "Okay, Daddy."

Daddy left his truck at a car rental place by the airport and continued on in a rental car that was more in keeping with his new persona. He chose a late model Toyota Prius and cruised his old neighborhood. He spotted the surveillance van. They were being much more careful this time. He wondered if they had entered the house and set either audio or video surveillance inside.

He pulled around to a parallel street and parked, then went in on foot to break into his own house from the back. He got inside with no trouble. He went immediately to his safe and extracted the ID's, passports, cash, and some weapons. He slung his Mossberg 500 pump shotgun over his shoulder.

He went upstairs and got some "toys" for Mia. He had a good time imagining if he got caught by any of Prescott's men.

Cash, check.

ID's, check.

Shotgun, check.

Vibrators?

What would a stone-cold criminal think of that? He looked around for anything that could incriminate him further.

This was the last time he would see this house for a while. Maybe ever. He enjoyed this house. His son had grown up here and if anything happened to him, his son would own it free and clear. It was a happy house. Full of good memories, good meals, and good times. He could still hear his son's laughter echoing through his mind. He and Mia had 'christened' every room, including the bathrooms. Except his son's room, of course.

He sat down at the Yamaha piano and had an almost uncontrollable urge to play the last song he and his son had played together. He remembered them dancing around the room, lost in the music.

Instead, he walked to the back door, opened it, stepped outside, and quietly shut the door on this chapter of his life.

"Three thousand jurisdictions across the U.S. are estimated to have had gang activity in 2001. In 2002, 32% of cities with a population of 25 to 50 thousand reported a gang-related homicide."

Bob Filner

Chapter 52

Flynn slowly rolled down Martin Luther King Bvld., scanning for someone. This specific someone had the skills and motivation for the job Prescott needed done. Truthfully, this was against Flynn's better judgment. He told himself that this was the last God damn favor he was doing for that rich prick, Prescott. He almost believed himself.

As he came to a stop at an intersection, he spotted his "friend." How could anyone miss him in that ugly, ostentatious piece of shit Caddy? It was an 80's model, white for fuck sake. He probably bought it off of Nick Nolte after they finished filming '48 hours.'

That wasn't the worst of it, though.

This wonderful member of society was a wannabe rapper. Just like all the other shit-for-brains wannabes, his ego was far bigger than his talent. *Why did they all want to be rappers?* thought Flynn, *the least they could do is pull up their pants.*

What Flynn couldn't figure out was how they thought they were supposed to look bad ass with the pants turned around and down around their ankles.

His car represented his ego perfectly; big on flash, small on substance. It had huge letters and graphics airbrushed over the entire thing. It was a moving advertisement for himself. There were the huge letters D.O.P. plastered over both doors and the hood. The wannabe idiot had named himself the "Duke of Pussy." The witty thug even put images of crowns and scepters on his car. If you took a minute to look hard enough, you could see that the heads of the scepters were female genitalia. Assuming he could even find feminine genitalia in person.

What a fucking class act, Flynn thought.

As he pulled up behind the Caddy. Flynn did a quick whoop-whoop with his siren and added lights, just to make a scene and maybe piss them off. He exited his patrol car, and two men tried getting out of the back.

"For your own safety, stay in the car."

They both shot him the look. The look said 'I have no problem shooting a cop's ass right here in public'.

Flynn gave them a look back that said 'go ahead. We'll see who wins.' That actually made Flynn smile while he walked around his car. He loved his job when it included fucking with dirt bags. Even so he undid the safety strap on his Glock.

"Dope! How the hell are you?" He loved the way mispronouncing his name got under his skin. This guy was just born to be someone's punch line. "Step out of the car, please."

"What the fuck you want?" Tavon Ward, aka D.O.P., threw his arms up, with added theatrics.

Flynn came to stand next to the young thug with his saggy jeans and straight-billed cap. Ward's friends, didn't listen, and got out of the car and backed up to join the rest of their small posse standing a few feet away.

"Dope, is that anyway to speak to your old friend?"

"It's D.O. motherfuckin' P., bitch!" Again, his arms flew around trying to look intimidating, but instead he almost dropped his low riding pants on the ground. Violent hand gestures gave way to pulling his pants back up.

The gang of men started to howl and holler. There was a "smack the shit out of this bitch" or two thrown around.

"All right, all right, Duke. We need to talk."

"We don't need to do shit mutherfucka."

"Okay, well I guess I'll just do all the talking then." Before the other man could react, Flynn grabbed him by the back of the neck, spun him and bent him over the hood of his gangsta-mobile. In one fluid motion, he bounced his head off the hood. Flynn used his other hand to pull his weapon and jam it into the Duke's ear. He could hear yelling and movement from the crowd.

"Now tell your shit-eatin' boys to stay put before my trigger finger gets a cramp. You know what could happen if it gets a cramp, don't you?"

The Duke swore under his breath, "Piece of shit." Louder, "Yo, yo, yo. Wait, fuckers."

Flynn heard the audience calm slightly. Most of the movement stopped.

"Now, that I think you are ready to listen. I have a job for you," Flynn growled into the man's ear.

"Why the fuck would I do anything for a punk ass cop?"

"Because you like my sense of style would be my guess," Flynn pressed the thug's face harder into the hood of his Caddy. "Or because I could take you in right now for the shit I'm sure is in your pockets and car. What would I find there, huh, Duke? And if I did take you in, I might accidentally mention how grateful we all were that you rolled on your boy last month. You remember, right? That shooting outside of the recording studio. I'm not sure we would have been able to solve that without your help. Maybe I could see to it you got a community service award you could hang on your rear-view mirror."

"You got some mutherfuckin nerve coming to my block and threatening me."

"Well, maybe your crew here would like to hear the story of Duke Of Snitch." Flynn raised his voice and directed it at the posse, "Hey guys! Did I ever tell you the story…"

"Fine, what the fuck do you need?"

"Be at the Third Street warehouse at eleven p.m. Then we can discuss the help I need. Oh, I will have friends around so don't even think of bringing the get-along-gang." With that, Flynn shoved the Duke's head one more time roughly into the airbrushed picture of a pussy scepter.

"Here Duke…eat some pussy."

The cop returned his weapon to its holster and nodded to the group of men. His smile quickly faded, however, as he got back into his patrol car.

Why the hell was he in this shit so deep? Fuck Prescott. Elder and Junior. Fuck them both.

"The genius of our ruling class is that it has kept a majority of the people from ever questioning the inequity of a system where most people drudge along, paying heavy taxes for which they get nothing in return."

Gore Vidal

Chapter 53

"You've been served," the process server slapped the papers in Jeffery Prescott's hand.

What new shit is this? he thought. He was sitting in the "Bar Exam," a watering hole for, you guessed it, lawyers, when the process server strolled in and walked right up to him. He didn't even bother asking Prescott to identify himself, which means he must have been getting a lot of press lately.

He was sitting with a group of lawyers and members of the planning board. None bothered to ask what the lawsuit was about. Getting served was as common as ordering a martini lunch. Jeffery Prescott accepted the envelope nonchalantly, and put it beside his drink.

"I think I've been able to answer all your concerns about this project," he continued smoothly, as though there had been no interruption, "furthermore, I don't see any reason we can't proceed on schedule. Do you, gentlemen?"

Every single person on the planning board had been bribed. Since they also had gotten smarter, and compared their bribes, adjustments had been made to include the lowest-paid members to the highest. In other words, everyone now had the feeling they were being screwed equally. Of course, no one alluded to the bad smell of corruption. It was the fart in the confessional no one wanted to talk about.

"Well, I wouldn't go so far, or so fast, Jeffery," said one of the senior members. "For example, you managed to evade the question of the 'no compete' contracts all going to the same contractor. If the city is giving this project a ten-year tax holiday, we have a right to want to open up the bidding to the best contractor."

You mean, one of your contractors, thought Prescott, instead he said, "I wouldn't characterize it as a 'no compete' contract. It simply represents the reality that all things taken into consideration, we can't go into an over-budget situation. While you may be giving us a tax holiday on the property tax, the city stands to gain over one hundred million dollars a year in tax revenue. I would call your end a 'holiday' long before mine." *You cheap fuck.*

Right then, the current mayor decided to amble over and grace the table with his presence. The city employees made a show of scraping and bowing. Each trying to outdo each other in bootlicking and bringing ass kissing to a whole new level. Prescott watched the show with interest. *This is how these same jackals will treat me once I'm elected,* he thought.

The Mayor finally got around to recognizing his opponent in the next election.

"Jeffery Prescott! How is your father doing?" *You privileged little dick-licker,* he didn't add.

"Mayor, it's good to see you," Jeffery stood up to shake his hand. *I'm going to stick my dick so far up your ass in the next election you'll think it took the place of one of your molars,* Prescott thought inwardly and smiled outwardly.

"Dad is fine. He wishes you'd come out to the house more."

"Well, I'd love to. It is barbecue season and all. Nothing like kicking back, having some brews, and watching a game." *I bet I could score an easy five hundred bucks off you, you little twit, by the time the game is over.*

"You know you're always welcome, Mayor." *Did I tell you I fucked your daughter?*

"Thank you, Jeff. Best of luck with the election. If you can unseat the incumbent you deserve the office." *I'm going to grind you into puppy dust, you little blow-dried, wife-beating, faggot.*

The table was quiet after the Mayor left. Jeffery Prescott thought that he had gotten out of all the awkward situations for the day, when Robert Nailer, one of the previously slighted planning board members took the opportunity to ask,

"Pity to hear about John Gilheart's suicide the other day. You just never know who you're dealing with, or what they're capable of. Has anything been heard about your wife? The shock of what that monster did must have been horrible for you."

Prescott looked at him and decided then and there, if he was elected he was going to crush this insolent little shit.

"Yes, it has been a shock. One I'd rather not talk about, if you don't mind."

"Of course, of course," said Nailer, "I do hope the police find those responsible."

Another planning board member, seeing the situation also chimed in.

"And this was a man teaching our children. Putting ill-deserving people in positions of responsibility is something which has got to stop." Leaving no doubt as to his meaning.

Okay, I guess I can't count on their votes, thought Prescott.

"Well, the present reality with our system as it stands is that sometimes ill-deserving people do get put into positions of responsibility. When that happens, a lot of *undeserving* people can certainly suffer," said Prescott, pointedly, standing up, looking at each member in turn. "Now, if you gentlemen will excuse me, I think our business is concluded, and I'll expect the planning board's approval by tomorrow. Good day, gentlemen."

Jeffery Prescott got back to his office, and slumped into his chair. Layla, his secretary came in with the missed calls, and put them on his desk, being sure to bend over far enough that her boss could see her nipples. Not getting the distraction she wanted, she went behind the desk so it would look to the world like she was just talking to her boss. She hiked her short skirt up high enough so he could stare at her shaved and smooth pussy.

"Is there anything I can get for you?"

"I think we'll be working late at my house again tonight. Are you available for overtime?"

"Of course I am, Boss."

Prescott nodded in dismissal, and opened the process server's envelope. It was a Petition for Dissolution of Marriage. That little bitch filed for divorce!

Which meant if she aired the dirty family laundry, it would kill any chances at the Mayor's office.

That little bitch, in one smooth motion, she held all the high cards.

"If the KKK was smart enough, they would've created gangsta rap because it's such a caricature of black culture and black masculinity."

Jackson Katz

Chapter 54

Flynn killed time calmly by the Third Street warehouse, waiting for DOP to arrive.

Normally in such a situation, he would be absolutely sure that DOP would try to set it up so he would be beaten. Killing a cop, of course, was dirty business. Even the gang bangers with all their puffery and playacting, didn't contemplate it lightly.

Even so, Flynn had a number of off-duty sharp-shooters he could call on for favors, who never asked questions. They were situated all around the open-air warehouse. Rifles zeroed, awaiting a command in their earpieces. They would have no hesitation in dropping them where they stood.

Twenty-five minutes past the agreed-upon time, Flynn could hear loud rap music in the distance growing closer. The DOP mobile rounded a corner by the edge of the warehouse, came forward, and stood idling with the headlights on.

Another intimidation tactic. Flynn was supposed to be blinded, while they could see. Flynn could smell, and see marijuana smoke rolling out of the car windows in clouds like in a Cheech and Chong movie.

Dipshits. Come to a firefight stoned, that's brilliant, thought Flynn.

"Yo, mothafucka. D.O.P. is in the house." DOP climbed out of the driver's side. Another home boy came out the passenger side, and three more out of the back. They all stood there, tough, fingering, and looking bad with guns in their belts.

I wonder how many gang bangers have shot their dicks off accidental-

ly? thought Flynn, *not enough for them to quit sticking their guns in the absolute worst place possible, I guess. I wonder how many of these clowns have the safety off?*

"What happened to coming alone? I thought I was pretty clear on that point."

"Me and my niggas are never caught slippin'. When you meet the Po Po, you be having some witnesses, you feel me, Flynn?"

"I don't feel a God damned thing, Dope."

"It's D.O.P. bitch. Check your fuckin' tone."

"Or what's gonna happen?"

"Shit, look at this ballsy cocksucka'. You want to find out?"

"Sure DOPE, let's give it a whirl." Flynn flicked the cigarette he was smoking in their direction, which was the signal. Bright-red laser dots appeared on the chest of every person present except Flynn.

"You still want to dance, DOPE?"

"What the fuck?"

"Yeah, shithead. Keep talking your shit and see what my boys think about it. I'm getting the feeling the Duke of Pussy doesn't trust me. That's good. Because I don't trust him either. Which gives us the basis of a good working relationship. You with me so far, or has pussy juice clogged up your ears?"

"Fuck you!"

"Oh, good. You do understand. Maybe you aren't as stupid as you look. Now be a good business partner and come over here so we can chat."

DOP shuffled over, pulling his pants up as he came. Flynn rolled his eyes. When he was out of earshot of his home boys, Flynn pulled him around so DOP's back was to them.

"I got a little job I need done."

"What kind of job?"

"A snatch and grab. Two people. One man, one woman."

"What's in it for me?"

"Spoken like a true urban hero. For openers, I'll let you keep on selling meth out of that whorehouse you call a recording studio."

"Dude, you don't fuckin' know me. I ain't be selling shit out of shit." He said this just loud enough for his boys to hear so they would think Flynn was rousting him.

"Shut the fuck up. Here's the way this is going to work. You'll take this phone. You'll get an address text. You do the deed, right then.

Not the next day. Right fuckin' then. Are we clear on this point?"

"Yeah, yeah, right then. Pronto, ASAP, and all that cop talk. So we be like level, then?"

"We 'be like' nothing. You do me a favor, and I do you one. If you don't fuck it completely up, I might have more. If you fuck it up, I'm coming down on you hard."

"Yeah, yeah."

"Another thing. You touch the woman, and I do mean, you so much as don't open a door for her, I will personally break your head open and feed you your brains. We need to be real clear on this point. No fun with the woman. No copping a feel. No sniffing her panties."

"What about the whitebread homey you want to snatch?"

"Who said he was a whitebread?"

"I'm not new to this fuckin' game, Officer. If it was a brotha' you wanted, any cop could swoop in."

"Right, I forgot how smart you are, Duke." Flynn snorted. "You can take your jollies out on him for all I care. But don't touch the woman."

Flynn looked over at the other gang bangers. The red laser dots were still on their chests. They were standing there like they were nailed into the ground.

"Since we now in bidness together and I'm sensing your generosity. I got…"

"I'm not feeling generous, DOP. I'm feeling mean as a snake, because I know you're going to fuck this up."

"No man, really. I be understandin' and all. Simple snatch and grab. Don't touch the woman. Me and my boys could do that any day of the week."

"Oh, by the way, I got to make this look good for your buddies and mine."

"Huh?"

Flynn decked him. A straight upper cut that came out of nowhere, that started under his solar plexus and continued up to his chin. It literally knocked DOP out of his pants and lifted him off the ground.

His posse surged forward as one. Muffled shots at their feet stopped them. Flynn wagged his finger back and forth at them. No, no.

"Man, what the fuck was that for? Here we be businessizing and all," said DOP, when he could catch his breath. He was rubbing his jaw, and cradling his gut, still sitting on his ass on the ground with his pants around his ankles.

"Just making sure you were awake. Pull your pants up for Christ's sake."

"Fuck you, Flynn."

"Fuck you too, Dope."

"I want my daughter to be proud of me and look up to me. I think early on in my pregnancy I realized that to be the mom I want to be, I had to change my life, and that's what I'm doing."

Holly Madison

Chapter 55

"Daddy, something's wrong."

"What do you mean?"

"I'm not feeling good."

"Are you saying Dr. McNasty needs to perform an examination?"

"Well, Dr. McNasty is always welcome, but I'm not joking. I haven't been feeling well."

"Okay, what's wrong?"

"I don't know. I've gotten sick the last couple of days. I thought it was something I ate. But now other things feel strange."

"I can assure you, Dr. McNasty's beef is one hundred percent USDA prime steak," Daddy said, smiling. "What else doesn't feel right, Baby?"

"My titties are sore. I think you were too rough with them last night."

"I wasn't rough with them."

"Yes, you were. I said so. I'm cramping, too. Like I'm getting my period, you know?"

"Well, not exactly, but I can imagine…"

"Daddy, be serious…"

"I am being serious! Stand up for me, okay?"

Mia stood, and Daddy sat on the edge of the bed and pulled her over so she stood between his legs. He put his hands over her kidneys, and pushed in.

"Does it hurt there?"

"No, not really."

"How about there?" He had moved his hands so that they were over her abdomen, around her navel.

"Yeah, kinda."

"When was the last time you got your period?"

"I don't remember, but it is always on time."

"Are you using birth control?"

"I thought you were snipped."

"Does that mean no?"

"Well, Daddy…"

Daddy hopped into his truck and cruised to the all-night drug store. His internal radar went off. He started looking around more closely but didn't see anything out of the ordinary, or anyone taking an unusual interest in him, so he dismissed it.

He walked the aisles, getting what he needed. He got more than was necessary, and different ones, so in case he was right he could check the conclusions of each and compare.

Daddy paid special attention going home, back-tracked, and re-traced in order to spot a tail, but still didn't see anything. Still, a nagging feeling.

Am I paranoid? he asked himself, living on the run will do it to you. He decided he was being overly cautious and slipped into the driveway.

Flynn sat down the street in a darkened city surveillance van, watching quietly.

Mia was still waiting on the bed where he left her.

"What did you get me?"

"Come on, Baby. Into the bathroom. Take your panties down and sit on the toilet. I want you to pee on this for me."

"Okay."

"Wait until I get the boxes open and pee on all three, okay?"

"Okay, hurry up because now I've got to go."

"Okay, go ahead."

Daddy held each under her warm stream. The warmth of the urine splashed across his fingers. He finished filling up each reservoir on each home pregnancy test kit, and set them aside. Then he washed his hands. Mia rearranged herself on the toilet, and spread her legs up and out, exposing her long thin legs, beautiful smooth pussy and ass. Which was completely too much visual input for Daddy.

Later, laying in bed after another marathon sex episode, Mia was contentedly laying in his arms, playing with the hair on Daddy's chest.

"Daddy? Can I ask you something?"

"Yes, Baby."

"Everything's perfect right now. Even this shitty apartment."

"This shitty apartment is keeping you safe."

"I know that Daddy."

"Oh shit! Wait a minute. I forgot."

Daddy got up out of bed naked and walked into the bathroom and got the three home pregnancy test kits. Mia liked looking at his cock swinging, knowing her juices were all over it. He walked back into the bedroom, and sat down on the bed.

"What do they say?"

"All three say you're pregnant, Baby. You're going to be a mother."

They sat there, looking at each other, as the importance of the news sank into each one differently.

"Let me see that," said Mia, taking them out of Daddy's hand. Mia put them down on the bed, then crawled into Daddy's lap, so they were facing each other.

"It's a part of me and you, Daddy, it's us…" a tear came down her face. "What do you want to do?"

"I know. I'm too old, Baby. You should be with a better man," Daddy said, softly.

"A better man? You are the ONLY man, I will EVER be with in this life. If you don't want it, then we should do…something, while we can."

"I didn't say that! Don't put words in my mouth."

"So then, you do want to have a baby with me," said Mia, smiling coyly, "I knew you did…"

Mia started laughing, looking at Daddy.

"I have Daddy's baby/I have Daddy's baby," she sing-songed.

"Even death is not to be feared by one who has lived wisely."

Buddha

Chapter 56

Flynn texted the address of Mia's safe house to DOP, then sat back waiting for news. *He had better not fuck this up,* he thought. He'd keep out of sight watching just in case.

DOP's cell phone went off, and he looked at the address.

"Yo! Bros, gather round. We's got a job to do." The homies stood around DOP all waiting for orders. "Now, this here's the way this has got to go down. We's gonna do a grab of some white bitch and cracker. No one is to touch the bitch, understands? No one. The honky we can have fun with."

DOP's crew looked at each other and shrugged. Their expressions said 'what's the big deal?'

"Why can't we fuck the bitch?"

"Cause I said so, stupid ass nigga. Don't touch her. Don't even so much as feel her titties, you feeling me?"

"Yeah, yeah." What was the point of stealing a white bitch if they couldn't all take turns fucking her?

"What we gonna do with 'em?"

"We take 'em to the old meat packing plant. So the plan is, we's get in, snatch 'em, put them both in the trunk and take 'em there. We can fuck up the whitebread though. Maybe we have fun and take turns with the baseball bat."

This appeased them somewhat.

Daddy heard the bells tinkling over his head. Which meant someone was coming up the stairs. He had attached a tripwire on the stairs and knew he had seconds to act.

"Run and hide, Baby," he said, as he pushed Mia off the bed. She looked at Daddy with big eyes. "Run! Just like we talked about."

He heard voices slamming up against the door. He had changed out the locks as well as put four-inch screws holding the lock in place in the door jam. They weren't going to kick that door open anytime soon. He heard black voices, and he was vaguely surprised he wasn't facing a Police SWAT team. The shotgun was loaded, so he started putting extra shells in his pocket.

Daddy moved to a defensive position, on the floor, facing the door. It wouldn't hold much longer. He racked the shotgun, to let them know he wasn't playing. The crowbar on the lock stopped momentarily as this new information got processed by even the dimmest lights outside the door. The first person through that door was going to die tonight.

The door blew inward, and Daddy let loose with the first round of buckshot, blowing a monster of a guy backwards. He rolled over to the other side of the door, just as shots from a .45 blew up the position where he had been moments before. He took down the second shooter. The muzzle blast from the shotgun revealed his position, so he had to move again.

He moved straight at them. Racking a load, and not even bothering to aim, he let loose. Racked another, and fired. Racked another and fired. Screams and body parts were all he could see in the momentary strobe light of the muzzle blasts.

Daddy was outnumbered, and he knew it. He was running out of ammo and didn't have time to reload. He wasn't going to win this.

It was time to die well.

I'm sorry, Baby, I did what I could, he thought, as he rammed the barrel of the shotgun into an attacker's throat, fired, and blew a hole all the way through one throat, and took out another attacker behind him with the same shot.

"Stand Back!" DOP yelled. His boy jogged to the left, and fired the taser into Daddy's chest. Daddy went down, jerking on the floor.

"Go get de bitch," DOP said, to the only man left standing. DOP looked down at the guy who took out five of the six soldiers he brought with him.

"Youse gonna pay, cracker, youse gonna die hard. Dem boys were my homies."

DOP kept the juice flowing. DOP couldn't believe the mayhem he saw around him. It looked like Beirut. Bodies were everywhere and none of them breathing. DOP, wisely, remained in back of his troops as the leader or he would have joined the others, he had no doubt.

DOP heard another gun off in another room, the five consecutive shots, then silence. Andre The Giant, brought in a kicking and screaming Mia, by the hair.

"Dis little bitch was armed too," he said, unbelievingly, like he didn't expect white people to fight back.

"Daddy!" Mia threw herself towards Daddy on the floor.

"Don't fight, Baby. Just go with them. They won't hurt you. I'll be coming for you."

"Get dat bitch out of here. Tape her mouth and hands. Remember what I said. No touching the bitch." DOP said.

The cell phone rang then.

"Wha?" DOP listened. "No, we got da bitch." Pause "No, she ain't hurt. You didn't tell me this cracker was trained. I lost five of my boys tonight, you lying pig."

DOP walked over to Daddy as he was talking and raised his boot to bring it down on the side of Daddy's head, knocking him out. Instead, Daddy reached up, grabbed his foot, and twisted it, rolling to the side as he did. DOP dropped the cell phone and had just enough time to put the juice back on the taser, stopping the assault.

"Mothafucka…"

Daddy had just enough time to think, *I hope I die well,* before his lights went out.

Flynn snapped the cell phone shut and pondered his next move. He was secretly glad he hadn't gone up against The Nameless Guy. It wasn't that he was afraid, but he had taken enough beatings in his life to know when to step aside. The place was going to be a mess. Already he heard units responding. The best course of action was to stay the fuck out of it and get the hell out of here. It will look like a drug hit gone wrong.

Five dead, Jesus Christ, he thought, *the shit is really going to hit the fan.* Flynn admitted to himself he had a grudging admiration and respect for the man. Whoever he was, he wasn't a shitbag. He asked for none of this. He was just trying to protect the woman he loved. Flynn wondered what it was like to have a love so great, so powerful, that your very own life is inconsequential. A love so powerful you would be willing to kill anyone who threatened it. He was a worthy adversary and a man of honor, deserving of respect.

Time to tell William Prescott his daughter-in-law would be joining them for a midnight snack.

"For me, my awakening came when I was kidnapped."

Patty Hearst

Chapter 57

Mia was slapped a couple of times by Andre The Giant, to make her shut up, then duct-taped. Multiple times around the mouth, and her arms, wrists, and ankles.

Mia was picked up, as though she weighed nothing, and put into the trunk of DOP's Caddy. There was plenty of room for her back there, and The Giant, was fairly gentle in putting her in.

Daddy was carried down next, duct taped, and put in beside her. Then DOP and Andre calmly drove away from the scene of the crime before the police arrived. Since this wasn't the best of neighborhoods, chances were small that they would be pulled over for "driving while black" in this part of town.

DOP and Andre hopped on the freeway without trouble and drove south. They exited the freeway, and made a right-hand turn into the old meat-packing plant. DOP drove in and told Andre to put the cracker in the room they prepared. So far, so good. Now to call Flynn and arrange the transfer.

"Yo? Come get the bitch," was all DOP said and disconnected. DOP could hear muffled shouts behind the duct-tape, as Mia kicked the inside of the trunk. He leaned against the trunk, unconcerned.

Soon enough, a shabby plumbing van pulled into the meat-packing plant side entrance. Flynn, in street clothes, jumped out.

"How'd it go?"

"Like we discussed. Dat boy of yours took out five of my brothers. You could have warned me."

"Yeah? And what would that have sounded like? Be careful of the fat, old, white guy. He'll probably kick your ass and take out five of the brothers? Something like that?"

"He gonna pay, you know dat, right?"

"Did you harm the girl?"

"Not a single hair on her pretty head."

"Let me see her." Flynn put on a black ski mask.

DOP popped the trunk. Mia wide-eyed and looking ready to tear someone's head off, stared defiantly back.

"She a wild cat, dat one."

"Get her out. Cut her loose."

DOP reached in with a Spyder knife and cut her leg restraints off. Then cut the ones binding her arms. He left the wrist restraints in place, and lifted her out of the trunk.

Flynn grabbed her upper arm tightly and started leading her toward the van. Mia dug her heels in and started twisting out of his grasp. DOP looked on in amusement.

Flynn stopped, looked at her then said very softly,

"Mia, I can take you hard, or take you easy. But you're going home. I won't hurt you. But if you keep fighting me, I'll knock you out cold with a shot." He lifted up a syringe.

"Your choice."

Mia looked at him with pleading eyes, and said something against her gag. Flynn imagined the words as 'Please, don't'.

"I don't have a choice, Mia," was all he said.

Flynn pulled up in front of Prescott Jr's. house, Mia's old home. The interior lights were on. He looked up and down the street, but all was quiet. He'd finish this job and then he was through with these rich scumbags.

He was disgusted with himself for what he was doing and thought about how far he had sunk as a human being. At least, the Nameless Guy had been protecting his woman. What was he doing? But delivering her back to the same hell she almost escaped from. Flynn rolled down the window and spat to get the bad taste out of his mouth.

Flynn got out, opened the back of the van, and took Mia out. Once she saw the house she started whipping her head back and forth. 'Oh no', she was trying to say. Flynn brought his mouth close to her ear.

"Walk, or I'll carry you."

Mia stopped struggling. Flynn watched as resolve came into her eyes. She straightened her shoulders, picked her chin up, and nodded her head. 'I'm ready', her eyes said.

Flynn looked at her with admiration. He could see why the Nameless Guy was ready to die for her. She was walking willingly, head up, towards her doom. She wasn't going to give him the satisfaction of seeing her flinch. He almost let her go, right then. Instead, he fought the urge, and walked up the path to the door.

The door opened instantly. Jeffery Prescott was there to greet them.

"Mia! I missed you!" he said.

Flynn brought her in. William Prescott was at the dining room table, drinking a scotch.

"Good work…"

"No names!" Flynn said before he could finish his sentence. "We're even. Don't call me again. I want no part of this."

"Oh, you're in deep now, I'm afraid," said William Prescott, calmly. "We own you. Don't you ever forget it. But you did a good job tonight, and I'm sure Jeff will be very grateful when he becomes Mayor. I'm thinking someone like you could be very handy as Police Commissioner. Of course, you'll have to come up through the ranks, but I think we'll be able to speed your career along."

"I don't think you heard me. I'm not interested."

"I don't think you heard me, Officer *Flynn*," saying his name for Mia's sake.

Flynn walked over and pushed one of the bedroom doors open. The mirrors were set up around the handcuffs hanging from the ceiling. Various paddles and whips were scattered about the room on tables. On one side, he saw an electric cattle prod. Another had a ping-pong paddle with small tacks embedded point side out.

"Would you like to stay and watch, Officer Flynn? Beating a woman is an acquired taste. However, once experienced it is very difficult to go back to plain Jane sex," said William Prescott. "I personally like to beat them until they are bloody. I love seeing blood trickle between their legs. Jeff here, is more of a belt kind of guy. He enjoys more sublime pleasures."

"You are both sick fucks."

Jeffery Prescott grabbed Mia by the hair and hauled her into the room, lifting her hands into the cuffs. The twisted pleasure in his eyes said he couldn't wait to get started. He ripped her dress off and let her swing naked in front of Flynn. Mia's eyes were looking right at him, resigned to her fate.

Flynn thought about shooting them both, right then and there. He could actually see it in his mind's eye. He could see the blood and brains blowing out the back of their heads. If he did he might even be able to welcome himself back to the human race.

William Prescott just looked at him, like he knew exactly what was going through his mind. He smiled slightly.

Sergeant Flynn, a man lost in his own moral abyss, turned and walked out the door. He got into the van, sickened with himself and flipped open the cell phone.

"Yeah?"

"Don't touch the white bread. Leave him for me."

"Well, the brothers are already softening him up with a baseball bat. He got a lot to answer fo."

Flynn could hear the muffled 'whumps' as the bat hit soft flesh in the background.

"He a tough fucker, I give him dat."

"No more fun. Stop it now."

DOP could be heard speaking away from the phone.

"Yo, yo! Stop fo a minute," then speaking back to Flynn, "I can't guarantee how long we be able to not wail on this boy, you feel me?"

"I'm on my way."

The least he could do, Flynn thought, was let him die like a man and not beaten like a piece of meat at the hands of animals.

"Violence is the last refuge of the incompetent."

Isaac Asimov

Chapter 58

Daddy came to and found he was hanging by his hands over a blood drain on the floor.

He looked about the room. It was an old, tiled room with one door leading into it. Judging from the hinges, the door opened inward, rather than outward. The floor was concrete, sloping to a large blood drain on the floor. The concrete was discolored in places with a rust color permanently etched into the concrete. There were a number of hooks hanging down, which rested on a ball-bearing track-like arrangement used for moving heavy hanging loads from one part of the room to another. There were also several rope pulleys suspended from the ceiling. One of which was holding him now.

He knew he was in the "killing room" of a slaughterhouse.

Okay, I know where I am. Time to take stock of my personal inventory, he thought, running through his options in his mind. He flexed each limb to see if there was any injury. None that he could feel. Good. He wasn't suspended above the ground, which was also good. He had no shoes and the concrete was cold on his feet. Another good sign. *Okay, I'm immobile, but uninjured,* he thought.

Okay, I'm in a slaughterhouse, which means I'm probably on the south side of town at one of the abandoned meat packing plants. Okay, take personal inventory, what's my current situation?

I'm uninjured. I'm on the south side of town. I'm in the killing room of a slaughterhouse which means there are probably makeshift weapons available if I can find them, or use what is handy. I'm suspended in the air, but my feet are touching the floor. I have no shoes.

"Yo, whitebread," DOP was sitting on a chair in back of him. He got up now, walking into Daddy's line of sight. "Youse got lots to answer fo."

Daddy said nothing.

The door to the killing room clanged open and a bunch of gang bangers came in. They were carrying baseball bats.

"Now we's gonna have a good old-fashioned game of baseball. Do you like baseball, cracker?"

DOP snapped his fingers and someone threw him a bat. He caught it and held it up.

"Louisville Slugger. These bats of course, ain't quite regulation, see? We fills the ends with lead. What chu think, Cracker?"

Daddy remained silent.

DOP waited a beat, then took careful aim, and let a wild swing go. Daddy had enough time to anticipate the swing and angle his body so that the bat hit nothing vital.

"Foul ball," said DOP. He sized Daddy up again and let loose another wild swing. Once again, Daddy could deflect the blow.

"I'd call dat one a strike," he looked over his shoulder at his boys, "what you think?"

DOP was getting angry. Daddy wasn't begging or pleading. He wasn't grunting in pain, or making any sound whatsoever. He just hung there looking at him. In fact, it was starting to creep DOP out a little. If he couldn't get this white bread to scream, he was going to lose face in front of his boys. Daddy looked at him and instantly knew what he was going to do next.

"Come on, homey's, come on over here. Wat dey call this in Mexico? A 'pin' something, I forget. It's Mexican for let's beat this cracker senseless."

Someone put on a boom box of loud rap music and cranked the volume to the max. The crowd surged forward to have fun. Daddy knew he had no choice but to take it and hope they didn't injure anything major. He knew he could take out the gang banger in front of him named DOP, but it wouldn't gain him anything. He'd still be trussed up and out numbered.

"Now, we be talking," the boys surged forward. A couple of their whores stood against the wall and watched. Their mouths hanging open in sick fascination.

The blows came out of nowhere and everywhere. Daddy had no other option but to disappear up inside his head and travel to another place. The Marines taught him how to handle pain a lifetime ago.

"Hey DOP! How come you don't let the ho's have a chance, uh?" said one of the hookers. "He took my man, maybe I take his 'man' too," said one of the women. She had a crazy look in her eye as she brought out a straight razor, leaving no doubt to her intent.

"Ooohhh…you hear dat, cracker? You went and pissed off one of dem bitches. As you know, you never, ever, piss off the kinder, gentler, sex, you feel me? Because, they say, 'hell ain't got no bitches, like a pissed off bitch,' or somethin' like dat."

"Let me try…" The skank walked up to Daddy and unzipped his fly, and pulled his cock out. They other guys backed off, watching this twisted treat about to play out.

She pulled Daddy's cock out into her hand and started stroking it.

"Oooohhhh…I think this look nice up on my trophy wall." She moved the straight razor over it. "Now, you see, if we cuts way up here, I be sure to get to the whole thing, and then…"

DOP's cell phone rang.

"Yeah?" DOP listened a minute. He motioned someone to turn down the music.

"Well, the brothers are already softening him up with a baseball bat. He got a lot to answer fo." DOP stuck a finger in his ear to hear better.

"He a tough fucker, I give him dat."

"Yo, yo! Stop fo a minute," DOP said, waving at his boys, then speaking back to Flynn. "I can't guarantee how long we be able to not wail on this boy, you feel me?"

DOP walked back over to Daddy.

"Yo bitch! Back off. The umps saying this game gonna have to go into overtime. I think youse a lucky cracker. Otherwise Lavonda here, she gonna take home a trophy."

"A lawyer with his briefcase can steal more
than a hundred men with guns."

Mario Puzo

Chapter 59

The Prescotts, Elder and Junior, watched a beaten and bruised Mia
swinging in front of the mirror.

They were siting at a table, both drinking whiskey, taking a well-
deserved break before resuming the fun.

"So what are we going to do with her boyfriend?" asked Junior.

"Kill him, of course. Do you see any other option?" Elder
Prescott, wiped Mia's blood off his hands with her torn dress and sat
down.

"He could still be useful. We're going to have to explain her disap-
pearance. It's kind of awkward right now. Gilheart, being the nice guy
that he was, took the fall for her abduction. Then she was abducted
again, poor girl, and brutalized by that fiend. Look at the condition
she's in. We'll need to explain it somehow."

"Well, I was careful. No marks we can't cover up."

"No, that isn't what I meant. I'm talking about political perception. I'm talking about getting the female sympathy vote," said Jeffery
Prescott, warming up to his subject. "If Hillary Clinton could do it
after Bill got a blow job in the Oval office, just by 'Standing By Her
Man' think what Mia could do."

"Okay, continue, I'm listening. What do you have in mind?"

"Like I said, we're going to have to explain the abduction somehow. What if the brave and heroic Sergeant Flynn, on his own ini-
tiative of course, were to rescue her? This would give us a reason to
promote Flynn as well."

"True, true, continue..."

"In the course of that heroic rescue, the abductor gets shot. No one can blame Flynn. His life was on the line. Mia gets rescued and brought home to her loving husband. Flynn gets a medal, and a key to the city and my life-long gratitude. Mia's boyfriend gets dead. We get the female sympathy vote. I get elected to the mayor's office."

"I can see, for once Jeffery, you've thought this out. It is however, going to need more back-up proof to sell, more than a dead kidnapper who can't contradict the story."

"That's why we'll need some semen from him before he dies, as well as a dirty doctor, who can perform the rape examination and repeat his findings on the witness stand. The Medical Examiner shouldn't be a problem, because he actually will get shot, and killed, the way Flynn said it went down. We'll have rock solid expert witness testimonies, DNA evidence gathered at the crime scene, as well as Mia's corroboration."

William Prescott drank his whiskey in silence, pondering the solution presented and looked for holes. He absently spun Mia around with the handle of a whip, absently inspecting her beaten body, probing with the whip handle into her orifices.

It could work, he thought.

"What do you think, Mia? Do you think that could work?"

Mia lifted her head, "I think Daddy is going to kill you both slowly."

Both men laughed.

"Mia, let me show you something."

Elder Prescott nodded to Jeffery, and Jeffery left the room and came back with a laptop computer. He opened it, punched some buttons and swung it around for Mia to see.

On the screen was a video being played in real time. Daddy was hung up on a meat hook over a blood drain and gang bangers were taking turns striking him with baseball bats. She watched as one of the skanks walked over and took his cock out rubbing it with a straight razor. Mia turned away.

"Still think he's going to come to your rescue?" said Elder Prescott. "Looks to me like he's found some new friends and is having quite a bit of fun without you."

William Prescott turned back to Jeffery. "It might work. Who do you have in mind to play the doctor?"

"I was hoping you could help me with that. Do you have any in your pocket?"

"Perhaps. Someone I do have in my pocket is a horse vet. I bet he's used to getting his stallions to spurt for breeding purposes."

"That might work."

"So it might work like this; we bring your lovely wife to the appropriate place with a syringe full of kidnapper juice, inject it into her pussy, then call in the calvary. Officer Flynn takes the credit, shoots a low-life in self-defense, and Mia takes an ambulance to the nearest hospital that can do a rape kit. We put out a press release, praise Officer Flynn, ask for privacy, and Mia disappears for a while."

"I like it," says Elder Prescott. "It wraps everything up in a nice little package. Let's give the good doctor a call, shall we?"

"He's probably asleep at the moment."

"So? What are money and power for?" Elder Prescott searched the numbers on his phone, found the one he was looking for and called.

"Denton? William Prescott. I hope I didn't wake you up." Prescott rolled his eyes for Jeffery's benefit. Silence, then,

"I've got a 'stallion' I'd like to stud, then put out to pasture. Is that something you can help with?" Prescott listened, then,

"Excellent, excellent. When can we do it? Sooner the better on this end." A final listening pause, then,

"I'll be expecting your call, then. Thanks again. Give my regards to Stella." He shut the phone.

"Done deal," he said to Jeffery.

"Dad? I haven't had a chance yet to try out this cattle prod. Its shape suggests so many different uses."

Elder Prescott picked it up, squeezed the button on the end to see if he could get it to charge. An electric bolt of blue lightening zapped between the two connectors. He touched it to Mia's nipple. She started jerking immediately.

"You're right, Jeff. It does have potential for fun. You're just full of good ideas tonight."

"The supreme art of war is to subdue the enemy without fighting."

Sun Tzu

Chapter 60

Denton Millstone had been an under-the-table veterinarian for William Prescott's horses for almost sixteen years.

His license had been revoked years ago, but Prescott still kept him around if he wanted to dope the horses, or hobble a competitor without being caught. Getting a call from him at three-thirty in the morning had unnerved him, but it wasn't altogether unusual. After all, horses and animals gave birth, got sick, and dropped dead at all hours of the day and night.

This job, he knew was going to be unusual right from the start. First, he was told to go out to the abandoned meat-packing plant on the South side of town. When he got there he was surrounded by a bunch of men with gang tats who started beating on his car with baseball bats when he didn't come out.

He was thinking of running them over and getting out of Dodge when some pimp mobile showed up. The gang banger in command seemed to be expecting him, so the others quieted down some. Denton got out of his car hesitantly.

"Yo, yo, hey dog doc, it's okay. My boys were just messin' with you a little. No harm done, am I right? Now bros…don't mess with the dog doc. Hes' got a job to do."

"So where is the animal to be treated?" asked Denton.

"Animal? Well, you could call him dat, but he might object, you feel me? You mind if the homeys and me watch? De hoes like this shit, you know."

"No, I guess not. It is a pretty straight-forward procedure."

"So what you call dis here, 'procedure'?"

"Electroejaculation."

"So, you like, gonna electro his jaculation?"

"Well, I guess that's one way of putting it."

"Okay, okay, now how's dis work?"

"An electric probe is inserted into the rectum adjacent to the prostate gland. The probe delivers an AC voltage, usually twelve to twenty-four -volts sine wave at a frequency of 60 Hz, although some devices can generate currents of up to one Amp. The probe is activated for one to two seconds, and is referred to as a stimulus cycle. Ejaculation usually occurs after two to three stimulus cycles."

"Wha' da fu? Was dat English?"

"I stick this up the animal's ass and shock his prostrate. How's that?"

"Yo, bros! Come take a look at this!" DOP said to his gang. They all gathered around, and DOP, ever the educated college professor, explained to his ignorant homeys exactly what was going to happen next.

"Yo, yo, check dis out. He gonna take dis here, and stick it up his ass, and then shock the shit out of him. To do what again?"

"To collect his semen."

"His wha?"

"His sperm," more noncomprehending looks.

"His cum?"

"Yo, yo, bros, he gonna collect his jizz! Why you wanna do dat?" They continued walking down the hall.

The vet was still not understanding the true reason for his involvement. Nor had DOP figured out they were talking about different things.

"Many people do it for artificially insemination of another animal."

"So den, let me get this straight, youse gonna get this brother's jizz, then go and get his bitch pregnant? In the hood, we be able to do dat ourselves without no dog doctor involved. You white people are strange. Okay, here we be. He's behind this door. Now you might want to be careful, doc, because he already kill five of my boys tonight."

"This animal has killed five people tonight?"

"True dat."

DOP opened the door. Daddy was still hanging over the drain, head down. Massive bruising on his face and body was starting to show. He lifted his head up, looking at the vet, but said nothing.

"Don't mind him, he don't talk much," said DOP, helpfully.

"Where's the animal?"

"What animal? He de animal! You milk the jizz out of DAT animal!"

"No, no, no. You can't do this to a human."

"Why? We wants to see. My hoes here are all worked up." It was true. The vet looked over and a couple of them were already rubbing the cocks of some of the soldiers.

"It would be too painful."

"Well, doc, that's de whole point! Let me put it this way. Either you do him, or we's gonna do you, ya feel me?" DOP pushed the vet inside the room. The vet walked around Daddy like he was a plague victim. Daddy just watched him calmly.

"This isn't my idea. I want you to know that. I don't have any choice in the matter."

"Who's idea was it?" Daddy spoke for the first time.

"William Prescott called me. Promised me a thousand dollars."

"So, do I have this right, you're going to electro stimulate me in order to collect my semen? Why does he need my semen?"

"He didn't include me in his plans."

"Okay. I see," said Daddy.

"So, you'll allow me to do it?" the vet asked with disbelief.

"Well no, I won't allow you to do it. But I won't kill you because you did. I understand you're a victim. But if I were you, I wouldn't hang around here very long after. Can you administer painkillers?"

"Yes, I can make it so you won't feel a thing. In fact, I can also make it so you won't feel anything these guys do to you either."

"Would it impair my motor control?"

"I don't understand."

"Would I still be able to fight?"

"I would think so. But it might impede depth perception as well as balance."

"Do you have any performance enhancers?"

"You mean like speed?"

"What I want is a cocktail. Both painkillers and performance enhancers, can you do that?"

"Yes, I think so."

"One last thing. Can you switch my semen with horse semen?"

"I don't understand."

"You're going to give my semen to Prescott, right? Maybe you could get them mixed up and give him horse semen instead."

"Yes, I could do that."

"Yo! Motherfucker! Quit talking. What you talking bout? Get on with it!" said DOP, "we be waiting."

"Go ahead, give them a show," said Daddy, "you have nothing to worry about. Do your job and go home, Doctor."

"You won't feel a thing, I promise."

DOP and his gang were thrilled by the performance. Several clapped their hands when the deed was done. All of DOP's soldiers got a blow job afterwards.

"Know thy self, know thy enemy. A thousand battles,
a thousand victories."

Sun Tzu

Chapter 61

Mia had two overriding thoughts in her mind. One, how to help Daddy, and two, how to protect their baby.

After beating and raping Mia, both Prescotts thought the best place for her would be at the estate. She could be watched and taken care of there with much fewer hassles.

Mia stood naked in front of a full-length mirror in her room at Prescott Manor. She was inspecting the bruises. Her breasts were becoming fuller. Her nipples were still sore and sensitive, they had been pinched and bitten last night. They were puckered and hardened.

She hadn't seen a lot of naked women so she didn't really know how her breasts compared. They were a little on the small side but she knew they were pretty good for a thin girl. Mia thought that her areolas were maybe just a tad big but they were a nice shade of dark pink.

Mia really liked the way her ass looked from the side. Her long thin legs ended at a perfectly round little ass. She took an extra minute just twisting and bending, looking at her backside. She liked how it then ran up into her slender waist and back. If it wasn't black and blue, she knew she had a nice ass.

Luckily, she wasn't showing yet. She slid her hand down her flat belly and wondered how long before the baby bump started to show.

Her mind was in overdrive. What was she was going to do once Jeffery found out she was pregnant? There was no doubt the baby was Daddy's. It was conceived during one of their very first moments together.

She knew this because she knew something even Jeffery didn't know; Jeffery was sterile. Mia hadn't used any birth control in over eight years. Prescott, of course, looked no further than placing the blame on her for their childless marriage. Mia knew better. It was also fine with her. The thought of having Prescott's child made her want to gag.

Daddy, however, was another story. Who knew he still had swimmers at his age? Mia giggled. Well, he wasn't *that* old. She recalled the look on his face when they were sitting on the bed just after making love. She could tell he was excited at the thought too. If they could just get free of the present problems, they could go somewhere together...

Mia slapped herself out of the daydream. She had to dress for an important political dinner and play the part as Jeffery Prescott's devoted wife. She had to stand beside him, grasp his hand, and look lovingly into his eyes as any proud wife would. It made her almost ill thinking about the charade she would have to play. She also knew if she didn't, Daddy would suffer.

Mia's future wasn't much better. As soon as it was politically convenient she would be killed and someone more suitable would take her place. If it wasn't for the baby and Daddy, she would have welcomed the idea. She had to figure out a way to help Daddy.

She decided then and there, if Daddy and her baby weren't a part of her future then she would just as soon be dead, and she would take Jeffery Prescott with her. Once that decision was made, and firmly planted in her heart, she felt much better, much calmer. No matter what, she knew, there was an end. An end she could accept the outcome either way. That was when Daddy's voice came into her mind, as though he were whispering into her ear.

Everything is going to be okay, Baby Doll. Everything is going to be all right, his voice said. The voice calmed her immediately.

Jeffery Prescott barged into the room just then, without knocking.

"How's my lovely wife this morning? I certainly hope the events of the last few days haven't put a damper on your mood, because tonight's a big night."

Mia turned around and looked at him, hating the sight of his false smile. She hated his blow-dried hair and polished teeth.

"Jeffery? Darling husband?" Mia put on her best, sexy kitten voice. "It's going to be a pleasure to kill you."

Prescott strode across the room and smacked her with an open hand.

"You think I'm afraid of you? Hey Jeff? I just wanted you to know…you've got a really small dick."

Prescott's rage filled his eyes, raised his hand, then closed his fist to let her have a good one.

"Go ahead, little dick, do it," Mia goaded.

"Jeffery? Now is not the time," Elder Prescott said from the doorway. "There will be plenty of time to deal with her later."

Ever since Mia got back, no, even before she left, there was a change in her. She was no longer afraid of him. It was like she was some sort of Samurai warrior. He remembered her standing in the living room of their house with a knife in her hand, and determination in her eyes. She wasn't afraid of pain, she wasn't even scared of death.

Which made Jeffery Prescott afraid of her.

Mia stood before the two men, naked, with her hand on her slender hip. Not the least bit self-conscious. Again, she heard Daddy's voice,

"You are their equal. You are mentally stronger than they are, and they know it. Battles are first won in the mind. Show them you aren't afraid of them, and they will fear you."

She stared at them both. She looked each in the eye, then said quietly,

"Daddy is coming for you. You will not beat him, and you will not beat me. We will take you down. We are going to destroy you both."

Both men looked at each other, then burst out laughing. However, their eyes said the laughter was forced, and fake.

William Prescott stepped up to Mia then, taking her chin roughly in his hand,

"Little girl, you have absolutely no idea who you are fucking with. As far as your 'Daddy' goes," he almost spat the word, "neither does he. Even so, don't you worry little one. I'm going to make you watch his execution. Which should be coming to a theater near you sooner than you think."

Mia didn't flinch. Instead, she swatted his hand away.

"I think you have one part of it right. I will be watching an execution soon. But I don't think it will be Daddy's."

Rage boiled up in Elder Prescott then. To be talked to in this fashion by this little whore was almost too much to control. He promised himself, when the time came, and he would make sure it came soon, he would personally put the bullet in her head.

Still Mia didn't flinch, she stared right into his eyes. She knew, she could see it. She WAS stronger.

"You have absolutely no idea the world of pain, awaiting you," Prescott said.

"You have it backwards," said Mia quietly. "You have no idea the pain awaiting you."

Elder Prescott lost it then and slapped her, sending Mia to the floor. What he didn't expect was when she got back up, went and stood at the place she had just occupied, and started laughing at him. Mia felt herself leaving her body and the warmth of Daddy surrounding her. She didn't know where it came from, or why she said it, but her next response was,

"I'm coming for you both."

"He who knows when he can fight and when he cannot,
will be victorious."

Sun Tzu

Chapter 62

The vet was good on his word.

He injected Daddy with enough painkillers to eliminate any pain. Then before he left, on the excuse he had to administer antibiotics, he injected him with something and Daddy felt strength returning. Daddy knew it was masking the pain and it would be short lived so he had to act fast.

After DOP and his boys got their jollies, they had pretty much left him alone, or maybe they were called off. It was time to act, and Daddy needed to figure out a plan.

Okay, what is binding me? he thought. He looked over his head at the rope and pulley and realized he was in luck.

Fucking amateurs, he thought.

The rope suspending him was hemp and/or manila. It wasn't a synthetic. Which means it will stretch. He put his weight on it by lifting his legs off the floor. Sure enough, it stretched. The rope bit into his wrists, but he blocked out the pain. He did that as long as the pain allowed, then put his legs back down. He gained about an inch of slack.

He took another breath, held it, and lifted his weight off the floor, putting his full 220 pounds on the rope. Each time he did it, he gained more slack, the rope trailing down his back, unseen to anyone coming through the door. Soon he would have enough slack he could chew through the ropes binding his hands.

Then, he heard voices outside the killing room.

"Yo, mothafucka. Bout time. Yo boy tied up in the room, there."

"You hurt him?"

"We fuck him up a bit. He's an old fat dude. He ain't so tough."

The "white" voice he recognized from somewhere. He'd heard it before. He stood up, letting all the slack he'd gathered from the rope hang down his back unseen. Judging by feel, he had three or four feet. He suspended his arms back up in the air so it would look like he was still hanging tight.

There was a scuffling sound outside the door then a large guy, wearing a black Balaclava, the kind terrorists and cops prefer, came in. Just his eyes were visible in a dark, cloth-covered face. He opened the door, and pulled a chair in with him. Then disappeared, and came back in carrying a car battery and jumper cables. Disappeared again, then came in carrying a five-gallon pail of what looked like water.

Okay, so I'm going to get tortured for information. Which means they need something from me, he thought. *Which means I still have a while to live.*

"Your name is Flynn, isn't it?" Daddy said to the figure in black.

The figure remained silent. Instead he sat down on the chair studying his victim.

"Yeah, I remember. We met when you pulled me over. You can hide your face Flynn, but you can't hide the eyes."

"What's your name?" Flynn asked.

"You can call me Daddy, if you want."

"A mystery man, uh?"

"No. I know who I am. It's no mystery to me. Flynn, what happened to you? This isn't your style."

"How do you know what my style is?"

"Letting girls get ass raped and beaten for the pleasure of sick fucks like Prescott is your style, Flynn? Is it a regular part of your job arranging kidnappings with the home boys? And when things get boring, moonlight as a torturer, and dirty cop for that ass Prescott? How long are you going to carry that boy's filthy laundry? You know he's going to fuck you over in the end, Flynn. It's his nature.

"What about when you pulled me over, Flynn, remember? You could have rousted me. Busted me on some bogus, bullshit charge. Beat the shit out of me for resisting. Splayed me out in the middle of the street in handcuffs, maced me, tazed me. But you didn't. You didn't use any low-class cop tactics. Instead, you played it smart. Played the game the way it was supposed to be played. You played it with *HONOR*," Daddy raised his voice on the last word. "So, I ask again, what the fuck happened to you?"

Flynn's resolve collapsed in on himself sitting in the chair. Daddy's words hit home. Flynn knew, from countless interrogations, the truth, people didn't want to face, worked every time. Even on himself.

"Fuck you."

"You're a cop, Flynn. I bet at one time, an honorable one. Did you join the force to be some rich boy's dirt bag?"

"It's not like that."

"It's *exactly* like that, and you know it!"

"We came up together. You know how it is. He helped me in the early years and we kept in touch. We traded favors back and forth, that sort of thing. This thing with you and Mia, it got out of hand."

"This 'thing' with Mia and me? Are you kidding me? I helped her get away from a sexual sadist! So now, you're going to torture me to get some information for your boss, is that it?"

"That's pretty much it, yeah. So why don't you just tell me your name. Save yourself the pain, and me the trouble."

"You're leaving out the best part, Flynn. It also means you're going to have to kill me because I know who you are. That's really why you're here isn't it? Now, it isn't trading favors back and forth. It's murder one. Are you telling me that sick suck ass is worth your pride, your honor, your pension? You'll murder for a scum bag like him?"

"Like I said, it wasn't always like that. Shit happens. Life happens, and…"

"And pretty soon you can't get off the merry-go-round. Am I right, Officer Flynn?"

"Yeah, that's pretty much it. It sucks and I'm sorry. You probably don't deserve it. But I'll make it quick."

Flynn stood up, hooked up the jumper cables to the battery and came over to Daddy. Using a large sponge, he soaked Daddy's chest in cold water. He dropped the sponge into the bucket and picked up the cables.

"What's your name?" Flynn said, advancing towards Daddy.

"Hey Flynn? I think you told me the truth just now. I think it was the first time in a long time, you'd been honest with yourself. I think it also felt good to tell the truth for a change. I think , deep down, you are a man of honor. For that reason, I'm going to let you live."

"You are one ballsy motherfuck…"

Daddy launched himself straight at Flynn's chest, wrapping his feet around his stomach. He whipped the rope slack two quick turns around Flynn's neck, then, in the same motion, pushed himself off Flynn with his feet and fell to the floor. The reflex action of suddenly losing his air supply made Flynn drop the jumper cables, and his hands flew to his neck.

Too late. The momentum of Daddy's fall to the floor jerked the rope tight, and hauled him partially in the air. Daddy rolled over the rope, keeping it taut as it stretched, slowly strangling Flynn. Both men stared at each other, Flynn thrashing, Daddy rolling taking up the slack with his body. Flynn made a final effort to kick Daddy in the face. Daddy took the blow and shook it off.

Daddy watched as the light dimmed in Flynn's protruding eyes, and his tongue started to extend. In case it was a fake, he held the line taut, past the time necessary, then dropped Flynn to the floor. He searched his pocket and found a knife and cut himself free, next checked Flynn's pulse on his neck.

No pulse. Fuck me, Flynn, thought Daddy. *You smoke too much.* He gave Flynn mouth to mouth. Still no pulse. *Don't you even think of dying on me.* He tried CPR, then switched to mouth to mouth again, then back to CPR. There, he got it. Flynn's pulse was thready and weak, but he was breathing and his heart pumping blood. Color returned to his face.

Now, you owe me, thought Daddy.

Daddy took Flynn's shoes and found his uniform with the Glock 17, and the spare magazine. He stuffed them in his pants pockets. Then, took the mace and the baton as well.

It was time to see if the Duke of Pussy, was a Duke, or a pussy.

"A fascist is one whose lust for money or power is combined with such an intensity of intolerance toward those of other races, parties, classes, religions, cultures, regions or nations as to make him ruthless in his use of deceit or violence to attain his ends."

Henry A. Wallace

Chapter 63

Denton Millstone came into the Prescott house and handed Jeffery Prescott a sealed test tube of semen. The package was received. He was paid, and he was dismissed.

"Okay, let's break this down in parts, so we don't miss anything," William Prescott said. "In order for this to work we have to consider the involvement of Flynn, Mia, the boyfriend, the medical examiner, and the press. Let's start with Flynn."

Flynn: Once given the green light, he would receive an anonymous tip, and go to the meat-packing plant where he would find Mia, and kill Daddy.

Mia: She would be found unconscious beaten and bruised. Semen would be injected into her body cavities. She would be taken to a local hospital where a rape kit would be performed.

Boyfriend: In the hospital, his DNA material would be found linking him to the brutal assault on Mia. He, of course, would be shot dead so his side of the story would be irrelevant.

The Medical Examiner and forensics: Would corroborate Flynn's and Mia's testimony.

The Press: Would be on hand recording the scene for public consumption as well as to leak various details after the fact designed to illicit public sympathy.

So the plan was this; they would give Sergeant Flynn the appropriate time and place, where he would bust in and find Daddy with a beaten Mia. Daddy of course would resist and be shot dead. After douching her thoroughly, they would inject enough Daddy juice into Mia's snatch and ass that conclusive DNA proof would be obtained. Mia would then corroborate the story about the abduction at the school, and the subsequent rapes and beatings. Salacious and sexual details would be leaked to the press in an effort to sway public opinion.

Prescotts Elder and Junior were seated in Elder Prescott's study. Both men had whiskeys. William preferred his neat, while Jeffery liked his with ice. Jeffery swirled the smoky amber liquid around in his glass as he thought through various aspects of the plan.

"How are we going to explain the massive bruising on his body?" asked Elder Prescott.

"Well, going up against an armed and trained police can't be too healthy. That is going to explain a large part of it."

"True, but he's been beaten with baseball bats. It won't explain all of it. I think the best course of action would be to have the ME make note of it, so it doesn't look suspicious, then ignore it. Or perhaps, not look too deeply. He'll just attribute it to trauma associated with death. Unless there is an independent autopsy, it shouldn't be called into question. Okay then, let's talk about Mia."

William Prescott didn't get to be the patriarch by virtue of being a fool, but by meticulous planning.

"What about her?"

"She's the weak link in the entire plan."

"How so?"

"If she doesn't go along with the story, it will all fall apart. We need some leverage. If we kill her boyfriend, what leverage do we have?"

Both men pondered this aspect.

"My police contacts said that three pregnancy tests were recovered at the apartment, all positive. Mia's pregnant. We can threaten to abort her baby. We'll have to any way of course when the time comes, but the threat alone should be enough to keep her in line."

"I think then, the less she knows the better. Her next beating should include some well placed kicks to the abdomen in the hope we can abort the fetus. We should knock her out, perform an anal and vaginal douche just in case. Then we squirt her full of her boyfriend's juice, take her unconscious body to the crime scene and leave her there with her boyfriend. Then have the good officer Flynn receive an anonymous tip. He rushes in and saves the day," wrapped up Elder Prescott.

Jeffery stroked his chin. "The police and press swarm the scene. We make sure we give Flynn a script to follow. Mia is filmed being taken away by ambulance. I like it."

"We'll also need some friendly reporters we can leak information too. Who do you know? We got any on the payroll?"

"Oh, sure. The press are whores. Give them something canned they don't need to investigate, that contains sex, drugs, or violence, and they eat it up with a spoon. That shouldn't be too hard."

"We need to make sure she only comes to after the forensic evidence has been obtained. If she starts with any wild stories, we can say she's been 'Stockholmed' by her abductor and is simply parroting lines he fed her. We let it leak last that she lost the baby. That should increase the female sympathy vote."

Both men sat lost in thought, looking at the various details from different angles.

"Actually, Jeff, if we play this right, there isn't any chances of you losing the election. Think about it. The press coverage will be all over the news. Beautiful young girl," Jeffery snorted at that, "kidnapped, raped, and beaten. Then comes a heroic officer to the rescue. The family, of course, asks for privacy in their time of grief and healing.

"We allow a few of the salacious details to escape, just to tantalize the public. Then, at the appropriate moment, we call a press conference. Parade Mia out, visibly pregnant with your baby. She parrots the party line about her horrendous abuse at the hands of Gilheart, then her abductor. There won't be a dry eye in the house. Then, right before the election, the poor girl loses the baby in a miscarriage.

"It will be so 'Kennedyeque' in its overtones, you'll almost be able to see John John saluting JFK's coffin. How could you NOT win the election?"

"What about Mia after the election?"

"She'll have to die, of course. She'll probably commit suicide from grief from losing the baby, or postpartum depression. We don't need that slutty little whore around anymore anyway."

"Well then, should we contact friendly officer Flynn and tell him the script?" Jeffery wanted to know.

"Now's a good a time as any."

Jeffery flipped open his cell phone and speed dialed. No Answer. He checked the number and tried again. Still no answer.

"Maybe he's busy."

Elder Prescott, however, didn't like the feel of it.

"Let's turn on the closed circuit TV and see what's happening."

Jeffery walked to the laptop computer and punched a few buttons. The screen immediately popped into view. They could see Flynn on the floor motionless, with rope wrapped around his neck. William and Jeffery looked at each other.

"Gimme that," said William Prescott, using the mouse to pan the camera.

He panned the camera and it looked like about a dozen dead gang bangers were piled up in the doorway as well as the hall.

"Oh, fuck me…" was all he said.

"I don't initiate violence, I retaliate."

Chuck Norris

Chapter 64

Daddy had to work fast, and he didn't have much time.

He put Flynn's shoes on, but they were much too big. So he grabbed some newspaper close by and stuffed the toes to make them fit better. The same with Flynn's uniform. He checked the pockets, getting what he thought might be useful, and using the knife he cut the pants to fit.

He looked around the kill room. There weren't any weapons other than Flynn's. He could hear the home boys down the hall and hoped they had satiated their blood lust enough that they wouldn't check in on Flynn. Next, he took the battery and jumper cables and carried them behind the door. Since the door opened inward, this gave him a place to hide.

Now, he had to think. The drugs may have deadened the pain, but it also hindered his thinking ability.

How many gang bangers? At least a dozen, maybe more.

What are my options? Very few. Sneak past them or fight.

Can I sneak out past them? There is only one way out, and it leads right past them.

What are my advantages? Right now, I have the element of surprise. I have weapons.

What are my disadvantages? I'm outnumbered, and outgunned.

Daddy weighed a bunch of plans in his mind, then discarded them for one reason or another. He had to use the element of surprise to take out a large number of them in the beginning. Then pick off pockets of resistance. For that, he needed them concentrated in one place.

Once he decided upon a plan, he put all the elements in place that he would need. Daddy took a bandanna, soaked it in water, and tied it over his eyes. He would need it when it came time to use the tear gas. He could still see, but his vision was obscured. No help for that.

He thought about the sound of Flynn's voice, and using his best imitation, he could come up with yelled,

"DOP, help me, hurry!"

Daddy heard a flurry of sound as feet and chairs scraped the floor, then the sound of weapons being grabbed. Next, he heard the sound of running feet as sneakers slapped the hall floor.

DOP rounded the door and stepped in, coming into the room while the others stood back in the hall.

"Wha de fuck..." Was all he could articulate as Daddy stepped from behind the door, and attached both cables, one to each side of his neck. DOP immediately went into a jittering dance the brothers haven't seen since 'Soul Train' went off the air.

Daddy stepped around the jitter dancing DOP, and sprayed mace with one hand while firing Flynn's Glock with the other. They were first blinded by the mace, and the brothers crowded in the doorway in confusion. As soon as one raised a weapon, Daddy shot him at point-blank range.

He emptied the clip, and the mace canister. He dropped the canister and ejected the clip on the floor. Reached into his pocket, and shoved another clip into the pistol grip of the Glock. Since the Glock had a seventeen round magazine, and this was close range, by the time the smoke cleared, it looked like an Auschwitz firing range.

Some of the brothers got away and were scrambling down the hall. Daddy took a quick peek around the door and saw two with their backs turned. He shot them both. One round literally picked the gang banger up and carried him on his tip toes right into the fire door blocking the exit. Daddy looked back into the room as DOP's afro spontaneously combusted and his head caught on fire. He turned back to the hallway.

Daddy could see the light on in the break room as well as hear more excited voices coming from there. He made his way silently down the hall, arm outstretched, gun aimed for the doorway.

A head poked around the corner and earned a head shot. The corpse dropped with a look of disbelief on his face, the back of his head missing.

Daddy had to get past the break room, and out the door. Unfortunately, his element of surprise was gone and he was now in the same position as the fallen gang bangers. He would be in the doorway, and they would be waiting for him.

He stood back to the wall against the door jamb.

"I knows you's there, Cracker, comes get what you came fo,'" this said by, he assumed, the girl with the straight razor. He looked down the hall and realized none of the bangers he shot were female. Which meant all the hoes had stayed back. One had to assume she had a better weapon than a straight razor now.

"All I want to do is get out that door," Daddy said, "you don't have to die tonight."

"Wha makes you think I be the one dying?"

"The big crowd of dead boyfriends on the floor, for one."

"So wha you suppose we do, Cracker?"

"How about you step out into the hall with your hands up?"

"So you can shoot us too?"

"It's either that or I come in there and shoot you."

He could hear the girls talking among themselves. Straight Razor was the leader and she was going down hard, no matter what. The other girls seemed to think living might be a better option.

Daddy took the baton he had shoved into his belt, weighed it in his hand, and let it fly as hard as he could towards the window of the break room. He hoped the window wasn't made of plexi-glass. The glass crashed inward with a bang, and Daddy stepped into the room. Straight Razor wheeled around with a gun in her hand. Daddy had no choice but to shoot her in the mouth.

Blood, teeth, and brains exited the back of her head all over the girls in back of her, then Straight Razor, fell in a heap on top of them. The two other girls had both hands over their mouths screaming, no guns or weapons in sight. They were no threat. So Daddy backed of out the room, and made for the door.

Daddy looked at the vehicles and decided the van must be Flynn's. He opened the back and climbed in. It was a surveillance van. He looked through the gear and realized, once again, he was in luck. He had surveillance and counter surveillance equipment. Both audio and video. This put a whole new wrinkle in this entire operation.

Daddy hopped in the driver's seat, put the van in gear, stirred up some dust on the gravel driveway and in minutes was heading North on the freeway.

Baby, I'm coming, he said to himself.

"Experience hath shewn, that even under the best forms of government, those entrusted with power have, in time, and by slow operations, perverted it into tyranny."

Thomas Jefferson

Chapter 65

William and Jeffery Prescott looked at CCTV in total disbelief.

They panned around the room with the camera. There was a river of blood flowing into the drain where Daddy had been tied. They saw movement and panned back towards it. Flynn was moving slightly at first, then sitting up shaking his head, trying to clear it.

"Well, at least Flynn's alive," said William, "we can take that as a small miracle."

"What the fuck happened? How could he possibly have outsmarted Flynn and gunned down all those gang bangers?"

"The last time we looked at it, he was being beaten to death with baseball bats!"

"Is there a recording function on that camera, is it just real time?"

"No, we can do a playback. Good thinking."

Jeffery pressed a few buttons, and rewound the tape back two hours. He stopped when he could see Flynn talking to the gang bangers.

"Try from here?"

"No, go back further. Let's see when Denton took his sample. Start from there."

Jeffery went back further until Denton appeared, shaking his head violently back and forth, gesturing at Daddy. Then the one they called DOP said something, and Denton walked around Daddy like he was walking around a rattlesnake. They appeared to be talking for a while. Denton, they could see, was visibly relaxing.

"I wonder what they are talking about? Does this system have audio?"

"No, unfortunately it doesn't."

Denton surreptitiously took out a syringe, loaded it, and shot Daddy in the ass.

"Look, he gave him a painkiller, I bet. Maybe that was what the conversation was about."

"Maybe."

They watched as Denton put a plastic sleeve over the end of Daddy's cock, then inserted the electro ejaculation device into his rectum.

"Man, that has just got to suck."

"It didn't suck enough, obviously."

Denton, went through a couple of cycles, then milked Daddy's testicles. Then he started the cycle over again.

The gang bangers just watched, their mouths hanging open. A couple of the hoes got down on their knees and with one eye watching the action and the other on their men, milked their cocks at the same time.

"What a bunch of animals."

Denton finished up, took the sleeve off Daddy's cock and stood up, putting his tools away.

"Freeze it right there!" said William Prescott.

"What the fuck is he doing?"

"He's giving him another shot. Why would he do that? Why give him a shot AFTER the procedure?"

"Okay, we've seen what we need to see. Fast-forward to when Flynn arrives."

Jeffery pressed some buttons and the figures moved forward in fast motion comically. In their rush they didn't see Daddy using his weight to get the slack from the rope. They stopped as Flynn was standing at the door in a black mask. They watched as he brought in the battery and jumper cables, then the five-gallon pail of water. Flynn was obviously talking. He pulled up a chair, and sat down. Flynn had his head down, so they couldn't see his lips. Then suddenly he stood up, sponged down his victim, and picked up the battery cables.

Neither man could believe their eyes when Daddy suddenly came alive from his beaten, submissive, posture, flew through the air and instantly wrapped the rope around Flynn's neck and then fell to the floor.

"Holy shit. Who is this guy?"

"Flynn said he had some sort of military background."

"Ya fuckin' think?"

Both men watched in awe as Daddy took the battery and cables, and set up an ambush. They watched in fascination as DOP came in and Daddy used the very same torture device meant for him and turned the tables on his attackers. They watched as he stepped from behind the door, spraying the gang bangers with yellow tear gas, and he calmly, and methodically, shot them all.

They sat looking at each other in silence.

"Well, that was quite some show."

"Too bad. After that, I'd like to hire him for my security detail."

"You realize this guy is now hunting us, right?"

"Yes, Jeffery, believe it not, that part didn't escape me."

"So what are you going to do?"

"I think we can continue with the plan. Instead of having him killed, which obviously would have been better, I think that a city-wide police manhunt for an escaped murderer might be in order. We'll get the public involved. Post a reward for information. To come after us, he has to move around. If anyone sees him, they contact the police and he, hopefully, goes down in a hail of gunfire. That puts time on our side. He can't stay invisible forever."

"That means we'll need to bring the Police Commissioner in on this. The more people involved, the weaker the plan."

"Let me worry about him."

"So then, how do we begin?"

"Let Flynn know we'll be bringing Mia down. We'll need to get rid of the gang bangers, or tie them in some way to this homicidal maniac. Let Flynn worry that detail."

"What do we do?"

"We need to get that kidnapped, abused wife of yours ready. If she'll go along with the plan, great. If not, knock her out and do it anyway. By the time she comes to, it will all be in motion."

"That's taking a hell of a gamble."

"Got any better ideas, Jeff?"

"Flynn is going to need some time to get his shit squared away."

"So? Give him twenty-four hours. After that, we have to move ahead."

"What about you? What are you going to do?"

"First, I have to square this entire fuck up with the commissioner.

Then, I think it is time we got some professionals involved to track this guy down."

"Professionals?"

"Yeah, professional mercenaries. Black Snake guys. They don't come cheap, believe me."

"What will you do with them?"

"Some we'll keep here as bodyguards. The others we send out as hunter-killer teams to track this fucker down. Between them, the police, and the public all looking for him, he won't stand a chance."

"Thus, what is of supreme importance in war
is to attack the enemy's strategy."

Sun Tzu

Chapter 66

Daddy took the freeway North, getting off at the Martin Luther King exit, then drove deep into the ghetto.

He knew the police would be looking for the van very soon and he had to ditch it. He wiped his prints off everything, then moved toward the back of the van and turned on the overhead light. There were all kinds of goodies back here. Obviously, the federal dollars were flowing into the local police departments. Some of the audio/video surveillance equipment was top of the line. Not as good as military tech, but better than the commercial variety.

The van also had weapons and night-vision equipment. He stuffed a knapsack full of everything he thought he would need and climbed out the back. He left the keys in the ignition.

"Yo Pops! I think you forgot yo ride." One of the toughs on the corner said to him as he passed.

"It's a gas hog. You can have it. Keys are in the ignition."

"No shit? You just gonna leave it?"

"I'm just going to leave it."

"Is it hot?"

"What do you think?" Daddy smiled. "But there are some goodies in the back you might like."

Daddy walked around the corner where there was a Seven-Eleven store and called a cab from a payphone. There were more gang bangers here, stumbling in and out of the store. Some gave him the stink-eye, most left him alone.

The cab came, an Indian driver, not looking too enthused to be in this part of town. He rolled down the passenger window.

"You call a cab?"

"Yes, I did."

The cabbie looked him up and down, still not sure if he wanted a fare from this section of the city.

"Where you going?"

"West side."

"Where on the West side?"

"Just get on the freeway and go west, I'll tell you where."

"Okay, get in."

Daddy got in the backseat and the cabbie hit the meter.

"I don't see many white faces in this neighborhood. You should be careful."

"It's all in your attitude. Most people don't want problems."

"If you don't mind me saying so, you look pretty bad. You want me to drop you at a hospital?"

"No, it looks worse than it is. I just need to get home."

They drove in silence. Daddy's familiar town seemed almost alien to him. He had to look at it in a different way. He had to look upon all things, and people, as potential threats, and how he would deal with them if they became one. The scary part was, how easily he could slide back into his old life.

His life before he had a child. He missed his son terribly. Nevertheless, he was also glad he wasn't here and a part of this.

"Okay, exit here at Jordan Creek, turn right, then turn left on University Ave. Then right on 156th St. After that, go north."

The cabbie silently followed directions.

"I'm going to need you to circle this block, and circle the blocks on either side of it, okay?"

"What am I getting myself into?"

"Absolutely nothing. I'm just not sure about the number."

"Or the street where you live?"

"Right."

The one thing Daddy knew was that they were down one surveillance van. But there were no vans of any kind on the street. Nor was anyone parked in cars, or out and about. Not even dog walkers, or joggers.

"You can let me out at the corner." Daddy rounded the fare up to the nearest twenty dollars and gave the whole thing to the cabbie. "Thanks, it's appreciated." Daddy got out of the cab.

Daddy had gotten out of the cab a few blocks from his house and did a walking reconnaissance over the area. Checking the backs of the houses facing his. Still nothing. No internal alarms going off. He felt no eyes. It very well could be if Prescott was paying for the surveillance, he didn't want to watch two empty houses, on the off chance he might turn up.

Of course, that didn't mean for a second that the house hadn't been rigged with internal devices. They could have silent alarms rigged to motion detectors. But that was just a chance he was going to have to take. There was no way to know until he got inside, in which case it would be too late anyway.

He cut through the backyard of a neighbor. He could hear a dog barking inside a house, but paid it no attention and came to his back door. He still had a key, so there was no reason to break in. He checked the door for wires and saw none. He made a quick check with a flash-light inside the house, but saw no motion detectors installed. So he opened the door and let himself in.

The familiar smell of his own house enveloped him as soon as he stepped inside. It reminded him, once again, of his son and all the good times they had had there. He made a beeline for the basement door and his office. The sooner he got away from the upstairs, the better.

Once downstairs and underground he felt better about turning on the light. It looked like nothing had been touched, or disturbed. Was it possible they completely ignored his house once they had a location on his other apartment?

He went to the gun safe and opened that. All his firearms were also still there. What a stroke of good fortune. But that didn't mean for a minute that luck would hold. One of the first things they should do now that he was on the run was come back here and see if anything would point to where he went.

It also meant he couldn't check his email, or use his computer, or his credit cards, or access any money from his bank accounts. He was going to need to use one of his identities and dive deep underground.

He was going to need a plan.

"Constantly choosing the lesser of two evils is still choosing evil."

Jerry Garcia

Chapter 67

"Momma, why have you put up with William's abuse all these years?"

Since their last showdown, both Prescotts having enough to attend to, largely left Mia alone in a locked bedroom. Her meals were brought to her. This time, Momma Prescott came and let her know that "the men" wanted to see her downstairs in the study. She was still covering up a black eye and half of her face was swollen. Mia looked at Momma Prescott and asked the question she had always wanted to ask.

Momma looked at Mia with sympathy in her eyes.

"Why did you?" she asked Mia right back.

"I never had a man treat me any differently. From the time I was a child on. I thought all men behaved this way. Then I learned, it is only the sick ones that do," said Mia.

"But you found a place to go. You found a person who loves you. How did that work out? They came and dragged you back, didn't they?"

"Did you ever try to leave?"

"And go where, child? There is nowhere in this town I could go. I have no relatives out of state, and even if I did, my family was the same as yours, they wouldn't care. They would have just beaten me some more and sent me back. I have no money of my own. William keeps it all. So where would I have gone?"

"Did you ever think about stopping William?"

"Of course. Like you, I used to dream about it. Take revenge. So many times. But I just don't have the courage. Besides, it is probably what I deserve anyway."

"No one deserves the way he treats you."

"He was not always like this, you know. In the beginning, he was very sweet."

"Now he is a monster. And he made his son into a monster. The son watched the father. Jeffery saw the way he treated you, and that power fed the monster in him."

"They will kill you if you fight them."

"One thing my Daddy taught me Momma, and that's my REAL Daddy, not the one I was born to. It is better to die fighting, than live as a slave in pain."

"Then, I fear, your life will be short."

"That may be, but at least it is a life I freely choose for myself. They didn't choose it for me," said Mia quietly.

Mia dressed quietly as her and Momma talked about the things they usually talked about. Jeffery's upcoming election, and how proud she'd be of her son. When Mia was ready, she was led downstairs and into the study. It was midday, so both men were sober.

Both men eyed her as she walked in. Elder Prescott looked at her with sexual longing. He still wanted to whip her some more for her earlier insolence. Jeffery looked at her with loathing. He would never touch her tenderly ever again. Not that he did that much anyway. His look said she was now unclean, and not to be touched. Of course, that didn't mean she couldn't be used for sport when the urge hit.

"Mia, Mia, please come in," said Elder Prescott.

"You look lovely, dear," Jeffery choked out.

Mia said nothing. She looked at them with no expression at all.

"Well, then, enough of the pleasantries, I guess," continued William Prescott. "As you know, you have a function within this family, and we just wanted to make sure you were up to it."

"That function would be to be beaten, and sexually abused?"

"If that is what we desire of you, Mia, yes. Of course, we don't have to take that road. We can put it all behind us. Start with a clean slate. What do you say?"

"What is it you want me to do?"

"That's much better, Mia. We want you to renounce this whole 'Daddy' business, make this divorce business go away, testify that he kidnapped, rape and beat you, and stand at Jeffery's side as the loyal, devoted wife when he is elected mayor."

Mia just looked at them. Daddy was right once again.

Through their weakness, she now had the power. She saw clearly they couldn't move forward without her. She also saw she could crush them both.

"I would much rather watch Daddy as he destroys you."

"You really think that is going to happen?"

"I know it is," said Mia, her faith in Daddy unshakable.

"Then let me show you something Mia."

Jeffery spun the laptop around so Mia could watch it. She could see Daddy hanging by his hands in the middle of the screen. The camera was mounted in back of him, so she could only see his back, but there was no doubt it was him. She watched as one gang banger after another came up to him and hit him with baseball bats.

"Oh, here, Mia, let me slow it down for you. It's much better in slow motion." Jeffery adjusted the speed of the film.

It was even more horrible to watch in slow motion. She could see the blows impact on his body. It was like she could almost hear the bones break. The gang bangers looked like they were playing some twisted game of baseball.

All of a sudden, they stopped and looked at the door, then hurried out. Daddy was left hanging there. She could see his body still swinging from side to side, from the blows. Jeffery fast forwarded the film, then stopped. After a while, another man came in, pulled his pants down around his ankles, and she had to watch his violation of him also in slow motion.

"He's receiving electro-shock therapy," both men snickered. "Yes, your 'Daddy' is quite the man taking it up the ass like a little faggot. He seems to enjoy it, don't you think so Jeff?"

"Oh, no doubt. I hear once they take it up the ass, they never really like going back to pussy."

Mia watched in horror as a man did unspeakable things to Daddy, then the man left. Jeffery fast forwarded the film again, this time to when Flynn entered the room. Flynn talked to Daddy awhile, then advanced towards him with the jumper cables.

Jeffery stopped it there.

"Seen enough, Mia? Or would you like to see his execution too?"

Mia was horrified beyond words at what she had just seen.

"What do you mean 'his execution'?"

"I mean exactly that. He's dead, Mia. He's not coming for you. No one is going to save you. So here are your choices; one, you can agree to do what we ask and your life will continue much the same as it has. Of course, Jeffery has a lot of anger to work out towards you so it probably won't be pleasant, but let's face it, you deserve it."

"What's the second option?"

"We kill your baby, first so that you know it was we who destroyed you, then the police find your body with that of your 'Daddy'. It will appear that he killed you, then committed suicide."

Book Three

Daddy

"A man who won't die for something is not fit to live."

Martin Luther King, Jr.

"Don't get the impression that you arouse my anger. You see, one can only be angry with those he respects."

Richard M. Nixon

Chapter 68

Mia could feel rage crawling up her spine.

It was the most intense feeling she had ever had, even compared to all the good things she had gotten from Daddy. She had just watched the video. Both men were standing there smugly. Looking at her, waiting to see what she would do. They were so used to holding all the high cards, and giving everyone else the orts and leavings from their table.

If Daddy was dead, she'd know it. They were so closely connected to each other, he would have reached out to her. She knew he would. Sometimes she could feel him all around her, even here. He wouldn't leave her. She felt, even now, he was coming for her.

"You fucking assholes!" Mia's arms were trembling as she leaned on the desk.

"I'm sorry. I must not have heard you correctly. Can you repeat that?" Jeffery's smug smile was oozing self-satisfaction.

"I'm going to fucking kill you."

"I don't think so, dear. You see now, that you're alone. You have no hope here." Jeffery stood from behind the desk and leaned on it, his face coming just inches from her face.

"Don't spit your lies at me. I'm different from the scared teenager that was forced to suck your cock. If Daddy was dead, you would have shown me. You just want me scared, and feeling defeated. It's not going to work, you piece of shit."

"Listen up, little girl." He spoke through clenched teeth. "I don't give a fuck if you believe it or not, but your Daddy is dead. He begged for his life just before we slit his throat."

Mia stood up straight as a smile lifted her lips.

"Now I know you are full of shit. My Daddy would never beg for his life, ever. Especially from a coward like you."

Mia saw just a bit of worry flicker in Jeffery's eyes. That was all she needed to see. She grabbed the laptop from the desk, that had featured Daddy's torture, and flung it towards her husband. He just barely ducked in time and the computer hit the wall. It made a loud cracking sound as pieces went flying.

"What the fu-"

Before he could finish, Mia crawled up onto the desk and jumped towards him. They both came down hard on the floor with Mia on top. She took all her rage and tried to put it into her arms as she swung repeatedly. Her small fists continually striking Jeffery in the face. One good hit had blood gushing from his nose.

Just like Daddy had told her, her husband was a coward. He tried to cover his face with his arms. Where was the man that took so much pleasure in hitting his wife? He could hit a defenseless girl but he couldn't fight a strong woman.

Mia was having so much fun punching her husband that she had momentarily forgotten that they weren't alone in the office. She was quickly reminded as something hard struck the side of her head. Pain exploded through her as she was knocked off Jeffery.

Laying on her side, Mia writhed in pain. She moaned softly as she lifted her hand to her head. When she pulled it down, it was covered in blood. She looked up with blurry vision to see Elder Prescott standing over her with a large object in his hand. She couldn't make out what it was, but it came down hard on her again, another shot to her head. Bright flashes erupted before her eyes. The pain instantly made her feel like she was going to vomit. Mia didn't see the next one coming. This time it hit her right in the stomach.

Mia screamed out and curled into a ball. More pain ripped through her. Her first thought was her baby. Her second thought was to escape or fight. In an instant, an image of Daddy's beaten body flashed into her mind and she had her answer. As she sensed the next blow coming, Mia rolled out of the way. She heard William swear loudly as the object hit the floor and he lost control of it.

She took this opportunity to get to her feet. Her vision was still slightly blurred and her legs wobbled. Mia felt the blood running down the sides of her face. After a few seconds, she turned her focus back to her husband. He was now kneeling, holding his nose as blood dripped from his hand.

Mia took the two steps to reach him and kicked him as hard as she could. Her foot landed solidly on Jeffery's chin. His arms flew into the air has he was knocked onto his back. Mia was satisfied with the loud cries of pain that was spilling from him. Again, this distracted her from the other attacker.

Something like a cord came from behind and wrapped around Mia's neck. It was pulled tighter and Mia couldn't take in her next breath. William yanked on it harder and Mia fell against his chest. She couldn't get any air, her vision started to become spotty.

"I can't wait to watch you die." The older man whispered in Mia's ear.

Mia had one more image of Daddy flash in her mind before everything went black, and she felt her whole body go limp.

"That little bitch broke my nose!" said Jeffery, wheezing through his mouth.

"Don't be a pussy. It's not broken. If it was it would be lying over on its side. You're going to have two nice shiners though. You better get an excuse ready to explain them."

Jeffery was still cupping his face in his hands, blood streaming through his fingers. He looked up at his father, then down at Mia lying at his feet.

"When the time comes, I get to kill her."

"Well, I think you at least deserve that much," said his father.

"Pretend inferiority and encourage his arrogance."

Sun Tzu

Chapter 69

"This is Dan Anderson with KTTO action news, and we have breaking news about the Mia Prescott kidnapping..."

The sun rose and Daddy watched the dust motes dance in the air as the sunlight came through the basement window. He needed to make a plan. However, this was a complex one as there were so many unknowns. It would require that he make a number of intuitive leaps in logic. The downside was, those leaps could turn out to be wrong, and he wouldn't know it until too late.

The first thing he needed was information. He knew he could probably turn on the TV downstairs without attracting attention.

"...we'll go to our news anchor on the spot. Cassandra, what can you tell us?"

"Dan, shocking details have emerged in the Mia Prescott kidnapping. I'd like to warn viewers right now, that some of our footage is graphic, and not intended for children or infirm viewers."

"Duly noted, Cassandra. What can you tell us?"

"The good news is that Mia Prescott has been found alive and relatively unharmed. Police aren't saying much but it appears she has been beaten and possibly sexually assaulted."

"How was she found, Cassandra?"

"By the tireless efforts of Sergeant Flynn of the Urbandale Police Department who took it upon himself to track her down even on his off hours. We have Sergeant Flynn with us. I think it best to let him describe it in his own words."

The camera widened to include an uncomfortable looking Flynn, thrust into the spotlight.

"Well Cassandra, I received an anonymous tip from a concerned citizen and followed up on it."

"And that tip led you here, an abandoned meat-packing plant?"

"Yes, it did."

"And what did you discover?"

"That there has obviously been a massacre here. It appears that a dozen or more members of a local gang stumbled upon where Mia Prescott was being held. They foolishly decided to take matters into their own hands and met with resistance. Many of them died as a result. This is the reason why we always caution citizens not to approach dangerous criminals."

"Then what happened?"

"There was a fire fight, and I barely escaped with my life."

"I can see you have a rope burn around your neck, Sergeant Flynn, can you tell us what happened there?"

"I'd rather not go into it at this time," said Flynn, modestly, leaving it up to the viewer to imagine it.

"We understand. How did you find Mia Prescott?"

"She was being kept in a separate room. When I was able, I made a sweep of the premises and found her."

"What was her condition?"

"She looked as though she had been assaulted."

"Do you mean physically, or sexually?"

"I'd rather not speculate."

The camera then cut to some earlier footage showing paramedic's wheeling a female out of the building. They held their hands up to the camera, and other officers on the scene pushed the reporters back. "Give us some room, give us some room!" One officer shouted at the cameraman.

The camera cut back to Flynn.

"Were you able to identify the person responsible?"

"No ma'am, I was not. However, with the help of Ms. Prescott, we could identify him as a 'James Peniwinkle.'" James Peniwinkle's driver's license photo was flashed up on the screen.

Daddy had added to his appearance from when the photo was taken so the likeness didn't resemble him at all anymore.

"Thank you very much for your service, Sergeant Flynn. I hope your heroic efforts will be rewarded."

"Thank you, Cassandra."

The camera cut back to the newsroom and Dan Anderson was saying,

"…Thank you, Cassandra. We've just learned that the Prescott family has issued a statement. They would like to say that they are grateful and overjoyed that Mia has been found alive. They would like to thank the Urbandale police department and Sergeant Flynn, in particular, for their heroic efforts. They are calling on the press and citizens of this city for privacy, to let Mia heal in peace. Another press release will be forthcoming in the near future."

Daddy clicked off the TV.

Okay, so what did he know?

He knew that the Prescotts had stepped up their game. Which could only mean William Prescott had taken over from Jeffery. Jeffery was far too much of an amateur to play at this level. It meant that a full-scale police manhunt was underway. This house wouldn't be safe much longer. He had to leave. It meant that Mia was in a hospital at least, her wounds were being treated, and she wouldn't be at peril for the time being, so that was good.

If I was William Prescott, with his money and power, what would I do? thought Daddy. *Given the set of circumstance he is faced with, I would call in professionals.*

What is their Achilles heel? Their weak link in all of this is Mia. If she doesn't go along with their plan, then it all unravels. What would they use as leverage to force compliance? They would tell her I was dead, and nothing could save her. If they find out about the baby, they could also use that against her. In any event, she is far too dangerous to them. Once she has outlived her usefulness, they'll have to kill her.

Daddy continued his line of thought.

What do I need most at this moment? I need weapons, and a place to hide to mount an attack. I also need more information.

What are my advantages? I have weapons. I have money, so I can find a place to hide.

What are my disadvantages? I need more information. I have the entire city looking for me, so if I'm spotted, I have to assume I'll be turned in.

What is the most important thing to do right now, before anything else? I need to get everything that I need, and get out of this house before it is raided. Once I'm safe, I need to put together a plan to gather more information.

With that, Daddy stood up and walked over to a hidden panel in the concrete basement wall. He had built a false wall here when he had moved in. It just stood out eighteen inches from the real wall, so unless someone used a tape measure and measured off the rooms with the blueprints in hand, it would never be spotted. He had never opened it once he stocked it. Indeed, it couldn't be "opened." He had to break through the concrete bricks.

Inside the wall, as a "fail safe" was more cash, more ID's, and his pride and joy, still looking as fresh and oiled as when he put it in there. A Barrett model M82 .50 caliber sniper rifle.

It was time to hunt.

Daddy's "Jihad" or Holy War, had begun.

"The object of war is not to die for your objective,
but to make the other bastard die for his."

George S. Patton

Chapter 70

Daddy packed everything he would need into the back of a rental
he had had delivered.

Luckily, his needs were few. Mostly, what he packed was gadgets
and gizmos as well as weapons and ammo. He would find a hotel for a
few hours sleep and tomorrow find a place to live.

Daddy made a last sweep of his house. He knew there was nothing
incriminating upstairs. But he didn't want them to know what he was
armed with. Let that piece of bad news come as a surprise.

He thought about Mia then. Who knows what she has had to
endure in his absence? He sent his intention out to her, and tried to
use every bit of strength he had to wrap her in his presence so that
she would know he was coming for her. He could feel her on the outer
edges of his consciousness. But something was wrong, and he couldn't
determine what it was. He had to move quickly for her sake, before her
strength failed.

He looked around his office. The pictures of his son comforted
him, and he took a few from their frames and put them in with his
personal things. By the time his family got back this would be over. He
wondered if he would ever see his son again. The thought of his son
growing up without his father made him sad. Another child lost to the
violence of his life.

He had an older son, who must be what, thirty-five by now? From
another marriage but he had never known him. He purposely stayed
out of his life. He kept tabs on him through the years, and knew he
lived in the same town. He was proud of him and he had done well

with his life. He would be a perfect guardian for Mia and the baby. However, that was a problem for another day.

He backed out of the driveway and headed away towards the suburbs where the auto body shops were. He saw a line of police cars going towards his house in the opposite direction and knew his luck was holding.

Next, he went to a Goodwill outlet and picked up some props he would need the next day. Then went looking for an apartment. He secured one in a "Micro-tel" near the freeway that offered monthly rates.

What he needed was intel on what the Prescotts were planning. The only way to get that would be to plant a bug in their office. He would need to get into their office to do that, and that was risky. It could be done with the right set up, but when he got there he wouldn't be leaving.

Which leaves putting a bug on someone going there. The only way to do that would be to plant the bug on Jeffery, or the old man.

He took the audio surveillance devices out of their cases and looked at them.

One looked promising. It was a combination GPS tracking system and wireless microphone. It looked like a watch battery. It was a stainless steel disk smaller than a dime. If he could get it into his pocket it might work. It was wireless so he'd have to have a set up where he could get close enough to intercept the transmissions. His gut feeling was Jeffery would hole up at William Prescott's estate. He'd run home to mommy. Which meant he'd need to surveil the family manor.

That was a stroke of luck as well as he knew the Prescott estate was surrounded by woods. He looked through the other gear and found what he was looking for. A laser sound surveillance system which he could gather sound impressions from a glass window. Between one or the other, or both, he might get some actionable intelligence.

His best chance, however, was getting the law enforcement unlock codes for Jeffery's cell phone, and using that as the surveillance device which would then transmit any sound to his cell phone.

He picked up his cell phone 'burner' and made a call he memorized from his bad 'ol days.

"ID number, please?"

"6154698KJX"

"One moment please...ID confirmed. Number, Please?"

"379-435-5555"

"Confirmed. Code is 987094366"

Daddy keyed the code into his cell phone and his burner instantly came alive with conversation. He recognized Jeffery Prescott's voice immediately.

"…why did you have to do that?"

"Because you've fucked this entire thing up, Jeff. I'm taking over."

"I hardly think that's necessary. We've got Mia back. The cops are hunting this guy. He's all over the news. He can't go anywhere without someone spotting him. It's only a matter of time before the police corner him and send in a SWAT team."

"That's your considered opinion, is it, Jeff?"

"Yes, it is."

"Then you're a bigger fool than I thought."

"So then, what's your answer?"

"I've called in a Black Snake team."

"You're giving this guy too much credit."

"I think you're not giving him enough."

"So how's this going to work?"

"I'm meeting the Black Snake agent tomorrow night outside the Ruan Cafe on Grand. This is costing me one point five mill, Jeff. You better be worth it. Tomorrow I will hand over the retainer. After that, we wait for confirmation."

"What time is the meeting?"

"Six o'clock."

"You want me to make the drop instead of you?"

"Truthfully Jeff, I don't trust you enough to not fuck it up."

"It's your show. I hope you know what you're doing."

Daddy had heard all he needed to hear. He had enough time to get ready.

"The only thing necessary for the triumph of evil
is for good men to do nothing."

Edmund Burke

Chapter 71

William Prescott sat outside the Ruan Cafe with a briefcase full of
cash.

Prescott looked like any of the other businessman having coffee
there. He also showed up early. Which indicated a street smart method
of conducting business, something Daddy hadn't expected from him.
Prescott had arranged the meeting on his terms, sitting where he wanted to sit, giving him a view that he wanted. Daddy had expected him to
arrive 'casually late' expecting his employee to be waiting for him.

I underestimated him, thought Daddy, filing that bit of information
away.

Daddy came next, in a business suit, tie pulled down and flopped
down in a chair not far away, at the back and left of Prescott. He ex-
uded the air of a tired businessman looking for a quick meal, then back
to the office for a late night. Prescott's eyes flicked over him, and dismissed him. Daddy brought out his iPod, put in the ear buds, angled
his chair so his back was to Prescott and directed the unidirectional
mic towards Prescott's table. He adjusted the sound and gain when the
waiter came over to take Prescott's order.

"Will you be having drinks or dinner tonight, sir?"

"Just drinks. I'll have a Black Velvet, on the rocks."

"Drinking alone?"

"No, I'm waiting for a business colleague."

"Very good, sir," the waiter said and left to get his drink.

Daddy could tell Prescott's 'colleague' had shown up simply by the sound of the crisp military walk that came in through the earbuds. He could almost see him in his mind's eye, wearing an expensive business suit. His hair was close-cropped, his back ram-rod straight. There was no hesitation in the visitor's manner. He knew exactly what he was doing.

Prescott looked up as he approached the table.

"Mr. Prescott, thank you for agreeing to this meet. Do I need to go over the rules for this conversation?"

"Probably not," said Prescott.

"Have you done this before?"

"Not with you."

"If we agree to handle your contract, once this meeting is over, there is nothing more for you to do except wait for a call from us confirming the delivery schedule. Once delivery has been made, the final payment will be expected immediately. Is there anything unclear about these conditions?"

"No, there isn't."

"I'd like you to take a look at our standard contract then." The man slid over a document. It looked like dozens of manufacturing contracts William Prescott had seen through the years. Both explicit and vague at the same time. The terms were outlined. There was a bland military baldness about this contract. There wasn't any dense legalese. It spelled itself out clearly. We do this, you do that.

"I'll also need a copy of this," said Prescott, signing his.

"I have one here."

"What's next?"

"Do you have the retainer?"

The waiter wandered over then. "Can I get you something?" he asked the new arrival.

"A glass of water, please." The waiter moved out of earshot.

"The retainer?"

"In the briefcase next to your feet. Simply pick it up when you leave."

"Excellent. Have you compiled a specification sheet on the part we need to manufacture?"

"Yes, it is in the briefcase."

"Then our business is concluded," Ram-Rod made ready to leave.

"Is there anything else you'll be requiring of me?" Prescott asked.

"Yes, approximately one week from today, the team will be touching down on your south pasture. We'll need a place to get our preliminary samples together. The barn near the south pasture should do. There is nothing you need to do, so this is just to let you know what to expect."

"Then our business is concluded."

The man got up and left without another word. His bottled water and glass were left untouched. Prescott realized later he had touched nothing on the table either, keeping his hands in his lap. He couldn't have gotten fingerprints if he had wanted to.

Prescott now had to see to the details of the party surrounding Jeffery's announcing his running for mayor.

Daddy had one week to heal, and to prepare.

"Murder begins where self-defense ends."

Georg Buchner

Chapter 72

"We need to discuss our little problem." William Prescott said, one week later, as he walked around an end table and took a seat near his son.

"Which problem is that?"

"The little problem that is growing inside your wife. You know it has to be dealt with. No spawn of 'Daddy' is going to even have the slightest chance of inheriting anything from this family."

"Oh, yes, that problem. That will soon be taken care of."

Jeffery stood and walked out of the room. He returned a few minutes later holding a small plastic container. He sat back down and opened it, showing his father the syringe inside.

"What the hell is that?"

"MTX."

"Isn't that a cancer drug?" William's face wrinkled in confusion.

"Yes, but it can also be used to terminate pregnancies." Jeffery smiled proudly. "One injection and my lovely wife will miscarriage. No fuss, no muss."

William sat back in his chair taking in the information.

"How long does it take to work?"

"She will lose the baby within the week, most likely."

"How did you get your hands on that?"

"I have friends. Anyway, that's not important. What is important, is that I will simply stick this needle into Mia and our problem will flush itself away." He made a disgusting gesture with his hands then closed the container.

"Jeffery, sometimes you can be useful, it seems." A crooked smile spread over the father's face. "When are you going to do it?"

"Right now."

Mia covered her mouth with her hand to stop the sound of her gasp reaching the men. Her eyes were wide with terror as she eavesdropped on their conversation outside the study door.

Mia ran back to her bedroom. She knew that she only had minutes until her husband descended on her with his abortion drug. Of course, she could fight him off this time or maybe the next few times but eventually he would succeed. Jeffery was going to find a way to kill her baby or her. It was only a matter of time. If it wasn't the drug, it would be something else.

Mia decided right then that she would end things first. She was going to kill him or die trying.

She scanned her bedroom looking for a quick weapon. There was a large lamp, a glass vase, and a fireplace poker. Perfect. She ran over to the fireplace and grabbed the would-be weapon. She quickly ran back to the door, standing off to the side so when the door was opened, she would be behind it.

She only had to wait a few moments before she heard footsteps. Mia was lucky, it seemed. Her husband was coming alone. There were only one set of shoes coming down the hall. She gripped the poker tightly and held it back, over her head.

Mia's heart was racing as the door slowly opened. She heard her husband cautiously enter the room. After he had taken a few steps in and was clear of the door, Mia kicked it shut. Then with no hesitation she stepped into her swing. The poker slammed against Jeffery's neck. As the hook part hit, Mia pulled back to inflict more damage.

Jeffery dropped the container he had been carrying and grabbed his throat. He fell to his knees gasping. Mia was pretty sure she had crushed his windpipe, or at least done severe damage. Still trying to inhale, he then crawled towards her. When he got to her feet, her husband grabbed her leg. Mia thought he looked almost cute begging for help. She stepped back roughly, pulling away from his hand.

Jeffery fell forward when Mia didn't grab his outstretched hand. When it came to rest on the floor, Mia lifted the poker high and stabbed it straight down with all her body weight. If he could breathe, she was sure the screams would have been award worthy. As it was, though, Jeffery's whole body was jerking back and forth as strange gurgling noises came from his mouth.

The poker hadn't stabbed through his hand but the puncture wound was deep. Blood spurted out and covered the floor. Mia pulled the poker back up, taking his hand with it for a few seconds. When he finally freed his hand, Jeffery fell back. He was grabbing his wounded hand and his face was now a deep shade of red.

Mia stood over him just watching. His face slowly turned blue. She hadn't realize that when people stop breathing, they really turn a purple-blue color. She thought it was just an expression. She was mesmerized by it for a few seconds.

Finally, she turned and bent down, retrieving the glass container from the floor. Mia took out the syringe and dropped the box. Laying the poker down, she got on her knees next to her husband. She stared into his eyes and saw his terror and pleading.

"You wanted to abort my baby. I'm going to abort you, instead. So in a way, this is just a very 'late term' abortion, Jeffery."

She kept watching as she lifted the drug. Mia brought the needle down, and injected the contents into Jeffery's carotid artery in his neck.

His whole body shook violently and his teeth clamped together in a rictus, trapping his tongue between them. Mia watched as in his pain and desperation, Jeffery bit through his own tongue. Blood flowed out his mouth and pooled underneath him.

Mia, sickened by what she had done, decided it was time to show a bit of mercy. She retrieved the poker and stood. With one final motion, she brought the metal poker down. The poker went through his teeth, entered his mouth and embedded deep into his skull.

"You were always so proud of your 'poker face', Jeffery," Mia said quietly, looking down at his corpse.

"There is no avoiding war; it can only be postponed
to the advantage of others."

Niccolo Machiavelli

Chapter 73

Daddy loved deer season. Not because he liked to hunt, he'd given that up years ago. But because he loved walking through the woods, enjoying the stillness of nature.

He drove a mile out of his way and parked off the road, and hiked in. He was twelve hours ahead of helicopter arrival. He was careful walking through the woods. He looked like any other hunter. His licenses were up to date, he had on hunter orange. He was legal in every sense of the word if he came across a game warden. He carried a 700 Remington 30.06 which would be considered an excellent deer rifle. It could also be considered an excellent sniper rifle as well. In fact, the military version of this same rifle was used as one.

The only thing unusual was he also carried a Barrett 50 caliber with a magazine of ten armor piercing shells and a ghillie suit. While none of the items are illegal or would call attention to themselves alone, the combination would make an attentive game warden curious.

A ghellie suit, typically, is a net or cloth garment covered in loose strips of burlap, cloth or twine, sometimes made to look like leaves and twigs, and optionally augmented with scraps of foliage from the area.

Snipers, hunters and nature photographers, wear ghillie suits to blend into their surroundings and conceal themselves from enemies or targets. The suit gives the wearer's outline a three-dimensional breakup, rather than a linear one. When manufactured correctly, the suits will move in the wind in the same way as surrounding foliage and are almost impossible to detect with the naked eye.

Daddy hiked all around the South Pasture. Keeping well back from the tree line. Once he found a high vantage point, he scanned the entire area with binoculars. He paid particular interest to any locations which would lend themselves to counter surveillance. If there were any watchers, he wanted to be the one watching them.

Next, he looked for any positions which would lend itself to being a sniper's position. He made a mental note of where the positions were, then set out to examine each one. He came up to each one from the rear, and downwind. None looked occupied, or had the appearance of a hasty departure. He sat in the last one, discarding the hunter orange vest and hat, put on his ghellie suit, and studied the surrounding country.

He was looking for, and trying to feel, anything out of place. A movement which didn't belong in the world of trees and animals. A flash of sunlight on a scope, a sound which didn't fit the surroundings. Finally, he probed the area with his mind, trying to pick up any hostile vibrations. Violence carried its own energy, and he knew the feeling well. He detected no threat, no movement which was out of place, or anything out of the ordinary.

He checked the direction of the wind and calculated the likely path of the helicopter on approach and take off. Lastly, he calculated where the sun would be at seven p.m. or nineteen hundred hours, military time. This last bit gave him an advantage as the spot he had chosen for the ambush would put the sun at his back, and in the eyes of the pilot.

He made his way quietly and carefully through the woods to his chosen spot and settled in for a long wait. It was still eight hours before the expected arrival of the helicopter. Since he had no spotter, he set everything up. One rifle on each side of him. Extra ammo of the correct size, loaded in spare magazines and within arms reach. He dug a depression into the ground, then used tree branches, cut at the "Y" intersection of one and stuck them into the ground to steady the barrels of each.

Once everything was prepared, he settled in for the long wait. Waiting quietly, silently, motionless for hours was an acquired skill. Many people he knew fell asleep. To remain alert and focused was far harder than most expected.

With four hours to go, he became hyper alert. This would probably be when an inexperienced, or lazy counter surveillance team would move into position. He wanted to be able to detect them long before they detected him.

There, he spotted it. The sun glinted off a glass scope. They moved into position exactly where he thought they would, the best position for counter surveillance and to watch the incoming helicopter, but not the best for an ambush. He watched them through his rifle scope. There were two of them, also to be expected. One on the gun, the other to work out targets. Since they would be in contact with the home team, he had to wait until the best time to take them out. Since this was more of a surgical execution, he chose the 700 Remington and slid it into position. Then he started watching their world through the Remington's scope.

Daddy glanced at his watch on the underside of his wrist. Fifteen minutes to show time. He stilled himself, then made a conscious effort to control his breathing as he had been taught so many years ago. With five minutes to go, he sighted carefully, inhaled, exhaled half a breath and gently squeezed the trigger. His shot was down, but took out the spotter in the throat. The sniper looked up from his rifle then, sensing his partner down, which gave Daddy just the opening he was looking for. He swung the rifle over in a gentle arc, and drilled a high-velocity bullet right through his forehead.

Now he grabbed the big Barrett .50 and pulled it into position. He checked the ammo, tapped the magazine once on the butt stock, and slapped it into the slot. He pulled back the bolt of the rifle, chambering a round and left the safety on. He was locked and loaded.

The helicopter was an Army surplus "Huey" made famous in the Vietnam War and still in wide circulation. It was a good, utilitarian chopper, expertly designed to do what it did well, which was infiltrations and extractions. It came in low and fast. Daddy watched it come in and prepare to land.

Daddy knew helicopters were at their most venerable when landing, and taking off. He couldn't wait for it to land and discharge its cargo of troops. He had to take it out while it was still in midair. While it was still five hundred feet up, and descending, he took careful aim, and put two quick shots into the pilot side windscreen. The helicopter made a flop as the copilot instantly took over the control and Daddy put two more armor piercing shells into the copilot.

The helicopter went into a death spiral with no one at the controls. Daddy saw his opportunity and quickly took out the tail rotor as well, watching pieces of metal fragment on impact of the bullets.

He lowered his weapon and watched what could only be described as a death ballet. The helicopter with no one alive at the control and the tail rotor blown to pieces, went into a slow motion dive. He saw one tropper with the presence of mind to jump out of the stricken aircraft, but it was still two hundred feet off the ground and doubted he survived the fall.

With the laziness of a slow motion train wreak, the Huey's long blades impacted with the top branches, shearing them off, then crashed into the trees, sending a huge fireball of orange and black flames upward as the aviation fuel ignited.

It was a perfectly executed ambush of a lone warrior against a superior and overwhelming force. Daddy felt no exaltation of a job well done. He felt only sadness at the lives wasted.

He bowed his head and wish the dead a speedy journey into the afterlife.

"There is no hunting like the hunting of man, and those who have hunted armed men long enough and liked it, never care for anything else thereafter."

Ernest Hemingway

Chapter 74

Daddy studied the crash site through his scope, then through the binoculars, and saw no movement.

He knew he wouldn't have much time before the team at the Prescott Estate rushed over. He left the Barrett .50 caliber where it was and walked down the hill, careful to keep out of sight. At the edge of the landing zone, he stopped and gave the area another sweep through his glasses.

He saw one team member who had jumped from the wreckage whose body was roughly the same size as he was and whose equipment was still intact. He hustled over to him, and checked his neck for a pulse. None. He picked him up in firemans carry and brought him back to the edge of the landing zone and reentered the tree-line.

He walked back to the crash site and picked up weapons and various materials and brought them back. He even found a sound suppressor for the pistol. He saw a severed arm from someone and brought that back too. He could hear sirens off in the distance coming closer and knew it was time to disappear. The first responders would be here soon.

Interesting that the Black Snake boys left at the estate didn't even bother to go see what happened to their teammates. They either thought he might be up on his rifle ready to pick them off if they did, or they were circling their wagons back at the ranch. Both of which were reasonable calls in their position. Whatever their reasoning, they now knew no reinforcements would be coming.

He dragged the corpse and gear up the side of the mountain and found a place to work. He stripped the corpse, then his own clothes, and put the corpse's clothes on. He smeared blood all over his face and neck from the severed arm, added the helmet and goggles and fixed other parts of the gear around his body. He now looked like a certified member of the Black Snake team. As long as no one noticed his age, he should be okay. The helmet and goggles should help with that.

Two members of the Black Snake team, and William Prescott stood on the porch watching a black, greasy, smoke plume rise above the trees. Moments before they had seen the chopper come in for a landing and while still five hundred feet off the ground, spiral out of control and crash. The resulting explosion had shook the windows in the manor. A fireball of orange and black flame had swept over the trees as the jet fuel blew. Since the wind was blowing away from them, they didn't hear the shots from the .50 caliber.

The two surviving members talked quietly among themselves. If either felt the loss, they didn't show it.

"Sir, this is now a combat situation and we have to get you inside," said the highest ranking squad leader.

"What do you mean a 'combat situation'?"

"We have to assume that aircraft was taken down intentionally."

"What is your next step?"

"We need to get you to a safe room inside the house."

"What about your teammates, aren't you going to see if they need help?"

"If we did sir, and if it was enemy action, he would pick us off as soon as we arrived."

"So you're just going to let them die?"

"No one would have survived that crash, sir. If you prefer we can go and examine the crash site. Of course, that means you'll be unprotected here."

That wasn't the situation Prescott was envisioning.

"Of course, I'll do whatever you say."

One man stayed on the porch in a defensive position scanning the tree line, the other led Prescott inside. Both men went into the study. The commando checked the window, then pulled drapes across it, shutting out the view from outside as well as the sunlight.

"You should be safe here, sir," said the squad leader.

"You actually don't think he'd be coming at us on the estate, do you?"

"Like it or not, we are on the defensive, sir. We are on our own. Black Snake headquarters has been sent word, and I assume, another chopper will be coming. However, that could take a while to get here. In the meantime, our best option is to hunker down here and wait for reinforcements to arrive."

Except the Black Snake team members were wrong. There was a survivor. One stumbled up to the gate, bloody, uniform torn and smoking. He buzzed the gate, then slumped against it. From the study, they could look at the surveillance cameras mounted outside the gate. They saw a wounded soldier in Black Snake uniform. He rang the buzzer again, then collapsed, blood streaming from several wounds. The squad leader keyed his mic.

"Unit two-unit one- there appears to be a surviving team member at the gate. Please check it out and proceed with caution."

"Copy that."

They could follow the Unit Two's progress up to the gate on the cameras. He took no chances. He opened the gate and checked the mercenary's pulse at his neck, then dragged him inside the compound and shut the gate. Once inside, he brought him over to a defensible position, out of view of the security cameras and checked his wounds. Several minutes passed.

"Unit two-unit one, report."

"Unit one-unit two, he didn't survive his wounds."

"Copy that. Return to base."

"Copy."

Unit Two, using the same exaggerated care, made his way back to the house. He walked into the house, and knocked on the study door. Unit One, opened it, and stood aside.

"Report."

"You're dead," Daddy said, and shot the remaining Black Snake member in the head, blowing blood and brains out the back of his head and all over the study. William Prescott looked on in horror.

Turning to Prescott, Daddy took off his helmet and goggles and said, "Now it's just you and me."

"Men should be either treated generously or destroyed, because they take revenge for slight injuries - for heavy ones they cannot."

Niccolo Machiavelli

Chapter 75

William Prescott recovered his composure quickly, and walked around to stand behind his desk.

"We meet at last," Prescott said.

"It appears we do."

Both men stood looking at each other. They were approximately the same age. Certainly, of the same generation which gave them a background in common.

"You do realize, of course, that you'll never get out of here alive, right?"

"I bet you thought I'd never get in here alive, either. You seem to have a flair for underestimating your opponent," said Daddy.

"So what do I call you?"

"You can call me 'Daddy' if you want, or 'hey you' also works."

Prescott snorted in derision. "A man of many names."

"Since, according to you, I'm not going to live that long. What do you care?"

"I don't, truthfully."

"Excellent. Now that we've got all the fake pleasantries out of the way, what do you say we get down to business?"

"What do you want?"

Daddy fished a paper out of his pocket. "I want you to call this number right here, and set up a general life insurance trust with Mia as the irrevocable trustee."

"You want me to set the little whore up for life, is that it?"

"This is your first and only warning. Do not disrespect her again," Daddy said calmly. He held out a piece of paper to Prescott.

"You realize, of course, it will do you no good. If the trust was set up by coercion, I'll be able to get all the money back."

"Really? Is that the way it works? Dial the number. Set it up and hand the phone to me."

"In what amount?"

"Fifty million, five hundred and forty-three thousand."

Prescott almost choked. "I haven't got that kind of…"

"Oh yes, you do. It's in this account right here," Daddy handed Prescott a bank statement from another pocket.

Prescott glared at Daddy with hate in his eyes. "It will bankrupt me."

"You're right, it will. Well, I am leaving you twenty dollars to keep the account open. Which if you look at it from my point of view is pretty generous of me. Make the call or die painfully."

Prescott dialed the numbers. A man answered the phone with precise English with a slight Germanic accent. Prescott watched Daddy the whole time. He told the banker the account number to withdraw the funds from, then handed the phone to Daddy.

"Satisfied?"

"Almost."

Daddy listened silently while the banker on the other end confirmed the deposit.

"Excellent, Jorge. Now please…" Daddy walked away from Prescott, to the other side of the room out of earshot and continued, "… split the account into three different trusts of equal amounts using Swiss Annuities. The beneficiaries of each account are the following…"

With his business concluded, Daddy walked back to the desk.

"I need you to do one more thing and I'll be leaving. Have your personal jet fueled up and ready to travel. Call now."

"You've got to be joking me. You really think you'll make it out of here?"

"That's my problem. Your problem is the amount of hurt I'll put on you if you don't do as I ask this minute."

Prescott picked up the phone, told them to fuel the jet and have it ready for immediate takeoff.

"They want to know the destination," Prescott said, with his hand over the mouthpiece.

"Tell them the destination is unknown at the moment, but will be revealed on takeoff."

Prescott went back to the phone and relayed the instructions. Once he was finished, Prescott spread both hands wide on his desk, leaning forward in his best 'King of the Kingdom' stance.

"Now that you've gotten what you want, why don't you take your whore and…"

Quicker than Prescott could react, Daddy took out two belt knives, one in each hand, concealed on his back belt, and drove them through both of Prescott's hands spread on the desk. The force of the blow drove the blade of the knives through his hands and sank the blade tips at least an inch into the top of the hardwood desk. Prescott screamed in surprise and pain.

"I warned you not to disrespect her."

Prescott tried to free his hands, but the knives only bit deeper. Daddy spun the intercom towards himself, and pushed the button for "whole house."

"Mia? Please, come to the study."

Mia was just finishing changing her blood-soaked clothes when she heard an explosion off in the distance. It had taken several minutes for her hands to stop shaking enough for them to work the buttons on her shirt. Mia looked at herself in the mirror, taking a deep calming breath. She couldn't believe all that had just happened.

It was necessary, she told herself, *he would have killed the baby.*

Just then the house intercom came alive. She hurried from the room. She couldn't wait to tell William Prescott about his first born.

Daddy heard the tentative knock on the door a few minutes later. He got behind the door so he wouldn't be a target and had a view through the door jamb when it opened.

"Baby, it's me Daddy. Open the door just enough to squeeze through and come in."

Mia squeezed through as instructed, closed the door, and stood looking at Daddy.

"Is it really you?"

"It's really me."

Mia looked over at Prescott, writhed in pain, both hands nailed to the desk.

"Daddy!" She screamed and flew into his arms. "I knew you'd come. They told me you were dead. I didn't believe them." She grabbed onto his neck and jumped into his arms wrapping her legs around his stomach.

"Listen to me, we don't have much time."

"Okay Daddy, anything you want," she said, she couldn't stop touching his face.

"First, is the baby okay?"

"Yes, Daddy. I protected her. Daddy, we're going to have a baby girl. I have the test results if you want to see it. Jeffery wanted to kill her. I killed him instead. He's upstairs dead on the floor."

"You do, what you got to do in this life. I can't say I'm going to miss him much."

"Listen to me now. You're going to leave here. I have everything set up for you to have the baby in Switzerland. They have the best clinics available. Everything is taken care of. You simply call this number here right before you get on the plane. When you arrive, they will take care of everything."

"What about you? You're coming aren't you?"

"I'm going to be there as soon as I can."

"Can you handle another girl?"

"A little girl. I always wanted a daughter. I want you to name the baby Mia Lynn. Can you do that for me?"

"Of course, Daddy. But we'll do it together, won't we?"

"I hope so, but I don't know how this is going to end. But I know how it is going to end for you and the baby. That's enough. Now, I want you to leave right now. You don't even need any clothes. Just go to the airport and get on a plane. Call me at the airport before you board, then call me again when you land."

"Daddy? Do you remember the time you told me that marriage and divorce were nothing more than a state of mind, and I could decide which one anytime I wanted?"

"Yes."

"Do you really believe that?"

"Yes, I do."

"Then I want to get married again, right now. Will you marry me, Daddy?"

"Of course, I will."

"We don't have rings."

"We'll manage," said Daddy smiling.

"So how do we do it?"

"We make a commitment to each other."

"I want to take your name, Daddy. I'm no longer a Prescott."

Daddy smiled at Mia, loving her. "Then you shall," he said simply.

"Then I am now Mia Cobalt."

Daddy kissed her. "And now I have kissed the bride. It's official."

"Do I have to go now, Daddy?"

"Baby, listen to me. You're about to go on a long journey. I've been preparing you for this journey since we met, and now you're ready. This is the journey you were meant to take. Now this is very important. I will ALWAYS be with you. I will always be standing right by your side. And I will be with you, and protect you forever."

"But Daddy…"

"Go Baby…fly like the wind. You don't have much time."

"I love you, Daddy."

"I love you too."

Mia spun on her heel, and was gone.

Ten minutes after Mia left, Daddy heard sirens in the distance growing closer, then tires squealing to a stop on the black top. He could hear voices and a whistle outside the window.

"Go! Go! Go!"

The SWAT team arrived.

"No trait is more justified than revenge in the right time and place."

Meir Kahane

Chapter 76

The SWAT team set up positions outside the estate.

Daddy knew their first priority would be to get 'eyes' inside the study in order to know who, how many, and what they were dealing with. Once they knew that, they would start negotiations. If they couldn't negotiate, then they would try to flush him out. If they couldn't flush him out, they would forcibly enter.

Daddy looked over at William Prescott still pinned to the desk by his hands.

"How you doing over there, Prescott? Have you wet yourself yet? Sorry to hear about your son. My guess is, he didn't die well."

"It's going to be a pleasure watching them kill you, I can tell you that," said Prescott, grimacing through the pain.

"After beating helpless girls, I bet watching a killing is right up your psychotic alley in terms of entertainment," said Daddy.

Daddy watched as a small telescoping camera was slipped under the door. He was ready for it and sprayed the lens with black paint, ruining it. It was withdrawn. They would try the ventilation system next.

His cell phone rang. "Yes?"

"I'm boarding the plane, Daddy," said Mia.

"Okay, good. Tell them once they get in the air, your destination is Geneva, Switzerland. Call the number I gave you now and call me when you land."

"Okay, Daddy. You're coming, right?"

"I'll be there one way or another, Baby," Daddy flipped his cell phone shut.

"That's so sweet," mocked Prescott, "'Daddy' and 'Baby.' I almost want to vomit."

"Go ahead. You're the one that will be standing in a stink of your own making. A feeling you should be familiar with by now."

"You realize of course, the longer I stay in this position, the bigger chance I have of bleeding to death."

"You realize of course, I don't really give a shit."

Right then, the phone on the desk rang. "I'd ask you to answer it, but I guess you're pinned down at the moment," said Daddy, nonchalantly. He picked it up without saying hello.

"I'm John Huntly, the police negotiator. Who am I talking to?"

"You can call me Daddy."

"Daddy?" The request clearly caught him off balance. Daddy grinned to himself, at the discomfort this was causing the negotiator. Tough to be a hard ass police negotiator, if you had to call your opponent "Daddy."

"Okay, 'Daddy,' do you have any immediate requests?"

"Just one. Is Officer Flynn among the able and willing out there?"

"He is."

"Send him in then. He's the only one I'll talk to." Daddy disconnected the call.

"Hey, Flynn, come here," ordered Flynn's immediate superior.

"Sir?" said Flynn.

"Your presence has been requested inside the mansion by the perp. I need to know the relationship you have with him and why he would request you."

"Here's what I know," began Flynn. "He's a professional and he's probably anticipating every move you make. He could have killed me, and he didn't. He goes into nothing without a planned entry and exit. And truthfully, even with the firepower you have here, you're probably out-matched."

"Well, thank you for the vote of confidence, Sergeant Flynn. He has requested you. Any idea why he would do that?"

"None," Flynn, of course, had an idea of why he had done it. However, this didn't feel like the right time to share that information.

"Well, he requested you go in. Do you want to go armed, or with body armor?"

"Did he say to go in unarmed?"

"He said nothing of the sort."

"Then it doesn't matter one way or the other. If he wanted me unarmed, he would have said so."

"I think we ought to outfit you with a camera and a wire."

"He's just going to find it."

"So what are you proposing?"

"Why don't I just go in there and see what he wants?"

Flynn knocked on the door.

"Is that you Flynn?" asked Daddy.

"Yes, sir, it is."

"I assume you're alone?"

"Yes, I am."

"Are you wearing a camera or a body mic?"

Flynn sighed, "No, I am not."

"Are you armed?"

"Yes, I am."

"Then enter slowly. Open the door just enough to squeeze through, no more."

Flynn opened the door slowly and squeezed through as instructed. Once inside, both men stood looking at each other. Daddy smiled, slightly.

"You look good, Flynn. I bet the rope scar around your neck hasn't hurt with the ladies. Chicks dig scars, for some reason."

Flynn smiled back. Perversely, there was an intimate connection between the two men now. Flynn knew perfectly well that by sparing his life, he owed a debt of obligation to Daddy. It was a strange relationship based on unspoken respect between warriors.

Flynn looked over at Prescott, still knifed to the top of the desk.

"Mr. Prescott," Flynn said, acknowledged him.

"Flynn, shoot this son of a bitch and get it over with," said Prescott.

"What do you think, sir, should I shoot you?"

Daddy shrugged his shoulders as though the question had no importance.

"Do what you have to do," Daddy said, "speaking of which, I wanted to give this back to you. I had to borrow it the last time we met, but I didn't want you to think I stole it. There's one in the throat, and sixteen in the magazine. The safety is on."

Daddy held out Flynn's Glock 17 to him, dangling it from his hand with one finger in the trigger guard.

"Does that leave you unarmed?" asked Flynn.

"It does."

"Are you giving yourself up?"

"No, not yet."

"But you're giving me your one and only weapon?"

"Sure, why not?" Daddy said, smiling.

Flynn took the weapon and looked at it. Looked at Daddy. He could end this right now, and be the hero of the day once again.

Instead, he flicked the safety off, turned, and shot William Prescott directly through the head. The bullet entered his forehead perfectly between the eyes and made a wide spray pattern of blood and brains on the wall behind him. Prescott collapsed, his hands still pinned to the desktop.

Flynn keyed his lapel mic at once, "Stand down, stand down. That was a misfire. This situation is under control."

"I've been wanting to do that for a long time," Flynn said. "Him and his son both are a total waste of the human race."

"I know the feeling. By the way, his son is dead upstairs as well. Mia said she wasted him."

"Good. I am, of course, going to blame both deaths on you. One in the throat, fifteen in the mag, safety is OFF." Flynn, reversed the grip on the gun, and held it out to Daddy. This time he was dangling the gun with one finger by the trigger guard.

"I'd be insulted if you didn't."

Daddy took the Glock, clicked the safety on, and motioned Flynn over to a table to sit down, putting the Glock on the polished wood.

"So what do we do now?" asked Flynn as both men sat down, and Daddy poured a shot of Prescott's whiskey for both.

"We wait, and drink Prescott's whiskey."

"Look," said Flynn. "You're going to have to give me your name because I'm not going to call you by the ridiculous name of 'Daddy.'"

Daddy laughed then. It struck him as completely funny. Both men started laughing, first chuckling, then guffawing, then out and out laughter as all the tension of the situation dissipated.

"My name is James Cobalt," said Daddy. "But anyone who knew

me by that name simply called me Cobalt."

"Is that your real name, or another alias?"

"It's my real name. You are among five people in the world who know it."

"So Cobalt, what do we do now?"

"You understand you owe me, right?"

"You didn't need to voice that."

"I know. Even so, I was making sure all the cards were on the table."

"They are. Name your ask."

"We wait for a call. When I get that call, which should be in about six hours, then you're going to kill me. I prefer a warrior's death. The same as you wasted on Prescott there, who didn't deserve it."

"Suicide by cop? It doesn't have to end that way. I can get you out of here, I could…"

"To what end?"

"To go be with your woman in peace. Disappear. It's what you do, isn't it?"

"No. It's what I *did*, a long time ago, not what I do. The journey ends here, Flynn. I'm tired. Mia is safe, she is taken care of. I did what I came to do. This is my last operation."

"I'm not sure I can accommodate that request, sir."

"You owe me, Flynn."

"Yes, I do. But it wouldn't be honorable."

"Ah, honor. Now we get to the crux of the matter, don't we?" said Cobalt.

"The lines on your face are your medals. You've earned them, so why shouldn't they be worn with honour?"

Cherie Lunghi

Chapter 77

The two men looked at each other in silence, drinking their whiskey.

"Have you lived an honorable life, Flynn?" asked Cobalt.

"I have tried, but I have slipped, as you well know. Have you lived an honorable life, Cobalt?"

Cobalt smiled. "I have tried but I have slipped as well."

"Try this on for size. I lead you out of here in handcuffs. I tell the team outside that part of the deal of giving yourself up included me and only me, bringing you in. Once we get out of here and away, you overpower me, maybe shoot me in the arm or something, and get away."

"I think it would work in the movies."

"Why won't it work?"

"I took out a Black Snake team. You think they are going to let me walk out of here? Those boys are going to want payback, and I'm sure there are snipers waiting out there now. As soon as I show, they will open fire. Your protection won't matter. It might even get you killed as well.

"Even if I get away, they will hunt me down extra judiciously. They will follow me no matter where I go and that will put Mia and the baby at risk all over again. I'm not going to do that."

"Mia's pregnant? I didn't know that. Congratulations!"

Cobalt got up from the table, walked to Prescott's desk, and got two cigars.

"Join me?" motioning to the cigar.

"Sure, why not."

Both men lit up their cigars. Cobalt poured another shot of whiskey, and they smoked in silence.

"Okay then," continued Flynn, "what if we faked your death?"

"They know all the same tricks I do. They are going to be watching for it. Flynn, I've thought this through. There's only one way out. I do need to do one thing while we're waiting though."

Flynn waved his hand in the air through the smoke as if to say 'Knock yourself out'.

Daddy walked to a corner, opened his cell phone and called Switzerland. He spoke out of earshot for a long while. Flynn smoked his cigar and ignored him. When Cobalt came back to the table, Flynn said,

"Do you have any idea how much bullshit I went through losing my service weapon AND a surveillance van?"

"Oh? And you think getting hung by your arms and beaten with baseball bats was a piece of cake?"

"True. You have me there. Why'd you let the vet stick that prod up your ass?"

"I told him in exchange for not killing him, to substitute my sperm with horse sperm."

"You've got to be shitting me?" Flynn said, laughing.

"No, I'm not. That was when I saw Prescott's whole plan unraveling. They wanted to pin Mia's rape and abduction on me. So, it was going to be pretty hard to do that unless the Mayor wanted to admit his wife like being fucked by horses. But you knew that. I thought you were in on that."

"I was hired help. No, they never shared their grand plans with me."

"And now, they never will."

The shadows started to deepen into late afternoon.

Flynn's shoulder mic came alive.

"Flynn? Report. Is everything still under control?"

Flynn keyed his shoulder microphone. "He's going to give himself up. Final preparations are being made now. Stand down." Looking at Cobalt he said, "I gotta tell them something to keep them from storming the castle."

Cobalt shrugged. Not real concerned, one way, or another.

"How do you feel about dying?" Flynn asked Cobalt.

"The same way I feel about living."

"It doesn't bother you?"

"How many dead people have you seen, Flynn?"

"Too many to count."

"Did any of them, and I mean any of them, look like they gave a fuck?"

"Some looked surprised. Some looked scared."

"How do you feel about it, Flynn?"

"It's not my time."

"There you have it. I feel it is my time. I'm getting older. I don't want to look forward to failing health, and a fading memory. I'd rather go now while the decision of when, where, and how is still in my hands."

"You're not afraid of death?"

"I'm more afraid of dying stupidly. I used to see people get killed in Asia. Many times, most times, it was because of something stupid. Some pointless detail they overlooked. Like not taking the safety off a weapon, or not cleaning it properly. I don't mind dying for something worthwhile, but I live in fear of wasting my life over something stupid. Like getting hit by a bus. This is a worthy reason to die. I can be at peace with that."

"What about your family?"

"I'm going to miss them. If I have any regrets, it is there. I don't want my son to grow up without a father. But if he has to, then I want him to know, his father died with honor, standing up for what he believed in."

Cobalt's cell phone rang then. He flipped it open.

"Yes?"

"I'm here, Daddy." Mia said, "It's cold. It is very beautiful. You'd like it. Lots of mountains. They met me at the airport just like you said they would. They are taking me to a hotel now, and tomorrow I will go meet a man you named."

"Very good. Remember, you're safe. You never have to worry about anything ever again, except making sure our daughter grows up properly. Teach her the things I taught you."

"You're scaring me, Daddy. Why don't you teach her?"

"I'm just saying she'll have lots of teachers."

"Daddy, it's so beautiful here. So quiet, and so clean."

"The Swiss are good people. You'll like them. You might have to learn a new language."

"When are you going to get here, Daddy?"

"As soon as I can."

"I love you, Daddy. Get here quick, because I want to share this with you."

"Okay, Baby. I love you too. Always remember that."

"I will, Daddy."

Cobalt flipped the cell phone shut. Knowing perfectly well it was the last time he would ever talk to her in this life.

Cobalt looked at Flynn. "You owe me."

"You saved my life in order to ask me to take yours?"

"Yes, I did. Well, among other reasons. I also saw a man of honor."

"As a man of honor, I refuse."

"I understand," Cobalt said quietly, "Then I ask this. Extend my debt to Mia and my sons. I have a full grown son who lives in town. the debt extends to him as well. Whatever they want, whatever they need, anytime, anywhere, for the rest of your life."

"That I can do."

Cobalt stood up. "Few men get a second chance at life, Flynn. I extended it to you because I felt you would use the gift wisely. I'm glad I wasn't disappointed. Live your life with honor."

"I intend to. Also, thank you for not killing me," Flynn said with a wry smile.

"My pleasure."

Cobalt walked toward the curtained, blacked out window, seemingly lost in thought. A random poem came into Daddy's head.

I was born the son of a blameless man,
I tried to right some wrongs,
With a gun in my hand.
I went too far and a bad man died.
A righteous jury,
And the witness lied.

I was tried and convicted,
And sentenced to hang.
But the hangman was conflicted,
When the church bells rang.
I was left alone and my heart evicted

When the reaper finally sang.

When he reached the window, he turned around and said,

"Please tell Mia when she calls that I will always be with her, and that everything will be all right. It was a pleasure knowing you…"

"Wait, don't…"

Cobalt opened the window curtains, his arms wide forming a crucifix in the window.

The shot came almost instantaneously.

The Black Snake sniper's aim was dead on.

The large caliber round hit Daddy in the forehead, knocking him backwards.

Daddy's spirit left his body before his corpse hit the floor.

"I've told my children that when I die, to release balloons in the sky to celebrate that I graduated. For me, death is a graduation."

Elisabeth Kubler-Ross

Chapter 78

Mia woke up from a sound sleep. Her stomach wrenched into a thousand knots and she knew.

Her Daddy was dead. She knew it beyond any doubt. She started crying softly.

Oh Daddy, she cried to herself, *why Daddy? Why?*

Mia was crushed with sudden, overwhelming grief. How could she possibly go forward without Daddy?

"It's okay Baby Doll. Everything is going to be all right."

She almost heard his voice. It was like Daddy was in her head. And in truth, she felt like he was there with her. She could almost feel his arms around her as he pulled her into his lap. She could smell him. It was like he was a small whiff of her imagination, but more solid than that. Or she was feeling the lingering after effects of a vivid daydream.

She should call him. He would answer the phone and tell her he was on his way. No matter what the situation was, Daddy could handle it, she was sure of it.

She got her phone and pressed the send button. She didn't need to even look at the number. Daddy had programmed it for her. There were the usual clicks and whirls as the call was routed overseas, then after a long minute, it began to ring. It rang twice and was picked up.

"This is Sergeant Flynn, who am I speaking to?"

"This is Mia Cobalt. I want to speak to James."

"Mia, I am so sorry…"

Mia dropped the phone, and fell back on the bed. She brought the pillow over her head and started to scream.

After what seemed like hours, but could only have been minutes, Mia realized Flynn was still on the phone. She picked it back up again and could hear him speaking.

"Officer Flynn, can you tell me what happened?"

"I can tell you he loved you very much. That his last words and thoughts were about you and the baby."

"How did he die?"

There was silence, then Flynn said, "He died the way a man like him would choose to die. It was quick and painless Mia. He also wanted me to give you a message.

"He said for me to tell you he would always be with you. That everything was going to be all right."

Mia cried silently.

"He also wanted me to tell you, that I was in his debt. He saved my life. Did you know that, Mia?"

"No, I didn't."

"He did. Because of that, I owe him a debt. He wanted me to transfer that debt to you. So if you ever need anything Mia, no matter what it is, or where you are, I will help you."

"I release you from that debt, Officer Flynn."

"It's not that simple, nor can you release me from it. Just remember my words, Mia. If you ever need anything. I will help."

"I will, Officer Flynn. Thank you for being there at the end. I'm sure he was comforted by your presence. I have to go. Thank you again."

Mia moved on autopilot. She knew she had a meeting with the banker today and she had to get ready. She found the strength and moved forward. One foot in front of the other, one step at a time. The way her Daddy taught her. She took a shower, comforted by the warm water, but her mind went back to the first time Daddy had given her a bath. The studious look on his face as he shaved her.

Why, Daddy, why…

Because it was the only way to keep you and the baby safe, came the answer.

She dressed, and promptly at eight the hotel called letting her know her car was waiting for her. She took the elevator down. She could smell Daddy in the elevator with her. She wondered if she was going mad.

She arrived at the banker's office. She was ushered in, had a seat on the couch and was asked if she wanted coffee, tea, or hot chocolate. She thought that strange, having hot chocolate first thing in the morning, and decided to try it. She was glad she did. It was strong, and sweet.

"Good morning, Ms. Cobalt. My name is Swen Antlier. We spoke on the phone."

The banker was smaller than she expected, thirty-five or so, he had pale, thinning, blond hair, and deep blue eyes. He sat down next to her in a chair.

"Good morning," said Mia.

"Is everything okay, Ms. Cobalt?" said Antlier, seeing the redness around Mia eyes.

"Yes, I'm sorry. I'm just emotional today. Please continue."

"Mr. Cobalt set up three trusts in what are called 'Swiss Annuity' trusts. These trusts are protected by Swiss law and no one can take them away from you. They are also self-servicing, meaning there is nothing you need to do. Mr. Cobalt set up three of them as I said. One for you, one for your baby, and one for his son. You are to be the trustee of all of them."

"What does a Trustee do?"

"In this case, nothing really. Except, perhaps, tell me where to send the checks."

"How much money are we talking about?" asked Mia.

"There is sixteen point six million in each trust. So your personal trust has over sixteen million US dollars. The interest alone on your trust will provide you with one point six million a year without ever touching the principle. My advice would be to reinvest the interest in the children's trust and they could conceivably be worth over sixty million in ten years. But you are in charge of it all. What would you like me to do?"

Mia almost swooned at the amount. This is what Daddy meant when he said we would never have to worry about anything ever again.

"Yes, of course, reinvest the children's trusts. Make James' son eligible to take it over when he reaches twenty-five, the same with Mia Lynn's."

"A couple more questions and we'll be done. For you, there will be approximately thirteen thousand, three hundred US dollars per month in interest on your trust. Would you like me to set a living account for you so that you can draw on it as necessary?"

"Yes, please do."

"Two final matters. These trusts, by Swiss Law, are outside the laws of the United States and not subject to violation or confiscation by anyone, including lawsuits, creditors, or government interference. This is a Swiss insurance product, not a banking product. Of course, the Swiss must maintain its banking in accordance with international banking law and legal agreements with the United States. Insurance products do not fall under that law.

"In order to ensure there is no coercion in any of your future dealings, all you have to do is say the words 'Swiss bank account' and that will be a code to us, that this instruction was made involuntarily or under coercion and is to be voided and not carried out. Do you understand what I'm telling you, Ms. Cobalt?"

"You're telling me if someone tries to take the money from me by legal means, all I have to say is 'Swiss bank account' and you won't process the transaction."

"Yes, that is correct."

"We only have one final item of business. Your husband recorded a tape recording yesterday and asked me to give it to you. I'll make arrangements for your transfers and allow you to listen to it in private. Please let the secretary know when you wish to leave. I would also like to tell you, your husband was an honorable man, and I'm very sorry for your loss."

The banker set the small handheld tape recorder down in front of Mia, stood up, gave her a half bow, and left the room.

"The fear of death follows from the fear of life. A man who lives
fully is prepared to die at any time."

Mark Twain

Chapter 79

"Hello, Baby," Daddy's voice came through the small recorder and
seemed to fill the room with his presence.

Once again, Mia felt as if Daddy was sitting right next to her. Mia
picked up the recorder and held it in her small hand. It felt so good to
hear his voice, and at the same time, grief wanted to engulf her.

*"I want to tell you how sorry I am for hurting you. If there was any
way I could have gotten you and the baby safe, and me free, I would be
with you right now. But there wasn't. It was a choice between getting
you and the baby safe, or us possibly running for the rest of our lives, in
constant danger. That is no way for a child to live. Please understand
the decision I made was the best possible one for all.*

*"I have so many things I want to tell you. The first one is that you
made my life complete, Mia. The happiest I have ever been was with
you. I don't regret any of my actions for a minute.*

*"I also want to tell you that you are now free. You're free of your
family, free of Prescott, and free to start your life over again. Free to live
your life the way you should have lived it..."*

"I don't want to start my life over again without you Daddy," Mia
cried at the recording.

*"Listen to me, Baby, you can do this. It is time for you to start your
own journey. You are no longer the scared girl that I met. You have the
power and ability to do anything you want. And here is what I want
you to do.*

*"I want you to stay in Switzerland until the baby is born. All the ar-
rangements have been made. You have more than enough money to live*

well and can afford anything you want. I have a doctor ready for you, and the hospitals there are first rate. Better than the US. You'll need to start your prenatal check-ups immediately.

"Swen Antlier is a good man and you can trust him. He will help you find an apartment and everything you need.

"Once the baby is born, and you feel up to it, I want you to start traveling. Where you go doesn't matter. Go wherever you want. Stay as long as you want. But always continue on, until you reach a place where the 'small voice' tells you to stop."

"Daddy I don't understand," said Mia out loud to the empty room, the same as if Daddy was in the room next to her. "I don't know what you mean by the 'small voice'. What small voice?"

"…The small voice is the voice deep inside your head," said Daddy, almost as though he heard her question, "when the other voices in your head are loud, this voice will be small. So tiny that if you aren't listening, you'll disregard it. You'll recognize the small voice because no matter what it says, it feels right. Do you understand, Baby Doll?"

"Yes, Daddy, I know the voice you mean," answered Mia.

"Always listen to that voice. The voice will tell you where you need to go."

"Why do I have to travel, Daddy?"

"You're going to meet people along your journey. However, you're going to keep traveling until you meet the right person. How will you know they are the right person? You will know. Listen to the small voice.

"The last thing I want to tell you is I will always be with you. I will always be right by your side. I will always protect you and the baby. Please believe that, and please trust it as the truth. Anytime you want to talk to me, go to where the small voice is, and I will hear you.

"Always know that I love you, and that you're my Baby, always."

The tape recorder clicked off on its own. Mia sat in the silence. She could feel her Daddy wrapped around her. She could feel his presence. She had no doubt if Daddy said he would be here and protect her, he would do exactly that. Even death itself, wouldn't stop her Daddy. She felt comforted by his words, but also a little bewildered and scared. How could she ever do this without her Daddy?

"Daddy, I miss you so much!" she cried out to her heart, and into the empty room.

"But I haven't gone anywhere, Baby," came the immediate reply.

"The only way to have a friend is to be one."

Ralph Waldo Emerson

Chapter 80

Mia stayed in Switzerland the full term of her pregnancy and gave birth to a healthy, happy, baby girl.

The first few months were hard having a newborn in a foreign country with no one to rely on. However, soon she found people she hardly knew would lend a hand. They would get her groceries, cook for her, bring her food, clean her apartment, do her laundry and just about anything else that needed done.

Mia was unprepared as well for the amount of joy Mia Lynn brought into her life. Mia Lynn had Daddy's eyes, a deep gray/green color, Mia's brunette hair, Daddy's nose and Mia's mouth. Mia would laugh when she held her up. She looked a lot like Daddy but was much prettier.

Mia missed Daddy almost as a physical pain. Like an arm or a leg was missing. But at the same time she was comforted in that she felt him close by. He kept his promise and never seemed to be far away. While he wasn't 'there' in the sense that she could reach out and touch him, he was there in the sense that she could talk to him.

However, now Daddy was different. He seemed much happier. He was always laughing and joking with her, like it used to be when they first got together at his house. He would tease her, then laugh uncontrollably, infinitely pleased.

She thought most of the people she knew thought her crazy. Mia sometimes would burst out laughing at the antics or practical jokes Daddy would play. While she couldn't 'see' him, she could see him in her mind's eye and he just looked so comical she would end up laughing too. When this happened in the outdoors at a cafe, she would have to get it under control, and point to the baby like 'they just do the darnedest things', or people would think she was crazy. More than once she thought maybe she was.

She was also unprepared by how much she enjoyed the Swiss, and Switzerland. It was clean, beautiful, the people were friendly, and most spoke English. The fact that she had a newborn baby meant that most Swiss went out of their way to help her. They gave up their seats on public trains, gave up their taxis on rainy days, held doors for her. They treated her like a queen.

And they treated Mia Lynn like a Goddess. When the people in her apartment building found out she was recently widowed, rather than unmarried, there was no end to their generosity. Mia never lacked for babysitters or company. The other women in the building simply showed up at her door and invited themselves in. For an American, used to their privacy, this was disconcerting at times. They would show up with hot chocolate, or tea, make it, and then do whatever chores needed to be done.

Sometimes if the wives noticed some small chore that needed to be done, their husbands would show up at the door, looking sheepish, and uncomfortable. They had a tool box in their hands, and would simply shrug their shoulders and fix whatever needed to be fixed. Always they would stop and play with Mia Lynn. Many of her neighbors simply adopted Mia Lynn on sight. Mia grew to love Switzerland, and the country's friendly people.

Swen Antiler was also usually in the background. Always efficient, taking care of matters before they even needed taking care of. It was him who gave her Swiss neighbors the 'low down' on her situation and asked them to watch out for her. He effortlessly handled any visa or immigration problems for her behind her back.

During one of his weekly visits after almost two years in Switzerland, she broached a subject with him that had been increasingly on her mind. Daddy was always silent on this subject so he hadn't been any help. But increasingly, slowly, she felt the urge to travel. Deep down, she knew, the Small Voice was calling. It was time to start her journey.

"Swen, I think it's time I returned to America."

"Do you think that's wise?"

"I think it is necessary."

Swen watched Mia Lynn now running around the flat, putting one thing after another into her mouth. He also marveled at Mia. When he met her almost two years ago, she had looked like a scared waif. Now she was a confident woman in her own right.

"Will you be coming back?"

"Of course, Swen. How could I stay away? Geneva is like home to me now."

"Then I will keep the flat for you. Don't worry about anything. I'll make all the arrangements for you. When would you like to leave?"

"Next week I think would be good. Thank you, Swen."

"I'm not afraid of death, but I'm in no hurry to die. I have so much I want to do first."

Stephen Hawking

Chapter 81

Mia, and Mia Lynn arrived at the airport after a long transatlantic flight. They went through Customs and Immigration with no problems. As soon as she stepped into the baggage claim area, she saw Flynn, standing there in street clothes, waiting for her. How he knew she would be arriving, she had no idea. Maybe Swen alerted him. He recognized her immediately and walked up to her.

"Ms. Cobalt, it is a pleasure to see you again," he said in his most polite and formal way.

"Officer Flynn, it's good to see you as well. And please, we are old friends, call me Mia."

Flynn nodded his head and then looked at Mia Lynn. "She is much prettier than her father. She takes after you. Please come this way. Swen Antlier made all the arrangements for you. You have a rental car as well as a hotel suite downtown. I also took time off and will be your personal driver."

"Officer Flynn, that's hardly necessary. I'm not an invalid."

"It's Lieutenant Flynn now, and it is necessary," he said seriously.

"Why? Am I in any danger?"

"No. Of course not," was all he said.

"As you wish. Tomorrow I'd like to visit James' grave. Now I'd just like to get to the hotel and sleep."

Flynn drove her to the hotel, carried her bags, then checked the room before allowing her and Mia Lynn to enter.

"I'll pick you up at nine a.m. in the morning," he said, handing her the key card.

"Why are you doing this? It's not necessary," asked Mia.

"I owe a debt to your husband, and it is very necessary. I told him I would, and I will. This was decided almost two years ago. With all due respect, Ms. Cobalt, you really have no say in the matter."

Mia sighed. She felt Daddy watching, nodding his head in agreement and satisfaction.

"As you wish."

Flynn picked Mia and Mia Lynn up exactly on time as she knew he would. He opened the door for her and insisted on placing Mia Lynn in the car seat himself. It was a beautiful fall day. The sun was out, the leaves changing color, and the temperature was perfect. Flynn drove in silence to the graveyard. Mia knew Daddy had wanted to be cremated, not buried, and his last wishes weren't carried out. He was buried instead. She wondered how he felt about that. She decided she would ask him later.

Flynn stood a ways off and let her have her privacy once they got to the graveyard. He pointed where she would find the marker and held Mia Lynn's tiny hand as she walked over alone. She walked up to the cold, granite marker. It simply said "Cobalt." No dates, no inscriptions. The grave was tended and clean. Small mementos had been left on it. Some, it looked, had been there for years. One was a small teddy bear. Another was a plastic flower, another was an envelope held down by a rock, stained and weathered.

"Oh Daddy, I miss you so much," she said, touching the cold gray stone.

"I miss him too," said a boy about ten years old. He had come to stand beside her without her hearing him. Mia looked up at him. His features were slightly Asian, but there was definitely Daddy in him. Mia looked up and saw an Asian woman standing a ways away, probably his mother. His mother stared at Mia with barely concealed hate in her eyes.

"Do you come here a lot?" Mia asked.

"Yes, it is close to my school. I feel good here. Daddy talks to me. Does he talk to you too?"

Tears came to Mia's eyes and dripped down her face. "Yes, he does."

"Don't cry. Daddy wouldn't want you to cry. He's happy now, you know. You were Daddy's friend, weren't you?"

"Yes, I was."

"That means you're my friend too."

"How did you know I would be here?"

"Daddy told me. He told me to come and meet you."

"Did he tell you anything else?"

"He said to tell you 'everything was going to be okay, Baby Doll. Everything is going to be all right.'"

Mia fell to her knees and broke down in great racking sobs then, unable to contain them any longer. The boy stepped up to her, held her and stroked Mia's head quietly, exactly as his father would have done. At that moment, Mia Lynn bounded over, unaware of her mother's grief, and both children held Mia, as she held both children.

"Is she my sister?"

"Yes, she is."

He got down on one knee and looked at her seriously, then held out his hand.

"Hi. I'm your big brother."

Mia Lynn shook his hand solemnly.

"What do you remember most about your Daddy?" Mia asked the boy.

"What I remember is that he always used to joke with me. He never got angry. He used to play the piano for me, you know. Sometimes, I can still hear it. Now, when I play, sometimes he sits down with me and we play together."

The three of them stayed sitting at Daddy's grave talking quietly. Soon, Mia was laughing. The boy had Daddy's off-beat sense of humor, and his mischievous grin.

"I have to go. I'm glad you were Daddy's friend. You made him very happy, you know."

He turned and walked away without another word. Out of the corner of her eye, she saw Flynn walk up to him as well. Flynn stuck out his hand and shook the boy's as an adult would do. He then gave the boy a business card. The boy looked at it, shook his head as if to say 'yes, I understand,' then Flynn shook his hand again.

When the boy got to the car, he turned around and looked at Mia and Mia Lynn. He waved once, and was gone.

Mia and Mia Lynn stayed at Daddy's grave the rest of the afternoon.

"Life and death are one thread, the same line
viewed from different sides."

Lao Tzu

Chapter 82

"Daddy, I've got to go now," Mia said getting up from his grave.

"Thank you Daddy for bringing me and Mia Lynn here to meet
your son. He is so much like you. I miss you, Daddy. I have to begin
my journey now."

Mia took Mia Lynn's hand and walked back to where Flynn was
waiting patiently.

"Flynn would you take me back to the hotel, so I can pack my
bags and then take me to the airport?"

"Of course. Where will you be going?"

"I don't know yet. I'm waiting for the small voice to tell me."

"Excuse me?"

"I'll decide when I get there. Did you ever get married, Lieutenant
Flynn?"

"No, ma'am, I did not."

"You should. You're a good man, Flynn."

"Most women don't feel the same way you do."

"Do you ever see Momma Prescott?"

"Occasionally. What was left of the Prescott estate was given to
her. She sold off all the business holdings, including the estate. She
took the money and started a number of charities. She came clean
about the years of abuse and publicly exonerated you. She said that
you acted in self-defense, and she had overheard Jeffery Prescott's
plan to kill you and the baby. Which was why no charges were ever
filed against you. The Grand Jury sided with you in absentia.

"Cobalt was charged with a number of crimes, including kidnapping and murder of William Prescott. However, since he was already dead there wasn't a whole lot the state could do. Everyone wanted to sweep the situation under the rug, and that was what they did. I was promoted. I almost quit in disgust. You tell Cobalt when you see him…" Flynn stopped, aware he was referring to Cobalt in the present tense, as if he were still alive.

"He talks to you too, doesn't he?"

"Yes…"

They were both silent. Neither comfortable talking about an impossible, and deeply private matter. Flynn dropped Mia off at the hotel, waited, then drove her to the airport.

"Mia, you and the little one are always welcome here," Flynn said, trying not to choke up.

"Thank you, Flynn," Mia said, kissing him softly on the cheek. Flynn watched as Mia walked away, Mia Lynn on her shoulder, big brown eyes, opening and closing her hand, in a child's wave of goodbye.

Mia walked up to the Air France desk and purchased a ticket for Paris. When they arrived in Paris, she and Mia Lynn sat under the Eiffel Tower in a small sidewalk cafe. Pictures didn't do the tower justice. It was huge. Its spider-like supports sweeping up into the air, spinning a metal web. Mia once thought she saw Daddy on one of the tourist platforms high up in the air, looking down at her and waving. She waved back.

Mia felt she was with Daddy quite a bit now that she was traveling. He seemed happy, full of jokes and laughter. She knew Mia Lynn felt his presence too. She wasn't scared in the slightest and took it as normal. Mia Lynn was walking and talking now. Frequently, out of the blue, she would say, "Daddy thinks we should go here…" or "Daddy said…"

In Venice, Italy, she saw Daddy go by in a Gondola. Her and Mia Lynn raced after it. However, when the passengers disembarked, Daddy was nowhere to be seen.

In London, she saw Daddy outside Buckingham Palace clowning in front of the stone-faced guards.

In Costa Rica, her and Mia Lynn went for a ride in a glass-bottom boat. The coral reef was beautiful. The water clear and turquoise. Mia Lynn loved all the bright-colored fish as they swam under the boat.

Mia could have sworn Daddy swam under the boat, in a mask and snorkel, tapped on the glass to get her attention, waved, then swam away.

They took a three-month world cruise, sailing all over the Mediterranean, coastal Africa, and finally Asia. Too many times to count she saw Daddy in the dining room, helping himself to lobster, or dressed as a crew member, even during the outing on shore.

Daddy was true to his word. He never left her. She talked to him nightly after putting Mia Lynn down for the night. She would sit down and quite naturally, she, or he would begin a conversation. Sometimes hours would pass and she would come to her senses and realize she was talking to herself, yet hearing Daddy's words in reply clearly in her mind. More than once, she wondered if she was going mad. Or had already gone mad, from the grief. But she didn't feel grief. She missed him yes, but she didn't grieve.

One night in St. Petersburg, Russia, with the snow falling quietly down outside, she asked,

"Daddy, what's it like to be dead?"

"It's like being alive, but much better," he replied.

"How is it better?"

"For one, I don't have to brush my teeth twice a day."

"Daddy, be serious."

"It is like everything is new and wonderful. Colors are more colorful. Smells, smell so good."

"How can I ever repay you, Daddy?"

"By giving someone else the love I gave to you."

"Will you always be here?"

"No, not always."

"When will you leave?"

"When the time comes, not before. I won't leave you, but there will be time for you to leave me."

"How come you don't leave now, and go to heaven, or wherever people go when they die?"

"I am in MY heaven, Baby. My heaven is you and Mia Lynn."

"I believe that dreams are more powerful than facts. That hope always triumphs over experience. That laughter is the only cure for grief. And I believe that love is stronger than death."

Robert Fulghum

Chapter 83

One year after starting her journey, Mia and Mia Lynn were touring Southeast Asia.

It was after Chinese New Year, and the weather was still cool. Mia was undecided. She didn't really know if she liked Asia. It was not only very foreign, but many parts had a 'rawness' that she wasn't comfortable with. Many other parts, like Bangkok and Singapore were so modern they put the US to shame. Singapore, especially.

Singapore with its sweeping skyscrapers was unbelievably clean for Asia. No other country, except Switzerland could match it. Bangkok was modern too, but not as clean as Singapore. Bangkok, and Thailand in general, were much more exotic.

Vietnam she didn't like. The people, while friendly and smiling, seemed to be hiding something. Their eyes held a different story. Most seemed to want to cheat you, or were looking for ways to scam you. Most of the other tourists grumbled about it too. Still though, the beaches and scenery were beautiful.

Cambodia and Laos were like taking a trip back in time fifty years. Phom Penh, the capital of Cambodia, was overlaid with colonial architecture. There were many places which told of the genocide there during the 1970's. Even Daddy said unhappy ghosts walked there, and she believed it. It had that feeling.

Which was how Mia and Mia Lynn ended up in Yangon, Myanmar, sitting on a park bench during the winter. No matter where they went in Asia, Asians were just goofy about children and Mia Lynn in particular. Mia watched Mia Lynn closely. She didn't fear for her, exactly. In truth, after traveling almost the entire world, the only place she felt in danger was in the US. Nowhere else had the tension she felt in all the major cities of the US.

Still, she was careful about her child the way any mother would be. The one thing she saw that she didn't see in other Asian cities was the army patrols of sullen child soldiers, walking the streets, daring anyone to cross eyes with them.

They sat on a bench in the sun. Mia had bought some food from a street vendor and Mia Lynn had pronounced that she liked it. Which meant digging into it with her fingers. It was a curry of some sort which meant that Mia Lynn was a mess in no time.

"Come here, Baby Doll, let me wipe your face," said Mia.

"It's pretty good Mommy."

"I can see that."

"Can we get some fruit after, the yellow one that stinks?"

Mia laughed. The fruit did stink. "Sure. Why do you want to try that one?"

"Daddy said it tasted like onion flavored ice cream. I never had onion flavored ice cream before, so I want to try it."

"Well, that sounds like your Daddy."

Together they walked over to the fruit vendor. The smell got worse as they neared it. But it didn't stop people from lining up to buy as much as they could. They got into line and waited patiently as any well brought up Western person would. However, people kept getting in front of them with no sense of order. Some people even pushed Mia out of the way to stand in her place, then pushed forward more, taking other people's places.

"These people aren't polite, Mommy," Mia Lynn said. They gave up and decided to wait until the crowd thinned before attempting again. They went back and sat down on their bench.

An elderly monk with a walking stick came along then and the crowd immediately parted and made way for him. Many people offered up their positions in line for him out of respect. Mia realized he must be an important man. All the people seemed to know him, and bowed and wai'd.

He went to the front of the line, chose the best fruit, and offered to pay. The vendor shook his head 'no' and refused payment. The monk nodded his head in thank you and went back the way he came. He sat down on the bench next to Mia and Mia Lynn.

Without asking, he offered the fruit to Mia Lynn. Mia Lynn looked at her mother for permission to accept it. Mia looked at the monk.

He appeared to be somewhere between forty and sixty, she couldn't really tell. He had a shaved head and wore the saffron robes of a Buddhist monk. He seemed harmless enough and she had watched him take the same fruit she herself was going to buy. So Mia nodded her head in approval, and Mia Lynn took the fruit from the monk and said thank you.

The monk smiled when she took it, and said, "You're welcome," in English. He sat back on the bench then and silently looked off into space. After a short while he said quietly,

"You have spirits around you."

Mia was taken aback. "Excuse me? I'm sorry. Did you say something to me?"

The monk looked at her calmly. "You have spirits around you," he repeated.

Mia looked at him. She felt a tug deep inside, the small voice was trying to be heard. Mia decided there was no sense in denying it.

"Yes, I do."

"Do you know why they stay?"

"He stays to protect us, and because he loves us."

"You are lucky to have such a strong spirit as your guide. Most people don't. That makes you special in some way."

Mia was silent. The monk was silent. Then abruptly he said,

"On this very bench a few years ago, I met a young man. He was seventeen at the time. He started his journey from this very bench. He became a man of power in his own right. It started right here."

Again, Mia felt the tug. The familiarity of the words 'he started his journey' the Small Voice was speaking. What was it trying to say?

"What is your name?" the monk asked.

"Mia Cobalt," she answered. "What's yours?"

"You can call me Monk."

"Well, at least it's consistent."

The Monk smiled. "I remember someone else saying the same thing. And this little Goddess, what is her name?" the Monk asked, indicating Mia Lynn.

The Small Voice grew louder.

"Mia Lynn."

"My Lin," the Monk repeated. He pronounced it differently

though. Saying 'MY ' instead of 'ME ah.'

"Of course it is," he said simply. "The Gods are having fun today, I think."

The tug was now a pull. The Small Voice rose in volume. Mia knew without a doubt this was the man Daddy had sent her to meet.

"You knew my Daddy, didn't you?" Mia Lynn asked, speaking for the first time.

"Yes, I did," the Monk said simply.

"Were you his teacher?" Mia asked.

"I would like to think I was one of his teachers. He had many."

"He led me to you, didn't he?"

"I don't know. I know the Gods led me here today, if that matters."

"What do we do now?"

"What do you want to do?"

"I don't know," said Mia, truthfully.

"What do you want to do, My Lynn?" the Monk asked.

Mia Lynn first looked at her mother, then did something she never did with strangers. She stood up, ran and jumped into the Monk's arms. The Monk laughed and held her easily and she looked over his shoulder at her mother.

"Please join us," the Monk said softly, holding out his hand, "you have nothing to fear. This is your journey."

Mia went and stood next to him without a word. Knowing this was where Daddy had led her and wanted her to go. The three of them set out for the monastery, and the long journey ahead.

Mia Lynn stayed in the Monk's arms, looking over his shoulder, looking backwards to the bench where they had just been sitting. She opened and closed her chubby hand in a child's gesture of goodbye at the empty space.

She saw her Daddy's spirit with tears of joy running down his face, thanking the merciful universe as he was left behind, and they started their own journey without him.

The End.

I see you've made it all the way to the end. I'm glad you liked it enough of it to finish.

If you liked the book, would you be open to leaving me a 4 or 5 star review?

You see, we're self published authors. We don't have big ad budgets, or editors, or a publishing house behind us or helping us.

All we have is readers like you.

When readers like you are able to give us positive reviews, it helps us out in a big way. In addition it is our readers which tell us what we did right, and what we did wrong. They tell us if we should continue a series, if they liked the characters, etc.

Readers like you are the only thing we have, and the only thing we need.

You can leave a review for me at Amazon here: <u>Leave a review for Mia's Journey,</u> where you bought the book. You can also contact me here: http://JohnRebell.com and you'll receive a personal reply.

It would really mean a lot to us.

All the best to you and your family,

John Rebell and Zee Ryan

About The Authors

John Rebell is an American expat splitting time between Southeast Asia and the US.

Merchant seaman, private investigator, biofuel consultant, writer, and teacher. He has written over 8 non-fiction books. His non-fiction books have been critically acclaimed and one a global bestseller.

His other fiction works include "Three Pagoda Pass" and "Bad Karma."

Zee Ryan is a published writer of erotic fiction under another pen name. This is her first collaboration. She is an University graduate with a degree in Education. She lives in the Midwest with her husband and son. When not writing she enjoys music, movies, and reading a good book.

"Mia's Journey" is their first collaboration. You can reach them with questions or comments at:

http://JohnRebell.com